The Bitcoin Gambit
By Jim Flynn Six

First ebook edition March 2021
First paperback edition March 2021

Contact the author at sincerejimmy942@gmail.com

Special Thanks to John R. Thomas, Colonel, U.S. Army Retired

Bitcoin:
In November, 2008, Satoshi Nakamoto published an academic paper: *Bitcoin: A Peer-to-Peer Electronic Cash System.* The system launched in January, 2009. Nine years later, the actual identity of Nakamoto-whether a person or a group-is still not known.

-Bradley, Foster & Sargent, Inc., January, 2018

Cyber Warfare
...while there is debate over how to define and use "cyberwarfare" as a term, many countries including the United States, United Kingdom, Russia, India, Pakistan, China, Israel, Iran and North Korea have active cyber capabilities for offensive and defensive operations.

-Wikipedia

Gambit:
(in chess) an opening in which a player makes a sacrifice, typically of a pawn, for the sake of some compensating advantage.

-Oxford English Dictionary

One
Spicewood, TX
The Hill Country
Yesterday

My head throbbed with shooting pain and I could see flashes of light. I was trapped inside something. My knees were up by my chest, and my shoulders pressed against the hard surface. When I tried to stretch I discovered I was in something round. The overpowering stench of oil made me gag.

I felt around with my hands. It was dark except for a few holes of light. I touched one of the holes and it had a sharp jagged edge that cut my fingertip. I jerked my hand back. Then I reached up over my head and found a flat hard cold metal surface.

I was imprisoned in an oil drum.

I pushed up hard with my hands. The lid didn't budge so I smacked the top of the can with the heels of both hands. I fought the urge to panic, then I thought *screw it, panic is appropriate sometimes, and it will give me more strength.* So I panicked. I went crazy. Smacking the top once created no result except for noise, so I smacked again and again, harder each time. Finally the top popped clean off, wobbling onto the floor. The act of raising my hands above my head created a terrible shooting pain in the right side of my ribcage. Were my ribs broken? I couldn't remember.

I tried to stand up straight, but I was exhausted by the sudden spurt of effort. The pulsing pain in my head grew worse. I was dizzy. My eyes tried to adjust to the sudden light. I realized I was in the back of a panel van and it was moving.

The commotion attracted the attention of a man and a woman who were accompanying me in the truck. The man, who was driving pulled the van over to the side of the road and stopped. The woman got out of her seat and climbed over the front console and approached the oil drum. I couldn't focus my eyes, but she looked familiar.

"I didn't think this jerk would be waking up so soon after you hit him in the head with the crowbar," she said to the man. I didn't recognize him.

My fingers gripped the rim of the oil drum as I attempted to steady myself. At least now I knew why my head hurt. I panted with my tongue hanging out. My racing heartbeat sent steady pulses of pain to my head and chest. The woman aimed a gun at me.

"Don't kill him," the man said in what sounded like a Russian accent.

That was good.

"I'll give you one more chance. Tell me what you know about Bitcoin, about Nakamoto," the woman said to me.

"I don't know anything," I said.

"Remember, if he doesn't talk, Turgenev wants him to be alive when we dump the oil drum in the water," the man continued.

That was not so good.

I saw the woman taking a vicious swing at my head with the butt of her gun. Then everything went black.

Two
Fort Meade, MD
U.S. Cyber Command
About three months ago

The Headquarters of U.S. Cyber Command was new
construction, the design of the building stated its mission. The
exterior was all aluminum, glass, and precast concrete. The
edifice would not be out of place in Silicon Valley.

Inside Toni Anne Laudano waited to be invited into the office
of the Commanding General A.B. "Buck" Goldstein. He was a
four star general, and nobody in the building addressed him as
anything other than his rank, or sir. Goldstein was the first
General to be recruited directly out of college to be in Cyber
Warfare and had never served in any of the traditional military
outfits.

The staff at Cyber Command included civilians and military
personnel. Among the military contingent the structure was
traditional hierarchy, but the civilians were rated differently. So
among the officers a major was outranked by a colonel, and the
colonel out ranked by a general, but the civilians were rated by
brain power. Most of the top intellectual talent was civilian.

So Toni Anne, who had dropped out of MIT as an undergrad
was the top rated civilian because she was smarter than
everybody else, including men who had several advanced
degrees in subjects like Computer Sciences, Software Design,
and Artificial Intelligence. While it was never formally stated
on any organization chart, Toni Anne Laudano was the de facto
second in command.

When she had first arrived at Cyber Command Laudano was
misjudged by many because she was so pretty. A lot of people
thought she looked like Mary Poppins, with her dark brown

hair in a bob and blue eyes courtesy of her English mother. Unlike many tech people of either sex, Toni Anne always was neatly attired. Her make-up was subtle but meticulously applied. She even dressed like a 1960s schoolgirl; her clothes gave just a hint of the terrific body beneath them.

She had a history of questioning academic authority, from the day in second grade when she had contradicted her startled teacher, and went on a substantial explanation that zero was conceptually different than and not a part of the set of cardinal numbers. Toni Anne had started her own company when her professor at MIT had told her that her Encryption Algorithms would never work. Laudano dropped out of MIT that day. Toni Anne's algorithms made her rich when she sold her company for $300 million six years later. Then she had presented herself to Cyber Command and demanded that she work for $1 per year. She also swore like a sailor, and did not suffer fools. Her first day at Cyber Command a scientist, mistaking her for a secretary, handed her a paper as she walked past his desk and told her to type it up.

"Type it up yourself, assface," Toni Anne had said with her charming smile, as though exchanging pleasantries, and handed it back to the man.

That guy, a double PhD, now reported to someone who reported to Toni Anne.

The General invited Laudano to sit in his office. "How are you doing on that new Russian threat?, he asked.

"We're halfway there, but the second half of the problem looks tough. Those friggin' Commies are good, we can't underrate them," Toni Anne said. She sometimes cleaned up her language a bit for General Goldstein, but not always.

"I've been talking to a new asset; this looks like a gift out of the blue. I want you to talk to him. We might be able to put together a very interesting plan," Goldstein said.

"Okay General," Toni Anne said.

"This stays just between us. Maybe we get the President involved if the asset checks out," Goldstein said.

"Yes sir," Toni Anne said.

"This could be spectacular. But the loop stays closed. Until we use the mole!" The General said.

"Sounds like you've got a plan," Toni Anne said.

"Yeah, but I'm going to need your genius to make it work," Goldstein said. "And we have to start thinking about getting the perfect Useful Idiot."

Three
Austin, TX
About three months ago

I had a serious crush on Gabrielle, a beautiful 6'3" Former
Army Ranger lesbian who twice in one evening had saved my
life by shooting and killing men who were trying to kill me.
Where was this relationship going? Even I realized that I had a
problem with commitments, because I had never made any. I
also pondered whether this was the time to stick out my neck
and try to make a commitment to a woman who might have no
interest in me.

I'm JR Johnson, a long-time resident of Austin, Texas.
Gabrielle was staying with me while she recovered from a near
fatal shooting. She had been shot in New York City.

JR Johnson. The J. stands for John, so my name is John
Johnson, as most recently a NYC female detective pointed out
to me, a few days before this very same detective shot and
wounded Gabrielle, and then killed Movie Star Lola Madison.
Lola was my client and sometime girlfriend, until she had
dumped me for her then bodyguard Gabrielle McHugh.

After the shooting I offered to bring Gabrielle home with me to
Austin while she recovered. Gabrielle was wildly overqualified
to for her position protecting Lola. I had asked her why she had
left a career as an Army officer to be a bodyguard, but she
brushed it off, and told me that was a story for another time.
When she first got here Gabrielle had made a phone call once
in a while. In the past few days Gab had been on her cellphone
a lot. She never told me the nature of the calls, and I didn't ask.

Then Gabrielle had appeared in my office. "JR, what are you
doing?

"I'm still deciding on what to do with Bitcoin," I told her. I had two computer screens going on my desk. I was looking at trading patterns on Bitcoin. I was tempted to get in and trade it for my own account. I could smell a sea change coming, and I didn't want to totally miss out.

"I thought you said that you'd never trade Bitcoin for your clients, and you didn't really understand it," Gabrielle said.

"First of all, it is way too risky for my clients. I'd just trade it in my own account. Second, I don't really understand it, but I don't think most people understand it. It doesn't seem to stop them from buying Bitcoin," I said.

"Oh. Well...JR... we need to discuss our relationship," she said. Then she left the room.

Where do women get that from? It's always the same phrase they say to me. Do they get a secret handbook when they reach puberty?

Not long before we'd been through an adventure, Gabrielle and me. Having men just feet away from you trying to kill you with guns, on two separate occasions within an hour, changes your perspective on life. It's not the same as a near miss car accident. These attempts were on purpose. Those villains wanted to kill *me*. If they had been successful I wouldn't have been able to play golf anymore, so I took it seriously.

While Gabrielle was physically recovering, I was thinking about the meaning of life. The only time I ever remembered reflecting on that subject before was once years ago when I was refilling my Dr. Pepper at a self-serve taco joint, but my deep thinking had been interrupted when the cup overflowed, and I never got back to it. Up until now I'd had a shallow, simple, yet happy existence. Maybe I was ready for a deeper, more complex, less happy life. Was the secret to long term happiness the willingness to face short term unhappiness? If not, at least that theory might be the basis for a phony but wildly popular self-help book.

I looked out the window of my house toward the pool, and there she was, sunning herself. Gabrielle was dressed in just her skimpy bra and panties. She had gone for a dip, and the undies took on a pleasant semi-transparent quality. I was admiring the bra especially, primarily for its cleverly designed mechanical support principles. At least I was trying to convince myself of that.

Gabrielle wasn't a person to lie still in the sun for long. You don't get to be third in your class at West Point and the first woman Army Ranger officer by having a lying-around-the-pool mindset. After a couple minutes in a lounge chair she got up and did push-ups and sit-ups. Then she got on all fours and did an exercise that I've forgotten the name of, supporting her weight on her arms while she alternated hopping her legs forward and back. *Was is called frog-something?* I hadn't done that particular activity since twelfth grade. But I was planning to increase the intensity and duration my own workouts, beginning any day now.

She wasn't just going through the motions. Gabrielle was working at it. She alternated the three above exercises and threw in some jumping jacks, which only served to increase my fascination with the mechanical support qualities of the undies. Isn't science great?

I tried to convince myself that it was just that Gab was the forbidden fruit, and I would become jaded about it if we ever did get intimate, but I knew deep down I was just kidding myself. Then again, Barbara Jean Parker was also in the picture. There was nothing ambivalent about Barb. She was all real flesh and blood Texas womanhood. Barbara Jean and I had gone out, off and on, when she was getting over her divorce. What kind of idiot am I? I had dated Movie Star Lola that I never saw, and now I was pining for Gabrielle the lesbian, when Barbara Jean was just about perfect and made no bones about wanting to marry me.

Maybe I was afraid of making a regular life, and maybe that went back to being estranged from my wealthy but peculiar family from the age of eighteen when I had declined to go the Medical School route and become a physician like every male member of my family since the Revolutionary War. Instead, I took a golf scholarship to the University of Texas and ended up on Wall Street for a while before coming back to Austin and working in the money business.

I couldn't figure out Gabrielle. Was she intentionally tempting me, or was it complacent, like two college roommates walking around in their underwear? I found it easier to be complacent back in the day when it was my potbellied college roomie Rex with a beer in his hand than the spectacular Gabrielle. I tried not to get caught staring.

It was autumn in Austin, Texas. I had lived in New York City for a while, and New Yorkers would consider the weather this day to be intolerably hot. Texas is hot. Before the invention of air conditioning only crazy people lived in Texas. But now with all the modern conveniences, it was just mostly crazy people.

My house guest seemed to be fond of me, but since I'm a guy that went just so far. Gabrielle not only outclassed me in toughness; she was also better looking and smarter than me. Not that I'm a human gargoyle or anything. I'm ok. But I have a lot of money, and that has made me attractive to women over the years. Maybe that would help.

Gabrielle had mentioned once that she was bi-sexual. I was unclear on the whole lesbian/bi-sexual thing. Lola had been vague in that area as well. Perhaps there was some wiggle room in the relationship after all. I'm open minded.

So what was with "JR, we need to talk."?

Four
Austin, TX

Conversations with women that start with them telling me that we need to talk don't end well for me.

Gabrielle and I had become internationally famous for even more than fifteen minutes when we had been involved in killing the New York Hedge Fund manager/Ponzi scheme operator Robert Stanton Banks who had defrauded many wealthy but financially naïve clients out of billions of dollars and ordered the death of my former client, girlfriend and Gabrielle's former girlfriend, Movie Star Lola Madison, who he was trying to swindle out of over $100 million. If that sounds complicated, it was.

Some hack writer wrote a best seller about the whole thing without our cooperation. He appears to have just made up some of the details. Netflix wants to make a six part series. Neither Gabrielle nor I are interested in cooperating with the production of the mini-series, and I've told Gab that she can have the rights to any royalties. I don't need the money, and she's broke. Of course if she married me that would change, and I had been thinking about it, but had not been able to summon up the courage to mention that to her.

So I'm in my forties and have never come close to getting married and here I was daydreaming about being married to a beautiful lesbian who seemed fond of me, but never expressed any lustful comments or actions in my direction. Call me old fashioned, but I think there should be some lust involved in a marriage. There were times when I let myself think that if Gabrielle married me, that would be all I'd want. I'd find happiness and meaning.

I'd never kissed her, but I wanted to. We held hands a few times when she was recovering in a hospital bed from her wounds. That sounds pathetic, but my life was stuck. I'm a normally active guy, have been intimate with a few women, including the deceased movie star. But so has Gabrielle. We have that in common. It's a puzzle.

Gabrielle had stolen my girlfriend Lola, but then Lola was killed. That's not really fair. Maybe it was Lola who initiated the relationship with Gab. I think.

Gabrielle got shot by the above mentioned New York female detective who was being paid by the Hedge Fund manager. The detective, Sierra Quinn, had apparently fled the U.S. At least that was what the police had said they suspected, but weren't positive.

Gab was recuperating in my compound in Austin. The complex consisted of a main house and a casita. Casita means "little house" in Spanish. Gabrielle lived in the casita, and routinely walked around in my presence in her skimpy bra and panties. I didn't know how to take that. Gab had a spectacular body. Unshared to anyone, I referred to her in my own mind as Xena the Warrior Princess. She had dark brown hair, piercing green eyes, and long legs even when considering that she was so tall. Gab had a flat stomach with well-defined abs. It was a striking combination.

I dated Lola for years and saw her in all stages of being dressed and undressed, but Gabrielle was more real, not just a movie icon.

Gab was more or less fully clothed when she walked in and told me we needed to have a talk, so it was easier to focus. Then she said it could wait for later and walked out of the room. Thanks. If there's something worse than Doom, it's Impending Doom.

Prior to Gabrielle coming to my house I had used the casita as my office, where I ran my money management business. I loved the casita; it was a single floor with one bedroom, a kitchen and a living area surrounded by glass that opened onto a deck that overlooked the pool. I'd be happy to just live there. It wasn't that I needed that much room to run my business, but it was easier to be disciplined to focus on work when I walked to the casita, which was separated from the main house by about 50 feet. The complex was behind a fence that gave us privacy. Looking at it from the street from left to right was a swimming pool with the casita behind it, and to the right of the pool was the main house.

Almost every day Gab sunbathed by the pool when I was working, then she'd knock and announce herself but come into the house without me saying anything. Gabrielle apparently equated her undies with swimwear, so she'd sometimes walk in the main house while still damp, toweling off from a dip in the pool. She wasn't top heavy, but was shapely enough. Her wet bikini panties and barely adequate bra maintained their slightly transparent qualities for several minutes after she got out of the pool, which made it hard to concentrate.

Did she think I was a eunuch?

Gabrielle had told me that a couple times that a blonde woman had been peeking through the slats of the fence that fronted my property, spying on her when she was by the pool. When Gab had started to approach the fence to confront the would be stalker, the blonde scurried into her yellow Corvette roadster and sped off. I was 100% sure who it was, but didn't share that with Gabrielle. Barbara Jean was the Corvette driver. There were times I thought I was in love with Barb. Why wouldn't I be? I needed to make up my mind.

"Is that typical behavior in Austin? Good looking blondes in Corvettes spying on your property? Would that hot babe be somebody that you know?" Gabrielle asked.

17

I thought about my answer for a second. Was Gabrielle somehow jealous? Jealous of what? I scratched my chin. "Well, I guess we do have some notoriety. People are curious."

"Hmmmm." She didn't buy my non-answer.

Gabrielle and I had been out in public a few times, to go to casual local restaurants, some of Austin's justifiably famous rib joints. We didn't hit the social scene, and pointedly did not go to the movies to see Lola's last film. I thought that the producers might pull the movie from circulation but as usual, greed won over good taste. The film was a big hit. Audiences around the world were said to stand up and cheer, with tears in their eyes, at the end of the movie. Lola played an assassin. Really.

Since all I needed was an internet connection and my cell phone, a spare bedroom in the main house had become my make-shift office. I didn't like it, but having Gabrielle as a companion more than made up for the business inconvenience.

When I returned to Austin after shooting the Ponzi Scheme phony in New York I was deluged by potential clients who wanted me to manage some of their money. Since my minimum account is $1 million, and the clients had to have at least $3 million in total assets and I'm very grumpy and strict about how I invest the money you'd wouldn't think I'd be that popular, but that wasn't the case. I don't need the business, and I just decided to tell people I wasn't taking new clients, but that just made them want me more. It's surprising how many people have three million, and not all of them are driving Mercedes Benzes and Teslas. Some of them are driving around in pickup trucks. More than one potential client used the line, "I want to do business with somebody who's made a killing on Wall Street."

Ha-ha. Not that I regret shooting the bastard, Robert Stanton Banks. He was responsible for the death of Lola and another long-time friend, and he was pointing a gun at me when I wounded him with a gunshot. After that Gabrielle finished him off. It was a close call. Another second and Banks would have killed me.

Gabrielle seemed about fully recovered. Not that I'm a doctor, but as I said, I'm from a long line of doctors, including my siblings. I'm the youngest, and my sister and two brothers are physicians. We don't get along. My last two conversations, years apart, with my older brother ended with me threatening to break his fingers. He's an eye surgeon.

Gab had resumed her grueling workout schedule, and looked even better in her undies than a month before. The first few weeks I didn't notice her on the phone that much. In the last few days she was on it constantly.

Later that day she walked in still dripping wet from the pool. "I'm going back in the Army," she announced.

Five
Moscow

Oleg Turgenev had been summoned without explanation for a
meeting the Russian President. The President now preferred to
be addressed as 'The Lider' or just 'Lider' which is Russian for
'Leader'. English speaking people pronounced it "LED-yuh"
the closest they could come to the Russian pronunciation.

Turgenev thought that term was reminiscent of 'Fuhrer', and
using that title hadn't ended well for that particular German.
This was a thought that he kept to himself.

The international press referred to Turgenev as an Oligarch.
Oleg thought of himself as a criminal, indeed the Russian
pronunciation of the word "oligarha" was guttural and sounded
more sinister, more like the Russian word for criminal.

Nobody really got close to knowing the Lider, but Oleg knew
him better than most. His favorite movie was *The Godfather,*
and he had used the Mafia structure portrayed in the picture to
build his criminal organization. He used a hierarchy of
subordinates to build plausible deniability, to give orders to
someone who gave orders to a subordinate and so on down the
line, so nothing could ever be tied back directly to him. It was
all a sham, certainly the western intelligence agencies knew the
exact identity of the crime boss of the Oligarchs, and knew
much of his illegal wealth.

One of Lider's favorite Oligarchs sponsored a vast private
army, complete with armored vehicles that rivaled the Russian
army in size. This private army had invaded the Ukraine, and
the Lider shrugged and told the West that he was powerless to
stop the invasion, it was just Ukrainian freedom fighters, which
was laughable. Only the most naïve believed him, but nobody
called him out. A succession of U.S. Presidents had made

occasional statements, but never did anything substantial about the situation. The Lider believed that aggression worked, and that philosophy was successful so far.

The Lider was a Great Russian. The Czar was a Great Russian, and Stalin was a Great Russian. Above everything else they were defenders of the Mother Russia. Germans may call their nation The Fatherland, the U.S. has Homeland Security, but since its founding Russians have thought of their country as The Motherland. It's part of the language. *Rodina,* Motherland.

A Fatherland can be an outward looking aggressor, but a Motherland must be defended against penetration from a foreign invader. That's why Stalin insisted on having the Soviet bloc countries surrounding Russia's western boundary after World War II. Never again would invaders' tanks be able to pull up unimpeded to Russia's border. The Soviet dominated countries like Poland, Czechoslovakia, Hungary would be in the way. After the collapse of Communism the threat of neighboring countries joining NATO alarmed the Russian people who looked for a strong man as a savior. The *Rodina* was being threatened. The Lider stepped into the leadership void.

The Lider was initially very popular with the Russian people. His popularity had waned somewhat, but he'd probably still win a free election by a wide margin. To avoid any potential upset his goons made sure the elections were rigged, but Russians didn't trust Democratic reformers all that much. Disappearance of crusading free speech reporters was something that had happened in Russia for hundreds of years, and the midnight knock on the door from the Secret Police continued unabated from the Czars, to the Communists, to the current regime of the Lider.

The western media didn't understand Russia, Oleg thought. The country hadn't changed for a thousand years. The Russian people craved a strong leader, and feared chaos over repression. In the reign of the Czar, the Emperor surrounded himself with the Boyars, the supposed nobility who lived in splendor, while the common folk lived pitiful existences. Russia still lived by the principles of Mercantilism, the old philosophy that there were a fixed amount of riches, and the strongest got the lion's share, leaving the crumbs to the masses. The Western democracies had gotten beyond that with a more modern belief that an expanding economy created more wealth that could lift more people into a middle class existence. Oleg knew in his heart that deep down a Russian would never accept the more modern theory.

Now the Lider was the Czar, and the Oligarchs were the Boyars. Any hope of democratic reform would be stamped out during the first hint of an economic downturn. Fifty generations of people had been bred to value cheap vodka and black Russian bread over free elections. The ruling class knew this and used the philosophy to loot as much of the Mother Country's resources as they could stuff in their pockets, or Swiss bank accounts.

It wasn't in a Russian's nature to be happy. Turgenev knew that the Lider was not content with being so wealthy and powerful. His contentment came from always acquiring more, and the Lider was far wealthier than any Czar. He stole Russia's wealth, just like the Czars, but being a modern man used it as leverage to steal from the world. More and more he was using the World Wide Web. It was so much more cost efficient to hire thousands of hackers for what would have been the cost of developing one new jet fighter system. Oleg got to go along for the ride.

Oleg was 6'4" and some considered him gaunt. He was lean and angular, and wouldn't have been instantly identified as a Russian. Turegnev had disdain for many fellow countrymen his age with their spreading bellies and puffy faces, results of vodka, over-eating and lack of exercise. In their too tight clothes the flabby fools thought of themselves as sex symbols to young women, who were attracted to them solely by their wallets. Turgenev worked out at a gym every day whether he was in Moscow or his more frequent home in Brooklyn. Oleg went through the training regimen of a boxer, and hit a heavy bag hard enough to scare onlookers, but when push came to shove he'd prefer not hitting an enemy when it was so much easier to just shoot them, or in more recent years, have one of his men shoot the opponent when there was no alternative solution.

The two met at the Lider's Moscow apartment, which more than 100 years before had been the living quarters of an Archduke, the uncle of the Czar. The Lider himself had directly called Oleg on his cellphone, which was his way in these private meetings. No secretary was involved. When The Lider called you wouldn't be late.

Years ago, the first time Oleg had entered the complex, he had been surprised by the lack of security. There wasn't any pat down by security personnel, and no apparent metal detector screening. It was much simpler on its face than entering the Manhattan office of an investment advisor.

It wasn't as though The Lider trusted anybody. But it had occurred to Turgenev that the people like himself who were invited to this less formal kind of meeting with The Lider were worldly enough to know that anyone doing harm to the Russian leader would suffer almost unimaginably horrible consequences, and that by itself was sufficient to provide security. The Lider had displayed to Oleg the embalmed head, in a jar, of a man who had been foolish enough to try to use a smattering of counterfeit $100 bills among the mostly genuine currency in a payment to consummate a business deal with the President.

To Oleg, The Lider's office looked like a baroque whorehouse with the ornate curtains and fancy white carved furniture with gold highlights, but in the interest of his own longevity Oleg pretended to be impressed. Turgenev now spent most of his time in New York and his apartment in Brooklyn was decorated in a clean modern style.

As always their meeting was just the two of them, no secretary or cronies of The Lider in attendance. In private the Russian leader didn't bother with the forced smiles he used before the TV cameras, but grim faced had gestured for Oleg to have a seat in his office, while he sat in a chair behind his desk that a Czar could have used as a portable throne.

"Now Oleg. You may have noticed there's some social unrest un Russia these days," The Lider started.

Turgenev noted The Lider's knack for understatement. People had been openly protesting and rioting in the streets of the big cities in Russia. Their main issue was the corruption in the The Lider's regime. They were tired of The Lider's extreme greed. Some stealing by the head of government was expected, but Russian President was lining his pockets at an unparalleled clip, and the regular folks were not seeing any improvement in their lives.

"Yes sir," Turgenev replied.

"I have a plan for calming the situation. It will be the biggest financial windfall in history. It will allow our government to send a substantial check to every Russian citizen. Of course, there will be a bit left over to reward me my fair share. I am thinking my fair share will be 50%." The Lider laughed.

The man does have balls. That's how he got where he is. "Mr. President, you are always five moves ahead of me," Turgenev said.

"Oleg," The Lider began, "The government of the United States has started to spend money quite recklessly. It used to be the Democrats who were the spenders, while the Republicans

24

showed some restraint. Now there's no restraint by either party. I have worked hard to cultivate chaos in their country, and it's succeeding beyond my initial hopes. Their lack of discipline had created inflation in the real world, if not yet fully reflected in the financial markets, and this sloppiness provides opportunities for us. An attacker always looks for a seam, a weakness, a moment when his opponent is preoccupied with something else."

Oleg Turgenev had been the audience of one for some of The Lider's speeches before. The man did like to pontificate, but he was a thinker. Others had tried to occupy the office The Lider had now consolidated, but they were short term men of action who didn't think things through, or clownish drunks like Yeltsin. The Lider always had a long range plan, and he used Oleg and others to listen to these plans.

The Lider went on, "The operation we now will commence against the Americans is something I have planned for many years. Compared to them, I am a Russian Chess Master and have plotted out many moves in advance, and those fools cannot even think one move ahead playing checkers! They're worried about the next congressional election. I have come up with a new phrase to describe our philosophy in the upcoming operation."

The Lider stopped speaking. It was quiet in the room. The Lider stared poker faced at Oleg. To break the tension Oleg asked, "Mr. President, what is the phrase?"

Now The Lider smiled, pleased with himself as he announced the codename for his new initiative:

"Trillion is the New Billion!"

Six
Austin, TX

I thought of saying to Gabrielle that if she wanted to have a serious discussion that she might want to get dressed, but decided to compromise and just maintain eye contact. That was a mixed success.

"I've decided to go back in. I get to have my old Army rank and seniority."

"You...uh... don't get shot enough in civilian life?" I asked.

"I'm not going back in the Rangers. No combat stuff. I'm going into Cyber Command."

"You mean stopping hackers, and like that?"

"Yeah, and a little more serious than that," Gab said, "There are some serious threats from enemy countries."

"How do you know about that stuff? Weren't you in the shooting people end of the business?" I asked.

Gab, soon again to be Captain Gabrielle McHugh, looked at me with tolerance. "I studied the Cyber stuff during downtime in the Rangers. There's a lot of downtime. I'm good at it. I was third in my Class at West Point, remember?"

"Hey, so what, I was sixth on the Golf Team at the University of Texas," I pointed out.

"Very impressive. If they have an opening for a golf pro at Fort Meade should I give them your name?" Gab said.

"Nah, I'm a terrible golf instructor. No patience. Fort Meade, that's in---"

Gab interrupted, "Fort Meade, is in Maryland, outside D.C."

"Yeah, now I remember. I grew up near there." I said.

"I'm going to work for Cyber Command. That's a joint task force that all the separate services ultimately report to. I can't tell you much about it---"

I laughed, and said in my best upper crust English accent 'yeah I know, it's all very hush-hush, and hoosh-hoosh."

"What?"

I tilted my head. "It's a line from one of my favorite old movies, *Mad, Mad---*"

"You and your movies. I never get any of your old movie references." Gabrielle was losing her patience at my irreverence when she was trying to be serious.

"Ok, sorry. I clown around when I get nervous," I answered.

"Why are *you* nervous?" Gabrielle asked.

"Gabrielle, I, well… I think I'm in love with you." As soon blurted it out I wished I could get it back. Not that I didn't mean it, but I had no idea of the repercussions. I was embarrassed.

She stood back and looked at me then came over and kissed me hard. On the lips, not a friend kiss, not a kiss from your sister, a very romantic kiss. Then she stood back again.

Seven
Moscow

The Lider looked pleased with himself. Why not, he had come from nothing and become perhaps the world's richest man. Now he had another plan to make vastly more money.

Oleg puzzled, "Mr. President, I don't really under—"

The Lider raised his hand, and Oleg stopped speaking in mid-word. "There are so many billionaires. You, of course, and deservedly so. But now there are these Silicon Valley punks in tee shirts and Chinese twenty five year-olds who have done nothing more than be aggressive in business for a couple years. I don't want to be lumped into their status. My plan will make me the first Trillionaire, several times over, in U.S. dollars of course."

Turgenev had carried a Zimbabwe One Hundred Trillion Dollar bill around in his wallet, and had once shown it to The Lider, but Oleg didn't think this was the time to take the bill out.

"Sir, I don't know how many pallets of one hundred dollar bills that would be."

The Lider and Turgenev had consummated a deal that entailed a payment by Oleg of over $6 billion, in one hundred dollar bills, stacked on pallets and transported around The Lider's warehouse by forklift trucks. The Russian President had boasted that he had the largest collection of $100 bills in the world, that he had taken so many out of circulation that the U.S. Treasury had to print many more than projected.

The Lider shook his head. "No, I'm getting out of the cash business. In fact, your fee for helping me in this transaction is the $6 billion in cash you paid me last year. I'm going all electronic. Bitcoin and some of the other cryptos are going to be my new currencies. I'll do Bitcoin first. I suggest you make the conversion.. after me."

Oleg understood. "Of course."

The Lider continued, "Do you know how many banks I will end up owning? My flagship bank in the U.S. will be.....Bank of America!"

The two stared at each other for a moment, then The Lider burst out laughing. "I'm bullish on America! I'll control their economy!"

Eight
Austin, TX

I've been kissed more than a few times. It's not like I'm a sixteen year old girl, I don't keep a kiss diary.

But that kiss from Gabrielle was the best, the Number One kiss I ever got in my life.

And what did I do to respond to this beautiful woman in dripping wet underwear when she kissed me? Nothing. I sat there like a dope, didn't know what to do.

Gabrielle stood back, smiling at me. "JR, I'm going back for a dip in the pool...don't follow me. That wasn't an invitation."

If I ever figure women out I'll write a book. The guys who write books about how women think are faking it.

"Ok, it wasn't an invitation. What was it then?" I asked.

Gabrielle shrugged. Observation: A beautiful woman in wet underwear looks even better when she shrugs.

We faced off in silence for a moment. Then Gabrielle said, "I'm confused about my feelings for you."

That was progress. I answered, "You probably have those feelings because I saved your life."

She laughed. "JR, I'm the one who saved *your* sorry ass."

"Well, I knew it was something like that," I said.

Nine
Austin, TX

The rest of that day I tried to pay attention to the Stock Market, but my mind kept coming back to Gabrielle. It was okay, the market was not to my liking, and I wasn't doing anything in the client accounts. The Tech sector was very hot, and so-called investors who considered five days to be long term investing were trading every headline on CNBC. I was a Value guy, and the market currently hated Value, it wanted stories about Tech stocks that were going to change the world.

I couldn't get too excited about how robot vacuum cleaners were going to usher in the new millennium, even though I had one of those gadgets, which I liked and called 'Milo', after the robot character in *Sleeper*. My housekeeper felt threatened by the robo-vacuum, and I think sabotaged it from time to time.

I looked at my messages. There was just one call I had to return, from Patrick, a long-time client. We had the same call every six months. Because I don't follow short term trends for client accounts, Patrick was always disappointed that he didn't own whatever was hot on CNBC that day.

I called. Patrick was disappointed that he didn't own Bitcoin.

"Ok Patrick, if you can explain it to me, I'll buy it for you," I told him.

"Well. It's up over 25% this week," he said.

"That's not much of an explanation," I said.

"I have a lot of money with you," he said.

"Yeah," I said. "If you're so rich, how come you're not smart?"

31

"That's a charming way you have about you," he said, "insulting your clients."

"Call me the next time you shoot under par. For 18 holes," I said. I knew that would be never.

I would never take the risk of buying Bitcoin for a client account. They trusted me to be conservative with their money. But I felt myself getting pulled in. There's something called "FOMO." It means 'Fear of Missing Out.' That's what I was experiencing. I decided to stick my toe in the water with Bitcoin. What was the worst that could happen?

Ten
Austin, TX

Gabrielle and I had to talk. When I had tidied up all my business for the day I walked over to the casita and knocked on the door. Gab answered. I stood on the stoop.

"How about if I make dinner tonight?" I asked.

"That would be fine, JR," Gabrielle answered.

"I'll grill us some chicken and make a nice salad. How's that?" As an afterthought I asked, "how long until you're leaving...to go back in the Army?"

"I'm leaving tomorrow morning," Gab said.

Oh.

When you live in Texas for a while you get to understand the difference between grilling and barbecuing. What people in New York call "barbecuing" is grilling. Just slathering on some sauce out of a bottle doesn't constitute barbecue. Poor folks invented proper barbecuing, taking a less expensive cut of meat and cooking it slowly. It requires skill, experience, and knowledge of spices. Flipping burgers is grilling, Brunswick Stew is barbecue.

My charcoal grill is out by the pool. I was grilling chicken legs bathed in Austin's own Leroy and Lewis sauce for Gabrielle, which she considered the height of fine cuisine. I had come to realize that the U.S. Army was good at many things, but educating their officers in the subtleties of fine dining was not one of them. Officers did get better cuts of meat than the enlisted personnel, Gabrielle explained, so sometimes the brass got prime rib when the privates got meat loaf.

Sophistication in food and investments were the two intellectual advantages I had over Gab, so I clung to them. She had me beat in just about everything else, including knowing how to kill people, which came in handy while we were in New York. It was a lot more expedient for Xena the Warrior Princess to shoot Robert Stanton Banks than for me to try to get him to choke to death on a pulled pork sandwich, for example.

Our entire dinner that evening consisted of several chicken legs and a salad of delicious local heirloom tomatoes and lettuce, accompanied by a few beers I had on ice in a cooler by the table. Gab didn't snack between meals, but when she did eat the woman was not shy about consumption. She would have eaten as many chicken legs as I cooked, and washed down the chicken with a couple beers.

Conversation during the meal was about Bitcoin. Gabrielle asked if I was getting in. I assumed she was making polite conversation, a way of putting off talking about our relationship.

"I bought some today," I admitted, "just for myself. I mostly did it out of boredom."

"Is this something you might invest a lot of money in?" she asked.

"I wouldn't necessarily call it investing," I answered. "We'll see what happens."

When we were done Gab's plate had a pile of chicken bones twice as big as mine. But she had such a high revving engine and great discipline that I thought she'd never put on any excess weight. When Gabrielle had been doing pushups maybe two weeks after being shot in the chest, I asked her if it was painful. "What do you think?" she said. End of discussion, and she kept doing the pushups.

Food finished, we sat facing each other across the patio table with our hands clasped. Gab chuckled at our matching poses, but still neither of us talked.

The thought stuck me that I wanted to grow up, to have somebody to share my life with, and if I could be persuasive enough I might stop Gabrielle from going back in the Army. It wasn't like me to go for broke in investing, in golf, or on the rare occasions that I participated in real life, but on the spur of the moment I blurted, "If you married me I'd take you to the Tour D'Argent on our honeymoon."

"What!" Gab said. "What are you taking about?" She sat back with her arms folded, the smile gone from her face.

"It's a restaurant in Paris, near Notre Dame. Kind of a tourist trap, but for rich tourists. The French go to more sophisticated places. The house specialty is duck," I explained. I was babbling like an idiot.

Still with her arms folded she took a deep breath. "I wasn't talking about the Tour Whatever. Married you?" she said.

"Yeah, I guess I just sort of skimmed over that part," I said.

"You want to marry me?" she asked.

I sat there not knowing what to say next. I wished I could read her mind, but she wasn't showing any emotion. She didn't seem to be taking this discussion all that seriously. Gab's expression was more like I had asked her if she wanted to go to the Dairy Queen for dessert. My hopes were deflating.

Finally she smiled. Gab was even more beautiful when she smiled. "Well, you're the first to ask me that. The first man, that is."

I scratched my chin. "Well, that's some feather in my cap," I said.

Eleven
Bali, Indonesia

"Thank you Annisa."

The Indonesia servant girl silently bowed and backed away without making eye contact with her mistress. Annisa was dressed in traditional local garb, called a kemben, a multicolored wraparound dress, this one primarily gold and blue batik. It exposed the shoulders and arms, ideal for the steamy Balinese climate.

The mistress of the abode mused to herself that she was wearing a version of the kemben, but hers was an oversized beach towel which she had donned when she emerged from her pool. The towel was tucked around her torso with nothing on beneath. Her naked sunbathing would have scandalized the nuns at her Catholic school back in Queens, but this was as far away from Queens as you could be on Earth.

She sat under a slatted trellis which supported a lavish climbing vine, what she thought of as wisteria, but she didn't know if that was something that grew in Bali. She didn't know much about the flora and fauna of Bali, just that there were way too many lizards. The slats and the vines only let dappled sunlight through, but she had a spectacular tan anyhow. She didn't think she could ever be this bronze. It was a different, more lasting tan than she used to get in the summers at Jones Beach. Those New York tans used to flake away unevenly in a couple days. Quinn was an exhibitionist, but there was nobody here she wanted to impress.

Annisa and her twin sister Surya were tiny, brown, and beautiful, and been sold by their parents to the previous master of the mansion in which they served. They had perfect complexions and smiles, and these features enabled their

37

parents to demand a high price when they were sold to corporation of the man who previously owned the premises. He was recently dead, and they now served this American woman, but only as domestic servants, not for the other types of duties that were assumed, but never having been demanded because the man was killed before he ever inhabited this Balinese mansion. The sisters were told by a Russian man that they remained part of the property, and they had pleasant and undemanding chores once their new mistress arrived.

The mistress tried to focus. This whole thing was unreal. Eight weeks before she might have been getting herself coffee from the messy break room in the Detective Bureau of the Manhattan South precinct. She used to tell macho cops who asked her to get them coffee to shove it. Now she had servants bringing whatever she wanted. It didn't seem like she ever was really here.

Sierra Quinn, mistress of all she surveyed, was bored stiff. She was having her second drink of the day, and it was only 12:30. Here she was living in a tropical paradise, with more money than she ever imagined she'd have, in a mansion with servants and she hated it.

A few months ago she had experienced the most exciting weeks of her life, and then she'd been ordered to go to Indonesia and the excitement stopped. But if she hadn't fled New York she's be dead or in jail awaiting trial by now.

Quinn had killed people in New York, some of them innocent, some of them scum, but felt no regret about any of it. She was a killer. Sierra got a powerful rush of adrenaline the first time she killed a man, this one being self-defense and in the line of duty, but she knew she would kill again, and not be bothered over whether it was justified. She had found her calling. The money was good for being a killer, but she admitted to herself that she'd do it for nothing. It wasn't the same as sex, it was better. After killing someone the satisfying feeling of power stayed with Quinn for days. Being on permanent vacation was a drag, she needed to have action.

She reflected on what had happened. Already a corrupt detective in Manhattan, and a part time hit-woman for criminal elements, Quinn had shot and killed Lola Madison, the movie star, and thought she had killed, but only wounded her bodyguard, Gabrielle McHugh at the behest of Money Manager Robert Stanton Banks. Also she had been a go-between in arranging a cash payment of over $6 billion from Banks to a Russian Oligarch named Oleg Turgenev, the cash laundered Columbian drug money through a Panamanian bank. She pretended not to know that the cash was ultimately a payoff of some kind from Turgenev to The Lider. She didn't think it was in her best interests to know the details.

That had been an exciting few weeks for a girl from Queens whose father was a beat cop. Quinn knew she had lost her soul, and didn't care. It was a bargain she'd made with herself. Sierra had made the observation that the successful people she had come in contact with all had one thing in common: they lived outside the normal rules. The Police and Political bigwigs in New York, The Russian crook, the Money Manager, the Movie Star all in their own ways existed as though the rules didn't apply for them. Quinn decided she'd live outside the rules too.

The dark side of life appealed to her, and her only right or wrong was whether she got what she wanted. People got killed every day and somebody was going to do it. Sierra had seen the daily grinding drudgery of the vast majority of peoples' lives, and the slimy corruption in Queens and Manhattan. The corrupt bosses seemed to have better lives than most, but she realized that it was more about power than money, and somebody from below was always trying to knock the bosses off their perches, so their lives were spent looking over their shoulders, worried about who was coming after them. But killing someone was the ultimate exercise of power, and she didn't have any whiny people reporting to her.

Quinn had been present at the transfer of the $6 billion at an airport in Panama. Six billion in one hundred dollar bills entails multiple pallets of cash, each so large that it had to be loaded by a forklift truck into the belly of a Russian military transport. It was literally tons of money.

After the money was loaded Oleg Turgenev came over to Quinn on the airport tarmac and handed her an envelope. "Open it," he said.

It was a First Class plane ticket to Jakarta, Indonesia, in the name Patricia Sizemore, the false passport name under which Sierra Quinn was traveling. She was confused, but knew that something from Turgenev was best considered an order, not a suggestion. Oleg Turgenev's criminal operatives in New York had put many who opposed them in 55 gallon drums and dumped them in the ocean. The 55 gallon drum had become Turgenev's criminal trademark, and she had no desire to be the occupant of one of the barrels. She hoped that if someday she had to go in the barrel at least they'd kill her before dumping her in the drink. It was said that Turgenev's men sometimes put living people in the barrels. This treatment was rumored to be reserved for miscreants who particularly irked the Russian.

"You are now the President of a vast resort in Bali. The former head of the resort is recently deceased. You'll be met at the airport in Jakarta and more will be explained at that time. I am about to embark on some ventures where your expertise, and your pleasant appearance might come in handy," Turgenev said matter-of-factly to Quinn, as though that was something that happened regularly.

By recently deceased, Turgenev meant the just shot dead, still warm Robert Stanton Banks, who had used the billions he had skimmed off from his Hedge Fund to build the resort in Bali.

Banks had intended to leave the U.S., have plastic surgery, get a new identity and passport, and end up as an Indonesian citizen. Just in case, Indonesia which includes Bali, had no extradition treaty with the U.S. The plan almost worked, except that JR Johnson had figured out his Ponzi scheme, and along with Gabrielle McHugh had shot and killed him just as he was about to fly out of New York for good.

Turgenev's criminal organization had uncovered Banks' plan, and had seized control of the corporation which was formed in the Cayman Islands. The Cayman Islands bank that had been used to create Banks' Indonesian resort sold Turgenev the resort for one dollar, after Turgenev had told them they would either make the sale or end up in oil drums at the bottom of the deep ocean shelves just of the coast of Grand Cayman Islands. The Resort was called Nitup.

"I am parking you in Bali," Turgenev had said. "I am saving you for important missions."

Turgenev continued, "I employ some very dangerous people, but none of them are attractive women who might be able to get access to areas I might find to be vital. Go to Bali and relax. It will be a while before I contact you."

Twelve
Bali, Indonesia

Quinn was now considered a missing person by the New York
Police Department, but they weren't spending any time looking
for her. The decomposed body of a female with Sierra's body
type was found in a shipping container in New Jersey, but the
DNA didn't match Quinn's and no other leads came along.
The usual street level police informants had nothing, not even a
rumor regarding her whereabouts. Police bosses vaguely
assumed that maybe Turgenev had put her in one of his oil
drums, but they weren't very interested in finding her alive. A
dead Sierra Quinn would have been no concern to them, but
alive and in New York would pose serious problems for the
brass.

Sierra Quinn was the rottenest of apples, and nobody in New
York law enforcement had any desire to put her on trial. Not
one official at One Police Plaza thought that having Quinn in a
court room and exposing the lack of supervision and beyond
rule-of-law criminality under which she had operated would do
any good for the reputation of New York's Finest, or help any
of them complete their tours of duty for the pension.

From time to time Quinn visited the General Manager of the
property. The manager, an Indonesian, had given her detailed
financial updates. Quinn didn't understand some of the
financial minutiae, but kept silent and nodded a lot.

During their first meeting Sierra said to the manager, "You do
understand who really controls this property?"

The Indonesian looked down at his hands. He was silent. Thin,
and meticulously dressed in his western businessman white
shirt and tie, he was sweating. The man had seemed nervous
when the discussion began, and now began shallow breathing.

Quinn was enjoying the moment. She had scheduled the meeting just for something to do, but it was obvious that the manager thought he was being audited somehow, maybe at the direction of the Russians.

"It's not necessary to discuss anyone specifically. But you understand that these are dangerous men?" Quinn asked.

"Yes. Yes, Mrs. Quinn."

She didn't bother correcting the manager. Her marital status was none of his business. "It's important for you to correctly account for every penny," she said.

The manager swallowed hard, and his face was bathed in sweat. "Mrs. Quinn, there are no irregularities. I swear this is completely accurate!"

Quinn had to bite down on her tongue to keep from smiling. This wasn't as good as shooting somebody, but she was enjoying torturing the man, an unplanned but amusing diversion. She kept a stern demeanor.

"That's good. As long as things stay that way, you won't have any problems," she said.

The manager nodded, but said nothing.

Quinn stood and said, "Until we meet again."

She was intentionally vague about the timing of another meeting because she wanted to keep the man off balance. Sierra mused that she might just be getting the hang of being an international criminal. It was better than walking a beat in Queens.

Thirteen
Bali, Indonesia
The Nitup Resort

Quinn had heard nothing from Turgenev. That morning she decided that it had been too long since she had a man in her bed, and resolved to take care of that situation.

Her mansion was part of the resort property, but walled off from access by the guests. Sierra had a driver, but that morning took the convertible Jeep, and had told her bodyguard that she'd be visiting the resort by herself, something she had done a few times.

This morning she drove past the hotel. Quinn had no interest in meeting the General Manager. She was going to the beach, looking for a man to bring back to her bed.

The Jeeps belonging to the resort were painted a custom aqua color, and when Sierra parked at the beach in a restricted area the lifeguards and other personnel knew better than to reprimand, or even make eye contact with Quinn. The beach was long and narrow with sand that was so white it looked unreal, some of it pure white marble dust that was trucked in from a mine and well mixed with the natural sand. The beach was dragged every morning to smooth out the footprints from the previous day and the water was a protected lagoon with a narrow opening in a breakwater to the open sea beyond. The whole effect was a man-made paradise. There were almost no waves, adventurous guests who wanted to surf went to other parts of the property.

This area was for sunning, sitting in groups by one of the several thatched roofed cabanas, drinking, and taking an occasional dip in the unthreatening tropical water, the point of the entire scene was preening for members of the opposite sex.

There were more men than women. The tourists were primarily Australians, with some Euros and a few Americans. The American men were easily distinguished by the relative modesty of their bathing suits, they just couldn't give in to the barely there stretch bikinis favored by the others, and the Aussie men unashamedly wore models that would have been considered daring in a gay bath house in Quinn's native New York.

Sex tourism is a popular draw in Bali, and many men at the resort who couldn't find women to hook up with during the day boarded buses at night for tours of the off-site sex compounds. Prostitution was banned at the resort, but the hotel ran regularly scheduled shuttles to the brothels.

Sierra, dressed in a modest short terry cloth robe and large sunglasses, walked from her Jeep to the beach and surveyed the area, looking for a candidate to bring back to her house. After a few minutes she saw a tall man with a thin, wiry, muscular body and a towel around his neck. Judging from the skimpiness of his bathing suit she guessed him an Aussie. He seemed to be by himself.

She walked up to him. "Hello, I'm...Sarah," she improvised.

He stuck out his hand and said, "Sarah, eh? I'm Lucky. Lucky Lidinski." They shook hands.

He had such a strong working class Australian accent she had a hard time understanding him.

Sierra didn't care, but did ask, "What's your real name?"

"Mark is my real name. Everybody calls me Lucky."

"Are you here by yourself?" Sierra asked.

"Yip."

Quinn said, "I'll be blunt. I'm looking for male companionship for the next hour. Then somebody who can keep their mouth shut."

Lidinski said, "I can keep my mouth shut *afterward*. I may have my mouth open some *during*."

He was enough of a macho slob to be a New York detective. But he did have a great body. Lucky was standing by a towel spread out on the sand. "Are those your clothes?" Quinn asked, pointing to a pair of shorts and a t-shirt.

"Yeah," he said.

"Put them on and meet me at the Jeep," she said pointing to the vehicle. The she turned and walked away.

A moment after she was behind the wheel, Lidinski let himself in the passenger side.

"Well Lucky," Quinn said, "you're about to live up to your nickname."

"I've always been Lucky," he said. Quinn drove away.

Fourteen
Bali, Indonesia

Sierra had driven fast partly in an attempt to make enough road noise with the open topped Jeep to avoid any small talk. The trip took less than five minutes.

She couldn't completely avoid conversation. Lidinski asked, "You're not a copper, are you?"

"No," she answered. *Not anymore.* "Why, are you a crook?"

"Not entirely," Lidinski answered.

"What does that mean?" Quinn asked.

"I run a used auto parts business," Lidinski said.

"So?" Quinn asked.

"From time to time the constabulary has questioned the legality of where the parts came from," he said.

"Oh, so you run a chop shop. You ever been in prison?" she asked. Quinn wasn't sure she needed a man bad enough to have sex with someone who'd done time. There were sexually transmitted diseases going around prisons for which medical science had yet to find cures.

"Nah. I've got a good barrister. He straightens out the misunderstandings," he said.

Once during the ride Lidinski openly stared at Quinn, checking out her body. There wasn't much to see with her cloth robe on except for her spectacular tanned legs. Their eyes met, then they looked away.

When the Jeep pulled in the circular driveway of the mansion Lidinski let out a low whistle. "You live here?" he asked.

"That's not important for you to know. In fact, you should forget it." Quinn said.

"No worries," he answered.

When they entered through the ornate engraved metal doorway and walked through the foyer there was no staff. It would seem to an outsider that they were alone. Lidinski followed Sierra up a short flight of stairs and though a hallway into her massive bedroom.

After Quinn closed the door she gestured for Lucky to stand where he was, then she walked the twenty feet over to the nightstand by her bed. She was relieved that she had stocked the drawer with condoms, especially with this character. It also held other protective equipment.

Sierra took off her robe, exposing the electric blue bikini she was wearing beneath. The color accentuated her tan. She took off her bikini top.

"What a wonderful world it is," said Lidinski, "for a trim looking Sheila to have such a great pair of Norks!"

Quinn had never heard that expression before, but did not require a translation. She had spent the last weeks sunbathing naked, so had no tan lines. The two of them were still twenty feet apart.

Lucky had been busy taking off his shirt and shorts, so he was down to just his skimpy swimsuit. "I got something to show you."

He dropped his bathing suit and was fully erect. It had been a while for Quinn and she was impressed by his manhood.

The cellphone rang on her nightstand.

"I have to answer this." Quinn said.

"Arrgh," Lucky said.

The call was from Turgenev. He told Sierra that he would be arriving at her home within an hour to discuss her next assignment. He hung up without any further conversation.

Quinn said, "Change in plans. You have to leave."

"I'm not bloody leaving! Give me fifteen minutes. It will be good for the both of us." Lucky started walking slowly toward Quinn.

Sierra turned to reach into her nightstand, and turned back to face Lidinski. She was holding a Glock 9mm with silencer, pointing it right at him. She slid back the action, chambering a round. Her face betrayed no emotion.

"I'm serious about you leaving," she said.

"Now drop the gun and drop your knickers! I'm not talking no for an answer at this point." He had a smirk on his face, confident that he would have his way with Quinn. Lidinski stepped more two paces toward her and now was no more than ten feet away.

Her right hand was steady. Sierra fired at Lucky's heart. The impact of the heavy round knocked him flat on his back. Still clad in just her bikini bottoms she bent over close to the Aussie, her feet on either side of his chest. He was still breathing, so she fired once more, into his forehead. Some of

49

his blood and brain matter splattered on Quinn's chest and legs. It excited her.

She stepped back and looked down at the dead man, and assumed he was still erect, since it was too soon for rigor mortis to have set in. That amused Quinn. She had not been able to have sex, but then she did get to kill someone.

"Now you're a Lucky stiff," Quinn said.

Fifteen
Bali, Indonesia
The Nitup Mansion

Quinn got dressed in clothes she thought more appropriate for her meeting with Turgenev, then walked in the hallway and called out to her driver. He appeared in seconds.

She waited until the driver was close enough so she could speak softly and be heard. "I need you to dispose of something for me. Come this way."

He followed her into the bedroom. When the driver saw Lidinski dead on the floor he betrayed no surprise.

"Do you have any special requests as to how the disposal be made?" he asked.

Quinn thought for a minute. "Get another guard that you trust. Wrap him up in the rug he's lying on and take him somewhere in the house out of the way. Then tonight take a boat, weigh him down, and dump him far enough out to sea that it won't create any problems."

Turgenev had hired the driver so Quinn assumed he would be trustworthy in this mission. "With your permission, we'll put him in an oil drum and dump that. It's a very effective solution. Is there anything else that you require?" he asked.

"The blood on the floor. Please clean that up." Quinn asked.

"Of course, ma'am." He said. "And ma'am?"

Quinn nodded.

"You can trust all the other guards. They'll never say a word," the driver said.

Sierra had gotten to shoot someone. One need fulfilled. She wondered about Turgenev. He was good looking man. Maybe this could work out to be a very good day.

Sixteen
Austin, TX

"Lola wanted to marry me," Gabrielle said.

"Oh." I said. "was that something that you wanted?"

"I had mixed feelings. It couldn't have happened for a while, because of Lola's career. We were talking about it," she said, "and I wasn't sure that I wanted to be a kept woman. I hadn't given up the idea of having my own career. I'm ashamed to admit that partly I thought about marrying Lola for the financial benefits. I wouldn't have ever worried about money again."

"You wouldn't be the first person to get married for that reason," I said. I thought for a second. "Besides, I knew Lola, she would have made you sign a prenup."

"We had already discussed that in general terms," Gab said.

I had pushed my chair back from the table. Gab then surprised me. She walked around to me and sat sideways on my lap. She ran her fingers through my hair.

I couldn't remember the last time a woman sat in my lap like that. It must have been in college. Lola had never done it, and Barbara Jean Parker hadn't either.

"Are you trying to drive me crazy?" I asked. "You're not a very convincing lesbian right now."

Gabrielle laughed, and tussled my hair. "I need to tell you about myself," she said, then stood up and went back to sit in her chair.

"I was an Army brat. My father was a colonel when he and my mother were killed in a car accident on the Autobahn. By then I was a junior in an American high school in Germany. We had lived in a million places," Gab explained.

"Were you close to your parents?, I asked.

"Yeah, I suppose. I was closer to my father, my mom was too subservient, like she was trying to be June Cleaver. I thought that was her idea, not like my father demanded it." she said. "Why do you ask?"

"Just curious," I said. "I wasn't that close to my family. My parents died about a year apart when I was in college."

"Oh," Gabrielle said. "Are you suggesting we have something in common?"

"No, I'm just blabbing. I'm sorry to interrupt," I said, "you were saying?"

"I'm trying to explain… why I am what I am," she said.

"And what is that, exactly?" I asked.

"How about I describe and you put a label on it?" Gab said.

"I'm not always the best label guy," I said. "That's not important. Please just tell me your story."

"After my parents died I went back to the states, to New Jersey. I lived with my mother's sister and her husband for the rest of high school.," Gab said.

"They were ok?" I asked.

"Oh yeah, they were nice. They could never have any kids, and I was only there for less than a year. They didn't know what to make of me. My aunt made up the spare bedroom for me, furnished like I was a nine year old girl. She even put a teddy bear on the bed. It was kind of quiet and lonely."

"Your uncle didn't.. you know, uh---," I stammered.

"Oh no! He was aloof, but nothing like that. When I left for West Point he shook hands with me. They pretty much just left me alone. They were even kind of cold toward each other, both of them had careers," Gab said.

"That must have been hard for you," I said.

"Remember that I was used to moving every couple of years, going to a new school. But this was different because none of the other kids had parents in the Army. I was just killing time. I had already applied to West Point. With my grades and extracurricular accomplishments I was going to get in, and any doubt of that was sealed when my father was killed. Military kids in that situation get special treatment."

"So, did you date…boys… in high school?" I asked.

"I was real naïve about sex. You probably can't relate, but in Germany I was the colonel's daughter, and a lot of the boys were intimidated by that. Plus I'm six foot three so that scared off the boys too."

"I have to admit that I was a bit intimidated when I first met you," I said. "But not so much that I wasn't attracted to you."

Gabrielle put her elbow on the table and rested her chin in her hand. She looked me right in the eye and smiled. "You're sweet, JR."

"Aw shucks, ma'am." I said.

She sat back and was quiet for a minute. Finally I said, "You don't have to tell me anything more."

"No, I'll tell you some more… but not everything just yet," she said.

"So, how did you discover your…feelings?" I was in over my head. I didn't want to embarrass Gabrielle. It was okay with me if she just stopped there.

"Did I ever tell you that I was an All American volleyball player in high school and college?" she asked.

"Nope."

"That doesn't have anything to do with this. I just dredged that up when I was trying to get my thoughts together about high school… You don't want to be on the other side of the net from me."

"I can see that." I said.

"Anyhow senior year in New Jersey this boy asked me to a dance and I went out. Afterwards we went to the make-out spot in his car and he got me in the backseat."

I wasn't sure if I wanted to hear the play-by-play details. "That's okay, you don't have to---"

Gabrielle plunged on, "he was naïve too. He started to grope me, to get his hand down my pants, but he was too aggressive and clumsy. I felt cold and afraid, so I told him to stop. He didn't at first, so I grabbed his wrist hard and asked him how he would explain it to his parents if he came home with a broken arm. That worked."

"So then what?" I asked.

"He was a nice boy, really. Afterwards I thought he was just doing that because he thought he was supposed to act that way," Gab said. "He drove me home and walked me to the door. I even gave him a little kiss on the forehead. He never bad mouthed me or lied about me in school or anything."

"That was it?" I asked.

"I walked in the house and told my aunt and uncle that I had a nice time and went up to my room. I turned on the TV and there was a music video on that changed my life. You know the Faith Hill song "Breathe"?"

"Yeah. Faith Hill's nice," I said.

"I thought so too. For the first time I admitted to myself that I would rather have Faith Hill kissing me, and touching me, than that boy," Gab said.

"As I said, Faith Hill's nice," I admitted.

"After that I got started with more than just music videos," she said. "I don't want to sound conceited, but if you're a good looking woman you get to have a lot of choices as partners. Part of the thrill is the forbidden pleasure. There are a lot of married women who are faking it, you know."

I'm smart enough to know that I don't know anything. This conversation reinforced that.

Seventeen
Austin, TX

After that revelation we both sat quietly for several minutes, I with my back to the street, Gabrielle facing the front. It was dusk and the temperature was just right. A perfect evening in Austin. I fished a beer out of the cooler, and offered it to Gab, but she declined. I opened it and took a long pull.

"Look at that," Gab said, pointing to the fence.

I turned around just in time to see a yellow Corvette convertible, top up, cruising slowly past the house. It was just dark enough that you couldn't get a good look at the driver.

"Hmmmm," said Gab.

I pretended not to notice. "So, tell me about your Army deal."

"Cyber Command is where the action is. A lot of the best minds think that's the next battleground. Why waste bombs and devastate property and lives when you can win with a few geniuses at computer keyboards?" Gab said.

"You've been on the phone making this deal. Who were you talking to?" I asked.

"Mostly I've been talking to my old CO, Colonel Powers," she said.

I laughed. "I can just picture Colonel Powers. An old guy with a crew cut and chomping on a cigar."

Gabrielle set her jaw and looked at me so sternly that I stopped smiling. "Colonel Powers is a woman. A …beautiful woman, and very ambitious. She's clever enough to have switched to Cyber Command, the fastest path to the top."

"Oh." I understood. Maybe.

"She and I have…. a history. This assignment is her way of…paying me back for a past injustice."

Eighteen
Austin, TX

Gabrielle had told me she'd take a taxi to the airport for her too early flight the next day, but I insisted I'd drive her. The alarm went off at 4:00 a.m., I took a quick shower and walked out to the pool.

I thought I'd have to knock on the door of the casita to get Gab, but she was standing there in her blue uniform with gold patches on the shoulders, like the old U.S. cavalry. She was wearing a black beret, and had her duffle bag next to her. Gab never slouched, but seemed to be standing even taller in her uniform. She didn't seem like the same Gabrielle of yesterday, the smiling woman sitting on my lap by the pool.

"I didn't realize that you'd wear your uniform for the flight," I said.

"I don't have to wear it, you just get a lot less shit when you travel in uniform," she said.

I couldn't imagine anybody giving Xena the Warrior Princess in her Army uniform even the smallest amount of shit. If the U.S. Army wanted to make a poster of what a woman officer should look like they'd be well advised to take a photo of Gabrielle standing there.

"You look great. I don't want to sound sappy, but you make me proud looking at you," I said.

"Yeah. Listen, when we get to the airport, it's not appropriate for you to give me a kiss. Just a little hug is okay," Gab said.

"Oh. All right," I answered.

"Give me a hug now," she said.

I went for an affectionate hug, but Gab was stiff and cold, giving me the Woman Leaning Forward Hug, so there can be no mutual pelvic touching. I hate that move. *What do you think, I'm gonna hump your leg like a dog? If you don't want to hug me, then just shake my hand.* She broke it off and stood back and picked up her duffel bag.

"Let's go," she said, "At least I didn't have to threaten to break your arm," she said.

"It's a strict guideline I live by. I never grope an officer in uniform," I said.

She didn't smile. I reached out to carry her duffel, but she stopped me with a withering look. "You carry your own bag," she snapped.

On the drive to the airport she asked, "So do you think you'll get strongly involved with Bitcoin?"

"I don't know. I could use a little excitement in my life," I said.

Gabrielle, who had never shown the slightest bit of curiosity about any of my other money maneuvering, asked "Does the Bitcoin trade on the Stock Exchange? What happens if someone outside the U.S. wants to trade Bitcoin when our markets are closed?"

"No it doesn't trade on a stock exchange. It's not a stock, it's a cryptocurrency. It never sleeps. You can find somewhere to trade it 24/7," I said. "Why the interest in Bitcoin?"

"It might be something I have to know about for my new job." She said.

"JR, as I told you, I'm confused about my feelings for you," Gab said. Then she contradicted her previous stated policy and gave me a big romantic kiss. "I….really don't know what to do."

"Well, I'm a little confused too," I said.

"I probably won't call you JR. It's not my way, and I'll be busy. You can call me if it's something important," meaning 'don't call if it's not important.'

She must have noticed the crestfallen look on my face. "JR, I'm going back to a different world. It's not a 9 to 5 job. I'm not saying don't call me. You can call me if it's important."

"I don't want you to leave. This is the first time in my life I didn't want to get rid of a woman. I always wanted Lola to leave," I said.

"I have to do this JR. We'll see what happens." Gab said.

Then she turned away and walked into the crowd going into the terminal. There were other soldiers going to flights, but they were all dressed in camo. Gab, Captain Gabrielle McHugh, was the only one in a more formal uniform. People got out of her way as she walked. The Warrior Princess was back in her element.

As she walked in the terminal I saw enlisted personnel notice her, and then snap to attention and salute. Unsmiling, she responded with the picture perfect salute of a West Pointer.

I absentmindedly walked back to my Ford F-150. She'd sit on my lap, then give me the sub-zero hug, give me a kiss, then tell me she wouldn't call me. I was the human ping pong ball of this relationship. *Was she just stringing me along? Why?* We hadn't resolved anything.

Nineteen
Austin, TX

The house felt empty the day after Gabrielle left. I thought that was strange. Empty was the normal status of the house. I lived there by myself for years, Gab was the only person who ever stayed for more than a few days. I felt lonesome. I had been pretty much alone in the world from the time I was eighteen years old, and this was the first time I felt lonesome.

I thought about how cold Gabrielle had been the morning I took her to the airport. Maybe she had to build that shell around herself, given how many times someone had to move during a military career, especially given her lifestyle. She didn't get to take the family along

It was always a relief when Lola had been there and left, but Gabrielle was different. We had interesting discussions, but now there was just me and my computer screens and the phone. I missed Gabrielle, but the smiling Gabrielle by the pool, not the cold eyed Captain McHugh of the final morning of her visit.

I had been meaning to call Barbara Jean Parker. We'd had a wild fling when we first went out, but I cooled it because I was still going out with Lola. Barb always told me that I was handsome, something that never seemed to occur to Lola to mention. Lola had spent a lot of time looking in the mirror.

I had no doubt that it was Barbara Jean spying through the fence. Also, she was a crack shot, had shooting contest medals hanging up in her den, and I thought she might take me on as a pupil. I called.

"Barb, how you doing?"

"Just fine and dandy, JR. I was wondering if you'd ever call me again," Barb answered.

"I was hoping I could come over sometime," I said.

"Sure. Is it just going to be you, or are you bringing the Viking assassin queen that's been staying with you?" Barb said pleasantly.

"How'd you know I had someone staying with me?" I asked.

No answer.

I continued, "it's just me. I was hoping you'd teach me how to handle a gun, to shoot better."

"Oh, you planning on shooting some more Hedge Fund boys?" Barb teased. Barbara Jean had a good honest laugh, and even on the phone you could picture her smiling. She always wore real red lipstick. It made her smile even more glamorous.

"Maybe. If I do shoot somebody again, I don't want them to be able to shoot back at me." When I had shot Banks in New York, I hit him in the neck, and although wounded he was able to raise his gun at me before Gabrielle, who I thought was dead, had sat up and finished him off.

"Sounds great. I've got all those trophies and medals, but you bagged a Wall Street tycoon. Maybe you can teach me about what it's like to actually shoot a person… I thought about shooting my ex-husband, or maybe *accidentally* running him over with the pickup truck, but I wanted to spend his money, not spend time on Death Row," Barb said.

"Oh c'mon Barb. Your lawyer would have been smart enough to have an all-male jury. You could have just worn a tight blouse and smiled at them. No way they'd convict you in Texas. Your husband done you wrong, and you're the church going former Homecoming Queen. Your finger just slipped on the trigger."

"Ooh, J. R. you sure know how to sweet talk a girl. Maybe you missed your calling. You could be one of those defense attorneys on the True Crime shows."

"Well Barb, you got all the cash and stocks. He kept the oil wells, and then the price of oil tanked. That was some pretty good revenge," I said.

"Yeah, and revenge is good," Barb said. "Just don't tell my minister I said that. I think the Bible is anti-revenge, the New Testament anyhow."

Barbara Jean's tone changed, "Are you serious about coming over and doing some shootin'?"

"Yeah…yes, I am. I want to get better at it," I said.

Barbara Jean lives on 100 acres in Spicewood, towards the real Hill Country to the West of Austin. It's about a half hour drive for me in my pickup truck, and maybe 20 minutes for Barb when she's driving her Corvette. She doesn't think that even the very flexible Texas speed limits apply to her.

Barb said, "Well you can come on over this evening. But remember, no drinking before shooting. Not even a beer. I'm real strict about that."

"Oh, I love it when you're strict! What time should I come over?" I asked.

"Could you come a little early, maybe five o'clock? Then maybe we'd have time for a little something else after the target practice," Barb said. "Is it going to be the old JR I was so fond of? Or is it going to be all talk, no action?"

"Uhh.," I cleverly replied. A little something else could be quite adventurous with Barbara Jean.

Twenty
Spicewood, TX

I drove up to the entrance of Barbara Jean's ranch. Framed by
sandstone columns, the gate was an imposing wrought iron
structure, with a custom made design, a circle in the middle
featuring Barb's cattle brand, a curly cue version of her initials,
BJP. The effect was grander than the stature of the ranch itself,
like entering Jurassic Park. You had to hit a buzzer and talk
through a speaker to get the gate buzzed open. It kept out the
riffraff. And Barbara Jean was a crack shot if someone
unwanted managed to get in.

The ranch was around 100 mixed acres, about half of it given
to grazing the 20 or so Black Angus cattle that Barbara Jean
raised. She had an old ranch hand take care of that operation,
which lost big money every year, and the whole deal was a tax
write-off. That was a pitiful number of cattle. Successful
cattlemen had properties of thousands of acres, with thousands
of head of cattle. But she had grown up in cattle country and
enjoyed having the herd. Not that you could get attached to an
individual animal, because when it was time the animal went to
the slaughterhouse. City folks thought the process was
distasteful, but then again they liked the Black Angus they ate
at Smith and Wollensky Steak House in New York, they just
didn't want to think about the process of how it got on their
plates.

Barbara Jean's house was a spectacular one story Spanish
influenced dwelling built by her ex-husband when he was
making millions in the Oil Business. The hand carved walnut
dual front doors with black wrought iron hinges were big
enough for a castle, and inside it had thick whitewashed stucco
walls and tile floors with a huge open living room complete
with a two-sided fireplace. It was too big for just Barb. She
talked about how her ranch hand Tommy lived with his wife

Alice in a comfortable suite of rooms in the horse barn, and how Barb would rather live there with three horses that the wife took care of, and Barb rode. Barbara Jean's son was away at Rice University, and her daughter attended Miss Porter's, a girl's prep school in Farmington, Connecticut. She lamented that they were both spoiled kids who knew how to play their father off their mother to get what they wanted, and there was no chance they'd ever return to live on the ranch.

I brought a bottle of Jack Daniels, because I didn't want to show up empty handed. Barb was strict about no drinking when shooting or riding the horses, but liked to kick back with a Jack and Ginger or two afterwards. I felt a little silly bringing the bottle, because there was a bar right there in the living room, always well stocked enough for an exclusive mid-sized hotel, but Barb was gracious about receiving the present. People do like to get presents, even people who don't need them.

Barbara Jean was old enough to have a son in college, but didn't look it. She had the same color blonde hair that she had decided on as a teenager, and I was pretty sure that her hair would always be that color, even if she made it to a hundred. It went just right with her blue eyes and her slightly weather-beaten tan. She was the kind of woman who filled out a blouse, and she was wearing one of those cowgirl snap-up numbers, tan with some red piping.

But Barb only wore a cowboy hat when she was riding a horse, even though she looked spectacular in her Stetson. She mostly wore a feed store baseball cap, her medium length hair pulled in a ponytail sticking out of the back of the adjustable hat. I hadn't seen women dressed like this in Manhattan, but even the best looking New York socialites weren't any more attractive than Barbara Jean, and the Gotham City ladies spent a lot more time and money on their looks. Barb cleaned up nice for Social Events in Austin, but no matter how she dressed there was always that sense of genuine country in Barb, and she could more than hold her own in conversation with the Billy Bobs if they tried to give her a hard time.

What most people noticed first was her smile. She smiled easily and it lit up a room. If you walked into a crowded party and didn't know Barbara Jean, the combination of her figure, her blonde hair, red lipstick and her smile would make you give her more than just a passing glance. She knew it, and used it to her benefit. I always told her she'd have been successful in the investment business. Every old horn toad in Texas would be falling all over her to give her their money.

Barbara Jean gave me that smile when I gave her the bottle of Jack Daniels. "Why thank you, JR, how thoughtful. I'll just put it up here on the bar so it'll be handy for us later." Her momma had taught her how to be the polite hostess. She mused for a minute. "You know, I like Jack Daniels better than all that fancy custom distilled stuff everybody's making such a big deal about these days."

"Well, you know me. I'd just as soon have a couple of Pearl beers when we're done shootin'," I said.

"My daddy calls Pearl beer 'Sod-y Pop'. Then again, that man can drink prodigious amounts of Jack Daniels and still be standing up," she said.

I wanted to ask Barbara Jean if that had been her spying between the fence posts, but I pretty much already knew the answer, and thought that subject would be better to discuss after we were done shooting.

"Yup, shooting is what we're going to be doing for the next hour or so. I've got three different pistols I'm going to give you a little tutoring on." She made her hand into the shape of a gun, just like a little kid does, and pulled the trigger a few times, but not pointing at me. Barb was really serious about gun safety, and wouldn't even point a loaded finger at another person.

That's one thing about country folks. They were brought up around guns, and they had a different attitude. Guns were just part of their lives and they were comfortable around the weapons, but were serious about safety. They wouldn't point a gun at another person just for fun, any more than a city person would hold a butcher knife at the throat of someone as a gag.

Barbara Jean learned how to hunt as a kid. Shooting a varmint like a coyote didn't bother her for one second. If she didn't shoot the coyote it would eat one of the chickens. It was like a city dweller swatting a fly.

We walked to Barbara's shooting range out behind the barn. There was a gully that served as a natural containment zone for bullets. Sometimes the shots would ricochet off rocks, but at enough distance to be harmless.

Barbara Jean held up a Colt.45 single action revolver. "They call this weapon 'The Peacemaker', at least in the movies."

"That's the model of gun I shot Banks with," I said, as though I was telling her something.

She looked at me impatiently. "Yeah, I read that in the papers."

I had taken the Colt off a dead lawyer who until the time Gabrielle shot him was my defense attorney. But then again he was trying to kill Gab and me, an apparent conflict of interest, even in New York. I had jammed the Colt under my belt and carried it on a drive in downtown Manhattan traffic and carried it unseen into Banks' office.

She gestured to the revolving chamber of the Colt. "they call this a six shooter, but you only load it with five bullets if you have any brains," Barbara Jean explained.

"Why is that?" I asked.

"Because it's a very old technology, and doesn't have a safety, so you leave one chamber unloaded. Then you have to cock the gun to revolve the chamber to have a bullet to shoot. You have to cock it for every shot."

"I didn't do that, I just pulled it out of my pants and shot Banks." I didn't know that you had to cock the gun between shots.

Barbara Jean thought about that for a second. "The lawyer must have had it cocked just before Gabrielle shot him, so when you picked it up it was ready to go. No safety or anything when you stuffed it in your pants. You're lucky you didn't shoot your dick off."

"Yeah, and it's such a big target," I added.

"I've seen bigger," Barbara retorted.

"Well, when you've seen thousands of them, there's bound to be a couple that are bigger," I said.

Barb just waved me off. "Very funny," she said.

We stood in the late day heat. The heat in this part of Texas was not the oppressive humid swampiness of Houston, or the dry desert oven outside of El Paso. It was a compromise between the two. A humid oven. You got used to it. It was quiet, especially in comparison to the concussive noise when we began shooting. I glanced around, and thought about how different this bleached out, barren landscape was than the humid green of the Maryland of my youth.

"Shut up and listen. I'm teaching you here." Barbara Jean was in Weapons Instructor mode and was now as serious as she gets.

"Here's the number one principle: don't put your finger on the trigger unless you intend to shoot" Barb said.
"Okay," I said.

For a minute a cold chill ran through me. First- I had recklessly driven quite a distance in Manhattan with a gun down my pants, aimed pretty much at my pecker, without knowing that the weapon was ready to go off. A fender bender could have been quite painful. Second- I had pulled the gun out and shot Banks by just pulling the trigger, not knowing that the gun had to be cocked between shots. So when I went to shoot him the second time, I thought the gun had jammed, but it was just that I didn't know how to use it. Gabrielle knew how to use her weapon and dropped Banks once and for all.

Barbara Jean looked pensive. "I wonder why the lawyer had the Colt single action. There are a lot better weapons for the job he was trying to do. It must have been a family heirloom or something."

Being a complete novice, I ventured no opinion.

Barb taught me how to load the Colt. It doesn't open up, but you load each bullet from the back as the cylinder revolves. I just put in five.

"OK, let's fire some rounds. JR, for the first shot, hold the weapon at hip level. Like in the cowboy movies, aim at the target and fire."

I did as instructed and completely missed the silhouette of a person was only about 25 yards away.

"Don't feel bad, pretty much nobody can hit anything shooting like that without a lot of practice. It just looks cool in the movies." Barbara Jean then showed me how to hold the Colt with two hands at eye level, and I pointed at the target and hit it, nowhere near the heart or head, but I did hit it.

It was surprising how loud each shot was, and how much the gun jerked up. The smell of gunpowder was strong. I thought back to New York. I hadn't noticed the noise or smell of the gunfire, but then again in Banks' office I had been involved in a mortal combat situation for the first time in my life, and my brain must have been functioning on a more primitive level.

Now I was just engaged in target practice. You really had to hold on tight to the Colt. I instinctively put my right foot back a bit to give me a more stable shooting platform. Each shot got progressively better and with the last I hit the target guy in the shoulder.

Another flashback happened as I thought back to shooting Banks. I had just whipped out the gun and pointed in his direction and managed to hit him in the neck. Lucky shot. At the time I had thought nothing of it, but now that I knew how hard it was, I realized it was maybe a ten percent chance.

My beautiful instructor gestured for me to put the Colt back down on the table. After I did that she reloaded, held the gun at waist level, cowboy movie style and shot the target three times out of five in the head, twice in the torso.

"I didn't say it was impossible to shoot in this manner, but I've had a lot of practice," Barb said. Then she reloaded again, this time shooting while holding the Colt with two hands at eye level. Results: five shots in the head, all close together.

"We call that a tight group." Barb said, pointing at her results on the target. Our conversation was shouted because we were wearing what I thought of as shooting earmuffs. "The Colt 45 is accurate in the hands of an expert at 100 yards, some specialists can even be accurate up to 200 yards, so that's something for a weapon designed over 125 years ago." She gestured for me to remove the ear protection.

The next several minutes were instruction only. She explained the similarities and differences on the two semi-automatic pistols on the table. Unlike the Colt, they were not revolvers and the ammunition was held in clips inserted into the gun from below. One of them held as many as seventeen rounds.

I interrupted, "I thought these were called automatic pistols---"

She cut me off, "There is some confusion about the terminology. But "automatic" has come to mean something else in weapons, basically a gun where you just hold the trigger and bullets come out until you stop squeezing or it runs out of ammo. A "semi-automatic" is a gun where you have to squeeze the trigger for each shot, but you don't have to cock it between shots. So these pistols are "semi-automatic," if you're being properly serious, which I always am when I'm talking about weapons. If you decide to get a pistol, I'll explain that specific model and teach you how to use it."

So back in New York, when Banks in his office was pointing his gun at me, that I thought was an automatic pistol, it was really a semi-automatic. Then again, he was more than "semi-dead."

We practiced loading and unloading the semi-automatic pistols, before Barb let me fire them at the targets. I wasn't a good shot with either of them.

"You just need practice," Barbara Jean pointed out. We spent the next several minutes picking up spent cartridges and tiding up the area.

A thought occurred to me. "You know, Barb, a lot of this is called "practice". Loading practice, target practice, practice range. But when you have to kill somebody, it's not practice."

Barbara Jean looked me right in the eyes. "You came through when you had to. Now we're just getting you ready in case you ever have to do it again."

"Yeah. I'm thinking about getting a gun. You know, for home protection." I wanted to sound like I knew what I was talking about.

"What keeps you safe is that everybody else in Texas already has at least one gun in their house. So the bad guys assume that you must have one. You can legally shoot anybody who breaks into your house, you know." Saying that made Barb smile.

"Does that apply to people just looking through the slats in my fence?" I decided it was a good time to bring that up to Barbara Jean.

"Why sir, whatever would you mean by that?" Barb said in her best Southern Belle impression. I thought she might get a case of the vapors.

"I was speaking hypothetically." I answered. It was a good opening salvo, but I thought I would get more specific when we were sitting down with some bourbon.

Twenty One
Spicewood, TX

Guns and ammo are heavy; heavier than I ever thought they'd
be, I noted as I helped Barbara Jean carry the three handguns
and the ammo back into her house. She locked all the stuff up
in her walk-in gun safe, more of a room, which had enough
weaponry in it to be considered an annex of the State Militia.
Besides a variety of handguns, she had several kinds of hunting
rifles, and a lot more shotguns than I judged to be necessary.
Some shotguns were pump action and looked to be anti-
personnel, as opposed to the sporty skeet shooting models. The
whole area was done up dark wood, and there were cabinets for
the ammo.

"What happens if there's a fire?" I asked.

Barb pointed to a sprinkler head. "It has a separate fire
suppression system. Doesn't use water, it has a much more
efficient chemical fire extinguishing spray."

"You know Barb, if this was the movies," I pointed to the wall
with the rifles, "and this closet was in the villain's lair, that
would be a false wall, and behind it would be automatic
weapons, machine guns, rocket launchers, stuff like that. You
got any of that, like hand grenades or something?"

Barbara Jean pursed her lips. "I've got some special equipment
in here, but you won't find that out unless you really disappoint
me. Or if you marry me and move in?" A statement and a
question all at once. It fits in with my theory that men are
simpletons and women operate in a whole different byzantine
mental world.

I thought it best to say nothing.

"Why don't I fix us a drink?" Barbara Jean said. We exited the private arsenal and walked out to the living room, and she gestured for me to have a seat in a big leather sofa, while she went to the bar.

"What do you want to drink?" she asked.

"I'll have what you're having."

She took the bottle of Jack Daniels that I brought and poured us a couple of Jack and Gingers with ice. That wouldn't have been my first choice, but it was okay.

Barbara Jean had a spectacular chest, and it just so happened that maybe the top three snaps of her cowgirl shirt had come undone. What a coincidence. She sat close, facing me. From the way she was sitting, it looked like another snap was in serious danger of releasing. There was a lot of mechanical stress on that one little snap.

I had seen this all before, but that didn't stop me from looking again and enjoying the view.

"Why JR, what are you looking at?" Miss Innocence.

"It's just that I have excellent peripheral vision, and I was trying to get in the complete picture. You know, to see you as an entire person. Holistically."

"Ha!" She held out her hand, and we clinked glasses. We both took good gulps.

She sat back a bit. I stood up, holding my drink, and walked to the other side of the coffee table.

"Barbara Jean, you are a beautiful, sexy, smart woman. And you can sure shoot a gun… but I didn't come up here tonight to, you know…"

She took another sip of her drink, so I did too. "You're in love with that tall girl, aren't you? Were you bangin' her?"

"Well, Barbara Jean! Do you talk that way when you're teaching Sunday school?"

"I don't teach Sunday school anymore," Barb sniffed.

I walked back around the coffee table and sat on it, facing Barbara Jean. "Well, it's really none of your business, but the answer is no, we didn't do anything."

"That girl could use a proper bathing suit. You should have called me. I would have taken her shopping." Barb said.

"So that *was* you peeking through the fence," I accused.

Barbara Jean laughed, "You already knew that!"

"You know what, Barb? I could really go for something to eat. You want to go out?" I asked.

"Nah, I'll just fix us something in the kitchen. How about some huevos rancheros?"

I brought the bottles of Jack Daniels and ginger ale and followed her into the equally spectacular kitchen. What an idiot her husband had been, abandoning this smart, beautiful woman and this ranch.

By the time we reached the kitchen, she had not been out of my sight, and was carrying her drink in one hand. Somehow two snaps on her cowboy shirt were re-snapped. Women are not only far cleverer than men, but they're also magicians. Maybe Barbara Jean could be the opening act for David Copperfield. Also, her hair was out of the ponytail, and just hung down, more ladylike. I hadn't noticed when that happened either. Maybe it was that way in the living room.

I love the smell of Tex-Mex cooking. The tangy combination of eggs, fried tortillas, refried beans, and Barb's homemade ranchero sauce went perfectly with the bourbon and ginger ale. It was one of those impromptu great meals that couldn't be recreated. Maybe the lingering smell of gunpowder on our clothes added to the mood.

We sat on stools on a kitchen island facing the stove. There wasn't any conversation for a few minutes, finally I asked.

"So what was with the Peeping Tom routine?"

Barbara Jean didn't say anything for a minute. "I just thought now with the Movie Star gone, it would be time for you and me to, you know, get serious. Then I go by and see that beautiful tall girl walking round the pool in her underwear. It was just… confusing."

"So you had to stop by and look through the fence a few more times?" I asked.

"I only did it twice in total… what difference does it make?" Barb said.

"It doesn't make any difference, Barbara Jean……. You know, if you're trying for any undercover spy work, you might want to ditch the yellow Corvette convertible."

We sat there self-consciously finishing up the scraps of food on our plates. I poured myself a little splash of bourbon and offered up the bottle to Barbara Jean. She nodded, and I poured a little in her glass. We clinked glasses again and downed the whiskey.

"I just have to tell you something, Mizz Parker."

She looked a little nervous.

"Your ex-husband… I never met him, but I have to tell you…
he's a real fool. How could he walk away from you? You must
have been a great wife."

She looked at me. "I could be a great wife for *you*."

Twenty Two
Spicewood, TX

Man, I walked right into that one.

"Yup. Yeah, Barbara Jean, that's right. I just have to get some things sorted out. I don't want to mislead you," I said.

"What's the matter with you? No other man has ever minded misleading me!"

I snorted. "Well, I'm just a man of higher principles than you're used to dealing with."

"That's a pretty low bar," she noted. "There are a lot of men around the Greater Austin area willing to tell me just about anything to get into these jeans." Barb stood up and swayed her hips to one side. She looked great in the jeans, weathered just so, and tailored I suspect.

"I'm sure that's true. It's just that I should run along home about now," I said.

"C'mon, JR. Why don't you stay over… No strings attached?"

Men tell women a lot of lies, but one of the big whoppers that women tell men is: No Strings Attached. There were strings alright, Barbara Jean was a black widow spider weaving a web. In previous circumstances I wouldn't have cared and just lived with the consequences, but things were different now. Something told me I had to just go home.

"Nope…. but Barb… "

She looked hopeful. "Yes, sweetie?"

"Could I have another shooting lesson? Maybe same time next week?"

"Yeah, great… just fine! Okay. I'll make sure I wear my chastity belt," Barb said.

Twenty Three
Moscow

"Bitcoin is an interesting phenomenon. Do you understand it?"
The Lider asked.

"No sir, I don't know anything about it. I followed your
example. American one hundred dollar bills are my currency,"
Turgenev said. "I thought Bitcoin was some foolishness,
something for the millennials to trade back and forth to each
other on their iPhones."

"That is what I thought at first, and crisp pictures of Benjamin
Franklin served us well, but the world changes. The real
fortunes belong to the people who see the changes coming and
take advantage of that," The Lider continued. "The Bitcoin,
and all the other cryptocurrencies are the rational marketplace
responding to the total lack of monetary discipline in the West,
especially the U.S. Bitcoin exists in a stateless world, much as
gold did for centuries. But gold is a relic.

"What do you mean, sir? Isn't gold what all the old wealthy
families in Europe have in vaults in Switzerland?" Oleg asked.

The Lider answered, "even for large holders the difference
between the price when you buy and what you get when you
sell is too big. It weighs too much, has to be physically stored
and moved. Gold suited the Czars 200 years ago, but it is not
designed for this new digital world. Transactions can be settled
using Bitcoin as currency in an instant anywhere in the world,
and then Bitcoin can be used again by the recipient in a flash
with the stroke of a computer keyboard, I think of Bitcoin as all
the gold reserves in the world that you can carry around on
your cellphone," The Lider said.

"But doesn't the U.S. dollar serve the purpose of being the world's de facto currency now?" Oleg asked.

"Yes, but the U.S. is debasing it's currency more and more every day. The financial community calls it 'printing money', but it's even simpler than that. The U.S. Treasury just creates money out of thin air. They don't have to print it, it's just electrons," The Lider said. "The buying power of one U.S. dollar in 1968 is now 10 cents."

"But isn't Bitcoin just electrons?" Turgenev asked.

"Yes, but there's a crucial difference," The Lider answered. "Bitcoin has discipline...that's one area I need to nail down before my plan goes too far down that path...did you ever hear of Satoshi Nakamoto?" The Lider asked.

Turgenev shook his head indicating 'no'.

"Nakamoto is the very mysterious creator of Bitcoin. Nobody has been able to find out who he is, or whether or not he's even a real person. As you know we have extensive intelligence resources, and we know nothing. The western governments know nothing."

"Why is it important that you get to know him?" Oleg asked.

"The thing that distinguishes Bitcoin from the fiat currencies of nations is that Nakamoto pledges that no more than 21 million Bitcoins will ever be created. No more. With a totally limited supply, Bitcoin can be a long term store of value. Their value should appreciate over time, unlike the dollar. We've got to get to know Mr. Nakamoto somehow to increase our comfort level. We have to make sure that he never issues any more Bitcoin than the original 21 million. This is where you come in," The Lider said. "Tomorrow we start phase one of the plan, but we don't need to worry about Bitcoin just yet. We're not planning on getting paid for this feint. It's just part of the Gambit."

Twenty Four
Fort Meade, MD
Cyber Command HQ

Captain Gabrielle McHugh reported early for her first day of duty at Cyber Command. She always reported early.

After some routine paperwork and issuance of new IDs she reported to the office of her Commanding Officer, Colonel Colleen Powers. The colonel had a male secretary, an E-5, who buzzed the commander and then told Gab to go ahead into the office.

Gab walked in, saluted and said, "Captain McHugh reporting for duty Ma'am."

The colonel was beautiful. She was 5'10" had green eyes and medium length red hair and the pale skin and freckles that went along with that hair color. She was dressed in camo, returned the salute with something like a wave in the vicinity of her head. Powers gestured to a chair and said, "have a seat Gabrielle."

When Gab was seated the Colonel spoke. "We aren't real big on saluting here. Most of the personnel are civilians who call me by my first name. The military people address each other by their ranks, and that's about as formal as it gets. What is important here is brains. You're the dumbest person here right now, and your job is to not be the dumbest person by the end of this week, and a month from now to be much smarter. I've laid on a special tutorial course for you with some of our best people. By best people, I mean smartest. They don't all have people skills, they don't care that you're an officer, and if you ask stupid questions some of them will tell you flat out. I know your work ethic and your intellect so I'm confident that you will succeed."

"I've been in hostile environments before, Colonel," Gab said.

"I know that Gabrielle, but this is different. You wouldn't be here if I didn't think you could handle it, and I wanted to get somebody from the outside," the Colonel said.

Gabrielle didn't respond.

 The Colonel went on, "I didn't tell you this on the phone, but this is my last day as a Colonel."

Gabrielle looked shocked, but Powers smiled. "Oh, I didn't mean it to sound that way! I'm not leaving, I'm being promoted to Brigadier General this morning."

Gab responded, "It's very well deserved Ma'am."

"I agree," the soon to be General said. "And there's another promotion being announced. You're becoming a Major as of next week."

"I'm not so sure that is well deserved Ma'am." Gabrielle almost called Powers 'General', but it wasn't time yet.

"That isn't your decision to make. You were up for Major before you…left under unusual circumstances, and the fact is that I need you to be a Major to do the job I have in mind for you. One of the things you're going to be doing is briefing people. I need somebody who can translate all the techno-talk into English. You're going to be in meeting with the Secretary of Defense, the National Security advisor, maybe the President. A Captain is somebody who holds the door open for these guys. Hell, I'd make you a Colonel if I could get away with it. General Goldstein agrees and has signed off on it. And don't disagree with your superiors."

General Buck Goldstein was the Four Star General, Commanding Officer of Cyber Command. He had the reputation as a genius, and had the devious mind it took to compete with America's adversaries.

"Ma'am could I ask you a question. Off the record?" Gab said.

"Yeah, you get one a month."

"How did General Goldstein get the nickname 'Buck'?" Gabrielle asked. "I mean this isn't exactly a rockin' sockin' Combat Outfit."

Colonel Powers paused. Finally she said, "You didn't hear this from me, but he's rumored to have a big...unit."

"Really? Gab asked.

"Yup. I know of no evidence either way except that I've met his wife several times, and she looks happy," Powers said. "That's enough of that topic, except to say that the General is very professional and there's never any hint of inappropriate behavior. Let's move on."

They both sat in silence for a minute. Their eyes met.

Finally Gab said, "Colleen, regarding inappropriate behavior—"

"We'll have to suppress anything like that. We're going to be busy, busier than you've ever been in your life, if some of the intel we're getting is any indication of what's brewing. And you should get used to calling me General. Ma'am is too much, and I think even the most non-conformist civilians will not call me Colleen anymore. Once you're a General, you're in a different class. Even Toni Anne calls General Goldstein 'General'."

"Toni Anne?" Gab said.

"Yeah, you'll get to meet her soon."

"Is it ok if I call you Colonel until you get the star pinned on? I'm superstitious," Gabrielle said.

"Sure. There is one more thing I just want to tell you to clear the air," Powers said. "My husband is finally divorcing me. That miserable son of a bitch has decided that a new wife will be better for his career. He's got one all picked out. He won't marry her until an appropriate amount of time has gone by. He's big on appearances, as you know."

Twenty Five
Austin, TX

Even though Gabrielle had vacated the premises, I just couldn't get past the inertia and move my work stuff back to the casita. I continued working in a spare bedroom of the house. Deep down I was hoping that if I left the casita empty, Gab would quit her Army job and return. But after the vibe she gave off when I drove her to the airport, I didn't think she'd be coming.

I liked being in the Central Time Zone but being linked to the stock market. The New York Stock Exchange opens at 8:30 CST which suits my habitual early rising schedule, and ends at 3:00, so I can get in nine holes sometimes after work. The markets trade around the clock these days, but somehow being around when the big exchange is open is psychologically important.

What most people don't understand is that the NYSE is just a TV studio, could blow away like a tumbleweed some night, and trading would just continue unhindered the next day on computers all over the world. CNBC just needs to have a place to broadcast from, and the whole operation is a pageant, complete with a balcony that the management of newly listed companies can stand on, ring a bell, and wave to a mostly empty room, and to the television audience. It's as phony as the set of a western movie, their streets lined with building fronts with no real buildings behind them.

I've been on the floor of the Exchange in recent times, and maybe it's just the male pig in me, but my overwhelming thought was: The Network women are even better looking in real life than they appear on television. I wondered, where do they get these beautiful women, who are also real smart and have the composure to be on live TV for hours at a time? It's not an easy job. As far as the men on CNBC goes: who cares?

Maybe they are chosen because they resemble the demographics of the largely male audience that watches the market every day, including me.

What would Karl Marx say about someone who sits in Austin, Texas and watches TV all day and once in a while hits a few computer buttons for a living? When I don't have much to do, thoughts like this occur to me, and I seldom have much to do.

As a business major at the University of Texas we had a class in Non-Capitalistic Economies, where we learned about Marxism. But it was Texas, so even the professors didn't like commies. We weren't as sophisticated or nuanced as the elite schools on the Coasts.

Some people consider the stock market gambling, but I don't. I know I'm going to win over time. You just have to make yourself greedy when everybody is afraid, and afraid when everybody is greedy. Buy for the Long Term, meaning years, not minutes. Sounds simple, but it's not. Then again, I do like to gamble, but on sports.

Football is the best sport to gamble on. Baseball is crazy and random, and NBA stands for Never Bet Anything as far as I'm concerned. I always bet on Pro football, but never anything big. But football season doesn't last all year and the games are mostly on Sundays.

Bitcoin was a whole new world for me. It was the trader's dream. Buy it when it goes down, sell it when it goes up. Don't kid yourself, trading is just gambling. And just like betting on a football game, there's a loser for every winner. I was just dabbling, not putting in any real money. Unlike football, with Bitcoin you could get action whenever you want it, 3am on Thursday, Tuesday 1 pm, Christmas Eve, Thanksgiving, any time, any day somewhere in the world you could hook up a trade. It was becoming a pastime, and I liked it a little too much. In the back of my mind I thought I had the capacity to get out of control. But I was okay for now.

One day I sat there watching CNBC in a half trance. Nothing that I cared about was happening. My cell rang. This was not my office phone, but my private number that very few only a few people had. I picked up.

"JR, his is Tom Jr."

It was Dr. Tom Good, Jr. son of my old mentor, legendary Texas broker Tom Good. Dr. Tom was now President of Baylor University after serving for years as the head of The Medical School at that institution. I couldn't for the life of me figure out why anybody would want to be President of a University. He made more money when he practiced medicine. Maybe it was a combination of appealing to his sense of duty and his ego.

"Dr. Tom, it's always good to hear your voice. What can I do for you?" I asked.

He usually called me to play golf in some charity fund raiser for the University. I always played, and it was a chore. For the uninitiated, charity tournaments are the most dreadful form of golf. You get teamed with big donors who couldn't hit a cow in the ass with a broom, let alone hit a golf ball, they cheat on just about every shot, and complain. They lie about their scores on every hole. The fat cats claim if they just had their new custom golf clubs that were on order they'd play a lot better. A lot of them smoke cigars. I hate smoke. The whole round takes a lot longer than a root canal. I braced myself for the invite. For Dr. Tom, the son of Tom Sr., I always showed up.

"I want to see if you can help me," he said. It wasn't his usual cordial manner coming through. "I've got a big problem."

"Is it something with the University's investments?," I asked. I avoided handling any money that involved reporting to a committee, which usually meant a group of well-heeled morons, some of whom always tried to show you up in front of the rest of the committee. I had one account like that years ago and gracefully got rid of them after a year. I hoped he wasn't going to ask me to handle part of the portfolio. Why else would he be calling me?

"No, it's nothing like that. It's ....worse," he said.

Twenty Six
Fort Meade, MD
Cyber Command

Gabrielle was promoted from Captain to Major one week after reporting to Cyber Command. She was working as many as 20 hours a day, impressing everyone who mattered, except for Toni Anne Laudano.

Gabrielle had finally met Toni Anne after a week. "You're the one who shot the Hedge Fund guy?" Laudano asked.

"Yes," Gabrielle answered.

"So, we have our very own Murder Bitch! Welcome aboard." Toni Anne said.

Toni Anne had christened her 'Murder Bitch' at a meeting with General Goldstein and Colonel Powers. It was clear that Goldstein not only tolerated Laudano's language, but that Toni Anne was the de facto second in command, regardless of any military hierarchy. Goldstein had said when introducing Toni Anne to Gabrielle that he considered Laudano the smartest person in the world. "She not only is the best at technical knowledge, but has the devious mind to excel at Game Theory. We're up against some very clever adversaries."

General Powers defended Gabrielle to Laudano by saying, "Major McHugh was third in her class at West Point."

"Third? Where's one and two? Laudano asked. "The Russians, the Chinese, the Iranians don't give a shit about your class rank at West Point. We gotta beat their brains in every day. As long as you understand that we'll get along fine."

General Goldstein made some comments about how crucial the mission of Cyber Command was, and the need for complete secrecy, then excused himself. "I'm on a call with the President in ten minutes. Please proceed, we'll talk later."

Toni Anne took over the meeting. "I understand that you're coming back in the military after being in civilian life for a while. That's unusual," she said, addressing Gabrielle.

'Yes, ma'am."

"You don't have to call me ma'am. I'm not an officer. But I am a patriotic American, and I'm dedicated to this job. Don't ever bullshit me and we'll get along," Toni Anne said.

Gabrielle said, "What should I call you, then?"

"Toni Anne. Just don't ever lie to me. Our mission is too critical for covering your ass. If you fuck up, admit it. And if you fuck up too many times, your ass is out of here. Nothing personal. You can go back to shooting people."

Powers spoke. It was clear that General Powers knew she was beneath Toni Anne in the unofficial Chain of Command. "Um, Toni Anne. Major McHugh had been in communication with me regarding getting back in the Army, after leaving in unusual circumstances. The situation that has come up regarding the Russian program that made me think it was best to get the Major back in the tent."

"Yeah, I know that, and frankly I'm familiar with the 'unusual circumstances' you referred to," Toni Anne said.

Powers swallowed hard. "She has a candidate for the Useful Idiot we need. And she thinks she can manipulate him into accepting the job," she said.

"So tell me Major McHugh. Who is your candidate, and why do you think he'll be the perfect Useful Idiot for our plan to divert Russian attention regarding Bitcoin?" Toni Anne asked.

"JR Johnson," Major Gabrielle McHugh said.

"The guy who was with you when you shot the Hedge Fund manager?" Toni Anne asked.

"Yes. He's perfect," McHugh said.

"Have you spoken to him?" Laudano asked.

"Not yet, but as we all know, but because of the current situation we've been monitoring the phone calls of the President of Baylor University, and he's right now speaking to Johnson, asking him to come onboard to help with their ransomware problem, We'll help out, make Johnson a hero, then he'll owe us," Gabrielle said.

Twenty Seven
Austin, TX

"Worse than some money manager losing a lot of your money?" I asked Dr. Tom.

"Yeah. All our money's at risk. Our entire endowment," Tom said.

"How much is that right now? Over a billion?" I asked.

"It's over $1.3 billion," he said.

"Well, what is going on? How could all your money be at risk?" I asked.

"It's a ransomware attack. Very sophisticated. It's not a fat guy in his parents' basement," Dr. Tom said.

A million wise guy answers occurred to me, like: it could be a very smart fat guy, but I wasn't going to say that to Dr. Tom. I was sure this was the most stressful day of his life. I asked, "Forgive me for asking the obvious, but don't you have people to take care of this sort of thing? What the hell are they doing?"

Dr. Tom lost his cool. "Of course we have people! In-house, and an outside consulting firm who's supposed to be the best in the country that receives a very sizable fee from us every year, and right now they're all completely friggin' useless. They are advising me to pay the ransom!"

"How much is the ransom?," I asked.

"Three hundred million," he answered.

I whistled. "That's a lot of charity golf tournaments. What happens if you don't pay the ransom?"

"If we don't pay, they claim they can take all the money. Right now they have every computer in the University locked up, except for the Hospital" he explained.

"Yeah. Fuck 'em. Don't pay. Buy some time. We'll think of something," I said. "I've read a bit about ransomware. The bad guys have their victims computers locked up, but I haven't heard of one that could actually take your money. Mostly they threaten to destroy all your data and not release their stranglehold on your computers."

"That's why I'm calling you. I'm not listening to these whiny nitwits who are supposed to be my experts. A month ago they gave me a presentation on just how safe we were from this sort of attack," Dr. Tom said.

"So what do you think I can do?" I asked.

"You're a sophisticated money guy. You have contacts in the banks, on Wall Street—"

I interrupted, "I don't know if you read the papers, but there are certain segments of the Hedge Fund industry where I'm not all that popular right now."

Dr. Tom laughed. It was a good, real laugh. He probably needed the release, but that's a Texan for you. He's the President of a University, has his entire endowment of $1.3 billion at serious risk and he's able to laugh. That's one of the reasons I love Texas. Try telling the President of Harvard a joke at that point and see if you get a laugh.

"Do you know anybody who can help me?" Tom asked.

"Let me make sure I understand this. The bad guys are not just saying they have your computer system hostage, and won't release it unless you pay, but they claim they can somehow electronically grab all your assets? Your money is scattered all over the place, a lot of different financial institutions are custodians for the investments. It's not just sitting at the Main Branch at the Waco National Bank. Do I understand that correctly?" I said.

"Yeah, that's about it," Tom said.

"Do your IT people think this is a credible threat?" I asked.

"They tell me this is a whole new level of ransomware, something that hasn't been seen. They are seeing signs of something like "protected capsules", smaller viruses embedded within in the viruses on our system that indicate a quantum leap in the level of sophistication. What they tell me is that ransomware up until now has been the work of very smart operators, maybe located in rogue states with the knowledge of their existence by the local government, but not to the level of State sponsored cyber threats. Our IT guys think this might be the direct work of a foreign government. China, Russia, Iran, North Korea, for example."

"Man what did Baylor do to piss off some foreign government? Are you sure it's not an attack from the NCAA? You've got a lot of violations in the past years," I said. Up until now Dr. Tom's biggest problem was the inheriting of rampant violations of NCAA rules and serious misconduct including violent felonies by members of the football and basketball teams that had occurred while his idiotic drunken predecessor had looked the other way. Dr. Good was just now getting a handle on the fallout from that situation, and now this ransomware thing was making that look like a church picnic.

"In my experience the NCAA isn't smart enough to organize a two car funeral," Tom said.

98

"I don't want to promise you anything, but I do have somebody I can call. Maybe they can at least point me in the right direction. In the meantime, can I make a suggestion?" I said.

"Sure."

"Call all your so-called experts into your big conference room, including the outside consultants, and absolutely tear them a new cornshoot. Threaten them. Tell them you've talked to outside counsel and they're all personally liable. Have some fun," I said.

"Yeah, that's tempting, but I can't do that," he said.

"You can see why I'd never be considered suitable material for a University President. Meanwhile, I'll get back to you as soon as I can. I'm not sure how fast I can get in touch with my contact," I said.

"Sure JR. Please express my sense of urgency when you get through," he said.

"I understand. This person I'm contacting may be in a meeting with, who knows, the President of the United States." I thought I was exaggerating. "But Dr. Tom, I do want one concession from you if I do manage to help you out of this mess."

"Anything. What is it?" he asked.

"I never want to play in one of your friggin' fund raiser golf tournaments again," I said.

"You bet," he said.

Twenty Eight
Fort Meade, MD
Cyber Command HQ

Gabrielle McHugh sat slumped in a chair in General Powers'
office. The General sat ramrod straight behind her desk.
Gabrielle could sense the power draining away from her CO
toward her. This outfit was based on brains, and Gabrielle had
more. Powers spoke less and less in meetings with General
Goldstein and Toni Anne, while Gab asserted herself with
confidence.

"Gabrielle, how do you know you can get Johnson onboard to
be the Useful Idiot?" Powers asked.

"Colleen, don't you get the dynamics going on?" McHugh
said. Calling the General by her first name was a sign of
borderline insubordination, but not mentioned by Powers.
Gabrielle wasn't bold or stupid enough to do it in public, but
by using the first name in private she was belittling the
General.

"I have to admit that I'm lost," Powers said.

"I know what Johnson will do. He'll call me today. If he
doesn't, I'll call him, but he won't suspect anything. He's still
stupid enough to think I'll be his girlfriend." Gabrielle said.

Twenty Nine
Austin, TX

It had been more than a month. Gabrielle hadn't called me.
Every day I pledged to myself that I wouldn't call her, but I
wanted to.

With Dr. Tom and Baylor in such deep trouble I had to give
Gab a call. I didn't think that Cyber Command got involved
with ransomware to a private institution. Gab would probably
just tell me to call the FBI.

I called Gab's cell. She surprised me by picking right up.

"Gab, it's me, JR," I said.

"I can see that. These phones are pretty smart, you know," she
replied.

"Well, Captain McHugh---"

"It's Major McHugh now. I got promoted," she said.

"Congratulations. This is important. It has to do with Cyber
stuff," I said.

"JR, it's great to hear your voice. But I have to tell you that
I'm working 18-20 hours a day, sometimes more. Go ahead,
but I have no patience. What is it?" she said.

"Don't cut me off. Let me finish. It's a ransomware situation,
but it's big, and different and may be something you folks want
to take a look at," I explained.

"We usually don't get involved with---"

"I know that. I told you this is different," I said. "I'm not calling you up just to say hello," I was a little pissed.

"Ok, Ok JR," Her voice was conciliatory. "To go forward with this. I need to know everything, and it has to be seen as a threat to national security. If the City of Austin, Texas is on the hook for a couple million to some hacker---"

"The ransom demand is $300 million, and if they don't pay the hacker says he'll take $1.3 billion," I said. "With a "B.""

"Oh!" It seemed like I got her attention. "Is it Austin?" she asked.

"No, it's Baylor University. Their entire endowment is $1.3 billion, the bad guys have already locked up their computers, and threaten not just to corrupt all of Baylor's data and destroy their computer network, but they claim to have the ability to grab all of Baylor's assets, wherever the assets are located, and take the money. All of it," I said.

"That might not be as far-fetched as it sounds," Gabrielle said. "We have seen…" She stopped. "I can't talk about it. Tell me more."

"Baylor has in-house and outside consultants who think the threat is credible. It has something to do with thousands of 'encapsulated mini-viruses' that are embedded in the main malware virus," I said. "Look, I don't know what that really means, I'm just parroting what the President of the University told me."

Gabrielle sighed. "Ok, JR. Just because it's you, and I owe you big time, here's what I'll do. I'll take it to my boss, who also got promoted and is now General Powers. I'm sure she'll call in our smartest colleague, who's really the second in command to General Goldstein."

"That's good, " I said.

"The good part is that this smart person, who's also a woman, might be the smartest person in the world. If not she's in the top five," Gab said. "The bad news is that this smart person is arrogant, rude… we don't get along. If she thinks this is a waste of her time, she'll call me 'Murder Bitch" which is her name for me"

"That's a good nickname. Have you thought of having vanity license plates made up?" I continued, "Well, that's better than getting shot at by Robert Stanton Banks," I said.

"The funny thing about this woman genius is that she looks like the sweetest person in the world, like Mary Poppins," Gab said.

"You mean she looks like Julie Andrews," I said.

"She looks like Julie Andrews playing Mary Poppins, and she dresses like Mary Poppins" Gabrielle said, "until she opens her mouth and calls me the Murder Bitch."

"That's the thing about appearances," I said, "for example, many people don't recognize me for the genius I am."

"JR I don't have time for your wit right now. Look, you're not working 20 hours a day at this pressure cooker. Around here it's intimidating. The brain power in this building is awesome. It's a good thing these people are on our side," Gabrielle said. "Say, JR, are you still trading Bitcoin?"

"Yeah. What does that have to do with this?" I asked.

"The two might be connected. I'll… see what I can do," Gabrielle said.

"Thanks," I said.

103

"JR, why are you involved in this?" Gab asked.

"Short version… The University President is a friend and client of mine," I said.

"One more question. Have they called the FBI?" she asked.

"No. The bad guys warned them not to do that, they claimed they have a mole at the FBI, and would know if Baylor called," I said.

"The bad guys may be helping Baylor with that advice. My turn to sound arrogant, but the FBI is great at this kind of thing if it's a couple teenagers in their parent's garage, or some stupid skinheads in Idaho, but if it's a sophisticated operation they can do more harm than good. This is Washington, so the FBI won't admit when they're in over their heads, because they want the credit for solving the cases. It's all about funding," Gabrielle said.

I didn't care about bureaucratic infighting, and wanted to say that, but I held my tongue.

"Sorry, JR. I don't want to drag you into that crap," Gabrielle said.

"Look Gabrielle, I really appreciate you sticking your neck out for me," I said.

"Yeah, well you might be sticking your neck out too," she said..

"What does that mean?" I asked.

"Umm..too early to say," Gabrielle said. "Alright, I'll try to help you, but I may be asking for help in return."

What could that possibly be?

"JR, you still there?" she asked.

"Yeah, sure."

"Look, I'll go see the General now. Stand by. If they think this story has credibility they'll probably want to talk to you," Gab explained.

"Jeez, I've never been questioned by a General," I said.

"That'll be the easy part," Gab said. "The genius' name is Toni Anne. If she questions you... well some of the guys around here say it's worse than a prostate exam."

"Toni Anne...that sounds like a friendly name," I said.

'Ha! That's a good one! Bend over. Put your hands on your knees. Brace yourself," Gab said.

Thirty
Fort Meade, MD
Cyber Command HQ

Gabrielle hung up. She had taken the call sitting in General Powers' office. Powers had just sat there listening, waiting for Gabrielle to explain the situation.

"I told you he'd call!" Gabrielle said.

"I'm lost...I don't understand," General Powers said.

"I know. Don't worry about it. I'll tell Toni Anne. We'll handle it from here." Gabrielle said.

Thirty One
Fort Meade, MD
Cyber Command

The status of Toni Anne Laudano as the smartest person at
Cyber Command was unchallenged, and she was so confident
in herself that when General Goldstein brought up the idea of
bringing in the special consultant, she was enthusiastic. That
was before Goldstein had told her the final reason. Toni Anne
couldn't believe this stroke of luck. If they just played their
cards right they'd trick the Russians into using the devastating
weapon they had been developing for years, but it would be
ineffective, and once they'd used it they'd be out of
ammunition for a long time. But the proposed candidate had to
be vetted for Above Top Secret clearance before anything more
could progress.

It was highly unusual for Toni Anne to respect anyone or defer
to someone else's expertise. But her first priority was winning,
and when someone else could help her win she was a realist.

Her ambition to be the best was as focused as say, Tiger
Woods or Michael Jordan, and she was as competitive as any
athlete or CEO. Toni Anne had been born with this gift and no
person or obstacle was going to stand in her way of
demonstrating it. She also was fiercely patriotic, and was
particularly distrustful of the Russians, who she never referred
to as anything except the "commies, except when for emphasis
she called them the 'fuckin' commies.'

Once in a joint meeting with Cyber Command and State
Department personnel, a mid-level diplomat pointed out to her
that the Russians were no longer technically Communists, Toni
Anne had told him that if he had any brains he'd know that

'The Lider is just a fuckin' commie who's discovered money'. That was the end of that discussion.

Unlike an academic institution, the pecking order at Cyber Command was not determined by someone's academic credentials. Lots of the best analysts had no formal degree. Some people are just savants regarding computers, their brains seeming to run in parallel to the way the machines are programmed to think. These people don't necessarily flourish in the traditional education system. Many of the maverick people without formal degrees had quirky personalities, and while different from each other in some aspect, they all shared one commonality: they worshipped Toni Anne. They wished they could get away with her arrogance and disrespect for authority, but in that way she was like Michael Jordan; there were special rules for Toni Anne because she was the best, and her behavior would be tolerated. Americans were safer because Toni Anne Laudano was at her post. The same couldn't be said for any of the lesser lights, they could be replaced.

The cyberthreat world is full of deception. It is common for Israel to make an attack on Iran while disguising it as an attack by North Korea, as a simple example. In the real world attacks could be multi-layered and much more complex to find the true origin of the attacker.

It was Toni Anne who had developed the useful theory of ascertaining the identity source of attack. To grossly oversimplify she likened it to handwriting analysis. Iran used blunt force; they'd throw thousands of attempts at a server thinking that just one had to get through. China was more math and algorithm based. North Korea was the least sophisticated, but making the fastest progress and managed to score at times. Israel was the most skilled at making an attack look like it came from any country other than themselves. But Russia was different than everybody else.

Russia's highest level attacks were based on Chess Strategy. It was way more layered and sophisticated than any other State actor. They'd make a feint in one direction, then withdraw and attack somewhere else, maybe eventually going back to the first attack. With the Russians it was tough to know if they were launching an attack that had short term goals or whether they were playing the Long Game. Toni Anne called it "Gambit Cyber'. So she wanted to get the best person in the world to combat the 'fuckin' commies', who she saw as the most dangerous threat. We weren't going to lose to them on her watch.

Thirty Two
Fort Meade, MD

Gabrielle told General Powers the outline of the situation.
Powers held up her hand, indicating it was time for Gab to stop
talking.

Powers picked up her phone and punched in Toni Anne's
number. "Toni Anne, we have a situation. It could be an
opportunity. I'd like to explain it to you. Maybe you'd like to
take it to General Goldstein." Powers said.

"This better be good," Toni Anne said, "I'm just indoctrinating
our newest asset."

"This might fit right in with that," Powers said.

Minutes later Toni Anne stomped into Powers' office, and
looked over to Gabrielle.

"Oh great, the Murder Bitch has a problem!" Addressing
Powers Toni Anne continued, "What, does she need help
upgrading the operating system on her iPhone?"

Powers ignored Toni Anne's comment. "I wouldn't ask for
your time unless I thought this was a situation we could
exploit."

Powers gestured for Gabrielle to brief Toni Anne. Surprising to
Gab, Toni Anne didn't interrupt. Gabrielle was an excellent
briefer, she naturally boiled down the situation to verbal bullet
points, and concluded in a couple minutes, "at the end of this
we might just have the Bitcoin diversion we've been looking
for."

Toni Anne, with folded hands, quietly addressed the General, "Yeah, you're right it's gotta be the Russians. We've just started seeing hints of these encapsulated mini-viruses in the last few days. Been waiting for a shoe to drop. This is a big escalation in capabilities, a threat to our financial system. Set up a conference call with Baylor. Have it start 90 minutes from now. I need to organize, but we've got to move fast." She looked at Gabrielle. "You did the right thing, Murder Bitch. You're not as stupid as I thought. You must be learning a few things hanging around here." Then Toni Anne surprised Gabrielle. Toni Anne smiled at Gab, shook her hand, and slapped her on the back.

"You mean they can just steal financial assets from institutions, no matter where the assets are held? General Powers asked.

"Yes. We had a meeting on it yesterday when you were at the Pentagon. I was going to brief you today. I've been thinking about counter-measures," Toni Anne said. She rose from her chair. "I've got to get the correct members of my team assembled in the conference room. Let's be ready in 60 minutes." She pointed to Gabrielle. "I suggest you have Murder Bitch sit in as well." Then, as Toni Anne exited the room, she turned back and said to Gabrielle,

"You're being pretty cold about setting up our Useful Idiot. Don't you have any loyalty to---"

"I have loyalty to our country, to our mission," Gabrielle said.

Laudano looked at Gabrielle without commenting, and left.

"What's with her?" Gab chose her words carefully, "You think she might, well, like me? You know—"

The General smiled. "No. You haven't heard? Toni Anne is a confirmed heterosexual. You haven't heard about her husband?"

"No."

"You know her husband, John Driscoll…" This got a shrug from Gab.

"You've been in meetings with him. He's a supervisor in the Control Room? Redheaded guy?" Powers said.

"Oh yeah, I know him," Gab said.

"Out of school?…That's her husband. Scuttlebutt has it that Toni Anne wakes him up every morning at 3 am, and demands that he screw her, she refers to him as 'Stud Pony'. Then they go to work. That's one of her two hobbies. The other one is that she watches baseball games. Keeps meticulous statistics."

Thirty Three
On the way to Waco, TX

Dr. Tom decided I needed to be at Baylor, so he arranged for me to be flown by Care Flite helicopter from University of Texas Hospital to the similar facility at Baylor. This was highly unusual since the service was reserved for only patients with a critical need to get to a hospital with the specialized care for their particular problem. The pilots on the flight were unfriendly to me, resentful that someone they considered a worthless but healthy one percenter was abusing the system. I didn't bother apologizing or trying to explain. If this hacking problem didn't get fixed there might not be gas money available for the helicopters in a few days. The flight took 40 minutes.

I got a call from Gabrielle during the flight. "My superiors are very concerned about the situation you described and directly phoned Dr. Tom Good at Baylor to arrange a conference call. But we thank you for bringing this up to us," she said.

"I happen to be on my way to Baylor right now, on a helicopter," I said.

"Oh. Why are you going to Baylor?" Gab asked.

"Dr. Tom wants me to be his advisor," I answered.

"No offense JR, but what do you know about this field?" Gab asked.

"Not much, but Dr. Tom trusts me. He doesn't have much faith in his tech people, who he blames for this mess, and I think he wants a confidant. Right now he has a room full of IT people who last month swore up and down that something like this could never happen," I said.

"The first thing Toni Anne Laudano is going to do on the conference call is read the Riot Act about Security and scare the hell out of people. We cannot have people talking about this," Gabrielle said.

"Okay…Hey Gabrielle it's me. I can be trusted, remember New York?" I said.

"Of course I remember. But Toni Anne doesn't know you…Look just listen to what Laudano says at the beginning of the call, and we'll see from there. You're walking into a field of landmines here," Gab said.

"Hey, I've got to be there. Dr. Tom needs me." I said.

"Okay. JR, I'll do my best to make you look good. But you're going to owe me," Gabrielle said.

Thirty Four
Waco, TX
Baylor University

Dr. Tom met me in a hallway outside the conference room where we were to meet.

"You look calm," I told him.

"We can only do our best. That's something you learn in medical school, sometimes the patient dies," Tom said. "I'm glad you're here. You are not walking into the friendliest environment. I told the IT personnel you'd be sitting in. Several of them mentioned that you're the guy who shot the Hedge Fund manager, and what qualifies you to be here?"

"What did you tell them," I asked.

"I told them that I trusted your judgement, that you had been smart enough to have uncovered the Ponzi scheme where many others of so-called experts had failed to do so, and if any of them had a problem with that they could leave before the meeting started," Dr. Good said.

"As you know, I shot Banks, but I didn't kill him. I do get credit for being a cold blooded killer sometimes in the press. Gabrielle, who did kill Banks is going to be on the other end of the conference call," I said.

"Small world," Tom said.

Thirty Five
Waco, TX

Dr. Tom's conference room was designed to host fat cat donors of the University in meetings designed to make them feel important, so it was fancier than the meeting places the techies who supported Baylor were used to. I walked in with Dr. Tom.

Dr. Wayne Flaggs, the President of the outside firm stared at me. "Who is this?," he asked, even though he knew the answer. This is a tactic I saw used on Wall Street, the big shot pretending not to know people he considered subordinate to himself.

"This is JR Johnson, which I suspect that you know. He's my special advisor," Dr. Tom said.

"I don't really see why he's here," Flaggs said. "I don't think it's necessary or desirable."

Dr. Tom was a person who didn't cuss except under extreme circumstances. He thought that 'gosh darn it', or 'goldang it' was borderline, so when he did swear it got people's attention.

"I don't really give a shit what you think, Wayne," Tom said. "Both of you have something in common. Neither one of you helped me avoid the current situation I am facing. Then again JR doesn't head a firm that Baylor pays a hefty fee to each year to fend off these kinds of problems, and he didn't sit in this room not a month ago making a ninety minute PowerPoint presentation on how the goatfuck we are presently faced with could never happen."

The room got real quiet at that point. Flaggs made no comment, but gripped down tighter on the yellow number two

116

pencil he was holding sideways with both hands. Flaggs and I looked each other in the eyes. I was guessing that we wouldn't be friends, and I thought that Baylor might just be looking for a new cyber security firm in the near future

Finally a man sitting next to Flaggs said "Well, Mr. Johnson might come in handy if we need to shoot someone."

I smiled at the man who made the comment. There are advantages to being the only person in a room who's a known killer. It's kind of like being Dirty Harry, and the advantages grow the longer you keep your mouth shut.

"Important distinction. He's only been known to shoot white collar personnel," Dr. Tom said. "Oh wait, I guess you could all be considered white collar employees." Nobody laughed.

Well, this is going to be one humdinger of a meeting.

Thirty Six
Waco, TX

We sat around the table in complete silence waiting for the call to come in from Cyber Command. There were four microphones placed on the table to pick up our comments, and a big video screen at the front of the room behind Dr. Tom, who sat at the head of the table. A voice came on the speaker.

"This is General Powers from Cyber Command in Fort Meade, Maryland. Right now I am accompanied only by Toni Anne Laudano, who is pretty much the smartest person in the world on the topic we are discussing today. We're going over some ground rules on security before we get started with the main meeting. Although this is a Skype meeting, it will be audio only, unless we choose to show you some graphics later. The reason for no video is to keep the identities of some of our personnel undisclosed. So far okay, Dr. Good?"

"Yes," Dr. Tom said.

General Powers went on, "I'm going to turn the floor over to Toni Anne Laudano. Toni Anne."

"This is Toni Anne Laudano. How many people are there on your end.?"

Dr. Tom looked around the table. "Thirteen, including myself."

"That's' too many," Toni Anne said. "Are any of the people there employees of Quantum Cyber?"

"Yes there are five of us, Ms. Laudano," Flaggs said before Dr. Tom could reply.

"Who is speaking?" Toni Anne asked.

"This is Dr. Wayne Flaggs, the CEO of Quantum Cyber---"

Toni Anne interrupted, "I was afraid of that. Just to get this out in the open, Flaggs and I have a history. He's the douchebag who was my professor at MIT who told me that the Encryption Algorithm I developed was garbage and would never work. So I quit MIT and started my own company. After I sold the company for $300 million I went to work full time for the Pentagon."

General Powers would never speak like Toni Anne had just spoken, but wanted all parties to understand the pecking order. "We're going to get the job done. Please understand that Toni Anne reports directly to General Goldstein, and that she has the President of the United States direct phone number, and permission to call him whenever she feels it is necessary. Are we clear on that, Dr. Good?"

"Yes."

"We needn't get personal, but I do want to make it clear that Toni Anne is the unquestioned decision maker in matters of technology. The reason you are all included in this meeting is not that we want any suggestions for solutions, but we need all the details you can provide of exactly what happened. Do your people understand that Dr. Good?" General Powers asked.

Dr. Tom visually surveyed the conference table and put his palms up. "Anybody got a problem so far?" he asked the group. No one spoke up.

"No problems here," Dr. Tom said.

"I want to make clear the matter of security. Anyone who stays in this meeting is subject to provisions of the Patriot Act and some other non-public Acts which allow us to monitor you. You are not to ever talk about anything that goes on in this room with anyone not in the room. To do so is a Federal Crime, and you will be prosecuted. If anybody there has a problem with that, you should leave the meeting now. But even if you do leave, your communications, electronic and otherwise, are subject to being monitored by the NSA and other government agencies," Toni Anne Laudano said.

I wondered if the NSA would be listening to the next conversation I had with my client Patrick when he called to whine about his account. But then again, I always assumed the government could be listening to my phone whenever they felt like it anyhow.

Wayne Flaggs snapped the pencil he had gripped so tightly in his hands. I couldn't tell if it was an act of passive aggressive defiance or if the tension had just gotten to him.

Toni Anne went on, "We're disconnecting the call for five minutes. You can discuss amongst yourselves if anyone would like to leave the process right now. We'll call back in five minutes."

Thirty Seven
Waco, TX
Conference Room of the University President

As promised, Toni Anne Laudano resumed the call in exactly
five minutes. This time instead of a blank screen behind Dr.
Tom Good was a slide of the impressive logo of U.S. Cyber
Command. The image reinforced the seriousness of the
meeting, and let us know that they were the big dogs, and we
were the little pups.

No one had left our conference room. There had been little
discussion, but somber looks all around the table. I smiled, but
maybe that was because I didn't know enough to be scared.

Toni Anne went on, "There are six people on this end of the
call including myself. Some people will ask you questions
without identifying themselves. Please identify yourself before
answering. Just to make it clear, we know who you are,
anyhow."

Thirty Eight
Waco, TX

I tried to pay attention for the next 20 minutes. The talk got
techno-heavy and I got lost in the details, but followed the
main plot, so in that way it was like the time when I worked in
New York and got dragged to Broadway to watch a
performance of Macbeth. Lady Macbeth was bad, right? So
were the ransomware people. I had the general concept.

The general tone of the conversation was: The Cyber
Command people were asking short questions, but getting long
answers. The employees of Quantum Cyber were especially
wordy, and beneath all their answers was the Cover-Your-Ass
mentality. 'we did everything right, how could you possibly
find us at fault'

The questioners at Cyber Command were even handed and not
attempting to assign blame, and a couple times when the
Quantum people went on too long with rambling alibis for
offenses with which they weren't even charged, Toni Anne cut
them off.

One time when the man who had mentioned that I could be
useful if we needed somebody shot gave a long-winded answer
way beyond what was necessary, Toni Anne said, "Why are
you still talking? Just answer the fuckin' question, then shut up.
Time is important here."

I had to admire Toni Anne. She could stop a blowhard faster
than anyone I had ever heard. I couldn't wait to meet her, the
foul mouthed Mary Poppins.

The meeting was brief, much shorter than I thought it would
be. At the conclusion Toni Anne said, "That's all we need for
you now. Here's what's going to happen. All the Quantum

122

Cyber people are dismissed. You have to leave, so go back to your office. I reiterate: do not discuss this situation with anyone. A federal law enforcement officer will be in your office tomorrow and go over the ramifications of the security protocols with which you are now faced."

Flaggs said, "That's outrageous. I---"

Laudano cut him off, "Be quiet Dr. Flaggs. We don't have the time for your dramatics. Let me make it clear that we do not find fault with your company, this threat is new, and could not have been anticipated by you. But let me also make it crystal clear—all Quantum personnel are to vacate the meeting immediately and go back to your corporate office in Austin. Dr. Good, please let me know when the Quantum people have left."

The Quantum personnel sat still and all looked to Flaggs for guidance. Dr. Tom gestured to Flaggs and said, "Wayne it's time for you all to go."

Flaggs rose and started to walk out, followed by his people. He paused near the door and looked over his shoulder at me. "I don't see why you're still here."

"Well, maybe because Dr. Tom trusts me not to just cover my ass," I said with a smile. Flaggs did not return my friendly gesture.

Dr. Tom waited for the door to close then said "All the Quantum people are gone. It's just Baylor IT people and myself. Well, then also my special advisor, JR Johnson."

"This is Toni Anne Laudano. JR Johnson, the guy who shot the Ponzi scheme manager along with our very own Murder Bitch? Why is he there?"

"JR has been an advisor to my family for many years, and I trust his independent judgement. He's staying," said Tom Good.

"Okay as long as he understands the security precautions I stated at the top of the meeting. Do you understand, Mr. Johnson?" Laudano asked.

"Yes," I said.

"Very well, we can proceed. The first thing you must now realize is that we here at Fort Meade will be seizing the control of your computer system. Your people should return to their workstations, and then we'll set up communications to go forward. Do so expeditiously," Toni Anne ordered. "Dr. Good, I will be leading the technical team here at Cyber Command. We will no longer be asking you for permission to do anything, and will not necessarily explain things as they go along, for two reasons: One-that takes too much time, and Two-we may well be able to solve your problem, but won't be telling you how we did so."

Thirty Nine
Fort Meade, MD
Cyber Command

That morning the newest member of Toni Anne's team had
arrived at work in an unusual way. A panel truck, with the
name "Mid Atlantic Vending" painted on the sides pulled up to
the loading dock area of Cyber Command. Two men in one
piece blue coveralls with the company name patch sewn to the
back and their own first names embroidered in script above
their right breast pocket stepped to the security desk for the
loading area. They each carried toolboxes, and had required
photo ID badges hung around their necks. After checking them
the guard let them pass.

One of the men, whose embroidered name said "Andy"
stopped at the first vending machine he encountered not far
from the loading area. The second man, "Gary", walked past
that machine and climbed a stairway and entered the second
floor though a steel fire door. He turned to a nearby alcove
which housed three vending machines. There were many
identical alcoves housing vending machines around the
building. This particular alcove was unique, because it had a
door on the wall opposite the machines with a sign reading
"Vending Machine Service Storage." Gary used one of the
dozens of keys on his giant keyring to open the storage door,
and closed it behind him. In the room were two racks of spare
parts and another unmarked door. Gary used the same key to
open this door.

Gary walked into a windowless room, maybe 30 by 30 feet.
There were four other people already there, and fifteen
computer screens. One of the people was Toni Anne Laudano.
"Good morning Yuri," she said. If Gary's blue one piece
coveralls had his real name embroidered over the pocket, it
would have said "Yuri" As in Yuri Sokolov, the Chess Grand

Master, a prominent defector and very vocal critic of The Lider.

Forty
Fort Meade, MD
Cyber Command

Two weeks before General Goldstein had come to Toni Anne after having interviewed and vetted a proposed new member of their team. It was Yuri Sokolov, now living in the U.S., after having moved from Russia, then recently from Bosnia for reasons of personal safety, was known as a dissident strongly opposed to The Lider, and had cooperated in other ways with U.S. Intelligence.

General Goldstein wondered if Sokolov could be brought in, for Cyber Command had the technical brains to go toe-to-toe with any other Cyber Warfare organization in the world, but the biggest current threat was the Russians. China was a strong second, but more easily understood because their tactics were all math based algorithms. The Russians were chess players, very skilled at making complex and convincing feints, parries, gambits in one direction while having a completely different real objective in mind. Only Israel had anything close to the Russian tactics, and they were known to have dissident former Russian chess players in Cyber roles.

Laudano had been very receptive to General Powers' idea. Both these two geniuses agreed that Toni Anne's supreme confidence in her own abilities made it possible for her to ask for specialized help when she needed it, for a lesser person might hesitate to admit they didn't have all the answers. Toni Anne just wanted to beat the 'fuckin' commies." Two weeks later Yuri Sokolov reported for his first day of work in blue coveralls, and now sat with the only three people besides Powers and General Goldstein who would know his identity. He wasn't expected to have technical solutions, the techno-babble would be translated to him. And he did have the secret weapon. Would the Russians fall for this?

The Group of Six, as it came to be known only by its members, sat at a table. Toni Anne began.

"Yuri, these people are as committed as you are to winning this war. At the risk of telling you what you already know, let's me go over a few things:

1) In cyberwarfare it is literally thousands of times simpler to attack than defend. In this way, cyber is similar to nuclear war. In the Cold War Era the U.S. and Russia had the capacity to completely obliterate the other side, but had no real capacity to stop their enemies from doing the same to them. So the policy of MAD, or Mutually Assured Destruction, prevented either side from ever launching.

2) In nuclear war one thing was certain: each side knew who would be launching an attack against them. This is the most important way that Cyber Warfare differs; an attacker can mask where the attack is coming from. In a simple example, Russia can route a Cyber attack through thousands of nodes around the world, making it look like an attack is coming from China. In a more complex example, Iran can make it look as though Israel is launching an attack while pretending to be the Russians. There are millions of multi-layered permutations of these strategies.

3) Another important way that Cyber Warfare is different is that any novel attack can only be used once against a sophisticated opponent. For example, North Korea's attack against Sony was dissected by all the other major players, and specific defenses were developed against it. So once you've shot a bullet, you have to develop a new bullet. Therefore any decent Cyber Warfare tactician saves their best ammunition for specific purposes, and launches attacks as probes to find weaknesses in their opponent's systems.

4) The U.S. maintains the best attack capabilities of all nations. We can, for example, turn off the power grid in

Russia, corrupt every data base in China, and disarm every sophisticated defense system in Iran in the next five minutes. We have also told every Cyber power in the world that we are taking no deterrent off the table, which means that we potentially will use every weapon in our arsenal, up to and including any Kinetic system. We have also stated that if in doubt where an attack is coming from, we will not rule out retaliating against some or all Cyber states simultaneously.

5) Because of this, any nation that makes a serious attack threatening the existence of the United States would have to: A-have the capability to launch a devastating attack so rapid that it wipe us out before we had the chance to retaliate, or B- have here-to-for unimagined defensive capabilities that could fend off any retaliatory Cyber capabilities of the U.S. and at the same time render our physical weapons systems useless."

"By Kinetic, you mean shit that blows up, yes?" Sokolov asked Toni Anne.

"Affirmative, Yuri. And I can see that we're going to get along," Laudano said. "Now, what we are up to: Russia is developing a new devastating multi-headed Cyber-attack system that we want to get them to launch against us----"

Forty One
Waco, TX
Office of Dr. Tom Good

Tom and I sat in his office while his team of IT professionals manned their workstations in an adjacent building. The doctor was calm, a trait that ran in his family.

"If this fix doesn't work, I'll have to resign," Tom said. "I'll go back in private practice. It will be tough, making more money and working half as many hours."

The mood reminded me of sitting in a hospital waiting room with a relative of someone undergoing surgery who wasn't supposed to make it. My mode of behavior in this circumstance was to make small talk, the subject being just about anything except discussing the monumental problem at hand.

"It would be nice to play golf with just you. You know, without having to drag along some lard ass that you're trying to hit up for a new library. Let's plan to do that no matter how this thing is resolved," I said.

"Okay, that's the best plan I've heard in a while," Tom said.

Tom had left his door open for the duration of the crisis, and instructed Jim Ed Langborn, his head of IT, to walk to his office and come in without knocking any time a situational update was necessary. The doctor had specifically dictated that Langborn was not to call on the phone. It was about a hundred yard walk for the overweight Langborn.

School was back in session and it was still hot and humid in Waco, so Langborn's shirt was soaked in sweat when he appeared in Tom's doorway, and despite his instructions stood in the opening and knocked.

"C'mon in Jim Ed," Tom said. "what's going on?"

Langborn stood in front of Tom's desk with his hands at his side, rubbing his thumbs against his forefingers and biting his lip. When it became evident that Jim Ed Langborn was not going to be seated without permission of the boss, Tom gestured and said, "Have a seat, Jim Ed"

Langborn moved fast for a man of his girth and sat facing Dr. Tom. Jim Ed looked straight at Tom, ignoring that I was present.

"First of all, Dr. Good, I'm getting a lot of pressure from the academic department heads that the computer systems are down--"

"For crying out loud, Jim Ed, I've been getting those calls too. You can't handle that! That's your biggest problem?" Tom said.

Jim Ed reached into his pocket for a handkerchief and mopped off his brow. He was so sweaty that I thought a beach towel would be a better, but still insufficient tool to dry him off.

"Of course not!" Langborn snapped, but then remembered who he was talking to. "Sir," he added, "or should I say doctor?"

Dr. Tom sat with his hands folded, then responded, "you should say what you're here to tell me. I hope you didn't come all this way to tell me about some whiny department heads."

Langborn repeatedly bit his upper lip while exposing his lower teeth. "It's just that we've relinquished all control. We're sitting at our workstations and the screens are being controlled remotely, from Cyber Command. The screens are blinking and moving faster than I thought possible."

"So?" Dr. Tom asked.

"So, what are we supposed to be doing, sir?" Langborn asked.

"You're supposed to be sitting at your machines, and ready to respond to any request that Cyber Command makes of you." Tom said.

"It just feels so helpless. Our fates are not in our own hands. What happens if—" Langborn blurted.

"What happens if we have to pay a $300 million ransom, or if the worst case and we lose $1.3 billion for the University?" Dr. Good asked.

"Yes, I..guess…that's my question," Langborn said.

"Well, for one thing it means that you and I will be getting new jobs. I'll go back to being a doctor, maybe on an Indian Reservation, and you'll be lucky to get a job programming the control arms that go up and down in a parking garage," Tom said.

"That's what I'm afraid of! It's not fair." Langborn said.

"Well, Jim Ed, you think if we lose $1.3 billion that people trusted us to keep safe we're not going to have to fall on our own swords? Tom said.

"It's … uh" Langborn searched for words and meanwhile took out his hanky again and dabbed his forehead. It looked like it was wet enough to wring out.

"Jim Ed go back to your department. Act confident. I don't think it's necessary to remind you that you are not to discuss this with anyone outside of your department. To do so would result in your immediate termination, and the FBI would be waiting at your door before you got home to explain the fifteen ways they're going to spy on you for the rest of your life." Tom said. "That's if they decide not to charge you for espionage. And you better not have any personal secrets that you don't want to be made public."

Langborn was hyperventilating through his nose, breathing faster and faster. He began to sound like a locomotive. His shirt was completely soaked in sweat. Dr. Tom walked around his desk and shook hands with Langborn, who stood and turned to leave.

Dr. Tom slapped him on the back. The doctor pulled his wet hand back and looked at it. "Do you have an extra shirt back at your office? It might help if you changed your clothes," Tom said.

Langborn slumped out of the office. When he reached the door Tom said, "Jim Ed, hold on a second. We're in the hands of the Cyber people. Let's hope our tax dollars have bought us the best brains at U.S. Cyber Command." Langborn turned away without comment and walked down the hall.

When I was sure that Langborn was out of earshot I said to Tom, "Was there some subtext there? Did I miss something?"

Tom grinned. "I was having some fun there. Yeah, Langborn is diddling one of the junior programmers in his department. He doesn't think I know about it. I'm told you can always tell that something went on when he wears a clean shirt home. He always wears the same style shirt white short sleeved dress shirt, so he thinks he's being clever."

"You did learn how to have fun from your old man," I said. Tom Good, Sr. had been my boss and mentor in the brokerage business. We both missed him.

"Never let a good crisis go to waste," Tom said.

That was something I'd heard his father say.

Forty Two
Fort Meade, MD
The Windowless Room

Laudano's team gathered at the modest table in the center of the room.

Sheldon raised his pencil in the direction of Toni Anne, a silent request for permission to speak. "Go ahead Sheldon," Toni Anne said.

"There are thousands of encapsulated micro-viruses in the data stream. That's the bad news. The good news is that all the micro-viruses are identical," Sheldon said.

"You sure of that?" Laudano asked.

"Yup," Sheldon said. Another man at the table nodded in agreement.

"So they're just showing us the Junior Varsity version. And you can get rid of the micro-viruses?" Tony Anne asked.

"It's was a little messy, but we've formulated a fix we can run right now," Sheldon said. "The rest of the virus is just standard high end hacker stuff. Not a problem for us."

"Are you sure that we're not overlooking something, that we're not creating a bigger problem by walking into a trap?" Laudano asked.

Sheldon paused for a minute. "Look boss, we've replicated the virus here, and have run the fix multiple times on our systems. We're 100% confident that this works as we planned."

Sheldon's compatriots all nodded vigorously.

"All right. I'll call General Goldstein, and explain the situation. It's his call. He's got to give the order to run the fix on Baylor's system."

Toni Anne called General Goldstein.

"How confident are you in this solution," Goldstein asked Toni Anne.

"One hundred percent confident, General." Toni Anne answered.

"This is just what we were expecting for Round One. Very well. I'm giving you the order to go ahead and execute the fix. Call me when you have an update."

"Yes sir," Toni Anne said, then hung up the phone. "I'm calling Dr. Good at Baylor as a courtesy before we execute," she explained.

After a brief call to Good, Toni Anne said to Sheldon, "Go ahead and execute the fix."

He walked to his computer keyboard, and paused.

"This always happens...I've forgotten which button to push," Sheldon said to general laughter, even by Toni Anne.

"Just send the friggin' command Sheldon," Laudano said.

With a few keystrokes Sheldon sent Cyber Command's fix to Baylor's computer system.

Forty Three
Waco, TX
Baylor University

Jim Ed Langborn was on the phone with Tom Good. "Jim Ed, Cyber Command just phoned me to say there would be running the fix to our system any minute now---"

"Holy shit!" Langborn said as his computer screen began to blink more rapidly than he thought possible, "Sir," he hastily added.

"I take it something is going on?" Dr. Good said.

"Yes, doctor, my computer screen looks like the Fourth of July is going on," Langborn said.

"Well, call me back when it stops blinking," Good said.

Baylor University has a special color green, designated as Pantone 3435u, along with gold as its school colors. Within five minutes after the fix was initiated, every computer on the Baylor System displayed a 3435u background, with gold letters stating: Baylor University Information Technology. It was as if nothing had happened, all systems were functioning normally.

Rather than call Dr. Tom, Jim Ed Langborn decided to run over to his office, and arrived breathless. He stood in Tom's doorway with his hands on his knees, panting. "It works! It works! It's fixed!"

"That's great Jim Ed" Tom said. "Now I know what it's like to be Delivered."

"Yeah!" Langborn said.

"Now that we've saved our jobs for a while, I've got two recommendations for you. Demands really." Tom said.

"Sure, anything," Langborn said.

"First, we've got to have a meeting with Quantum Cyber tomorrow morning. I think it's best to keep them, but let's scare them a little bit first. Set that meeting up, will you?" Tom said.

"Yes sir. And what else?" Langborn asked.

"It's time for you to stop diddling that young girl on your staff. And make sure her career goes along as she deserves, nothing better or worse than that." Tom said.

Forty Four
Fort Meade, MD
Windowless Room

Toni Anne got off the phone with Tom Good. "Baylor University is very pleased with our services," she told her group.

Nobody said anything. Toni Anne looked around. "Okay, what was wrong with this scenario?"

Sokolov raised his hand in a gesture to keep everyone silent. "May I venture a guess?" he asked.

"Certainly," Toni Anne said.

"It was too easy. The problem was complex, but not complex enough to really strain the intellectual capacities sitting around this table?," Sokolov said.

Sheldon answered, "You're right. Too easy."

"What does that tell you," Toni Anne asked Sokolov.

Yuri Sokolov looked around the other faces sitting at the table. "I take it you all have played some Chess?"

"I think it's safe to say that everyone here was President of their High School Chess Club, but we're not even remotely on your level. That's why you're here. What is your assessment of the situation?" Toni Anne asked.

"I think what we just saw was a Gambit, which is, you'll recall, an opening move in which a minor piece is sacrificed to gain a strategic advantage." Sokolov said. "There are two levels of Gambits, the simple one being the sacrifice of a pawn at the very beginning of a match, to see how the opponent responds, and the more complex of which is better disguised and intended to create a sense of over-confidence in the opposition. I think what we just saw was the latter." Sokolov said.

"Very interesting," Toni Anne said. "Let me ask you this, Yuri. Given your uniform, can you also fix the vending machine? I could use a friggin' Kit Kat right now."

"Have you tried slamming the side of the machine with your palm?" Sokolov asked, "It usually works for me."

Toni Anne laughed. "I'll table that discussion for now. So if the commies think they have made us over-confident, they have another move to make. What might that be?"

Sokolov said, "I think they have more than one tactical strike planned. Just what we want."

Forty Five
Nitup Resort
Bali, Indonesia

"You shouldn't kill unless it is necessary," Oleg said to Quinn.

"It was necessary," Quinn answered.

Oleg shrugged. "That's one thing that I found is the same in every country. There is an international standard size of oil drums. My men will be using one this evening. This situation won't be a problem, but please be careful in the future."

Quinn felt the cold shiver of a threat. Her experience in New York taught her that the blowhards who shouted threats were nothing, but the quiet powerful men who hinted danger were the lethal ones. She knew that Turgenev wouldn't hesitate to kill her if he felt it was in his best interests.

"We are sending you back to the United States. An attractive woman may help us get the information my, well boss, The Lider, needs," Turgenev said.

"What information is that?" Quinn asked.

"Do you know anything about Bitcoin?" Turgenev asked.

Forty Six
Waco, TX
Baylor University
Office of the President

Dr. Tom Good Jr. and I sat in his massive office. The Ransomware crisis was over for a few hours, the University's computer system ran just as though nothing had ever been wrong. I had just returned from the Executive dining room where I had dined alone.

"So Dr. Tom, when are we going to, just you and I, go out and play golf? I asked.

"How much you want to play for?" Tom asked.

"How about $1.3 billion?" I asked.

"That's a little rich for my blood," Tom said.

"Well then, how about our standard bet, a $1 Nassau?" I said.

For those unfamiliar with golf betting a $1 Nassau, even with all sorts of side bets, might result in a potential loss of up to seven or eight dollars.

"That's more like---" Dr, Tom was cut off by his intercom, and he picked up his phone. The next couple minutes were filled with him listening with a couple of "I understand" s and "I agree" s.

"That was the Chair of our Art Department. He was outraged that our computer system was down for so long. Something like that never happened when he was at Vanderbilt," Tom explained.

"I would have taken his crap for about two seconds," I said. "Then I would have threatened to take away his box of Crayolas."

Tom pondered for a minute. He put his hands on his desk and made an inverse V shape with his fingers. "I've said it before. I don't think you'd make a good University President," he told me.

"No shit," I said.

"Our golf match is going to have to wait awhile. I've got some tidying up to do around here," Tom said.

"Which means it's never going to happen," I said. "Can you get me back down to Austin?"

"Sure, but I can't get the Medical helicopter to take you. I've already gotten a call criticizing me for abusing that system," Tom said. "I'm certain you realize we can't let any details of this near disaster go public, so I can't explain why you got the helicopter ride."

"Oh sure, when you need me you're willing to break all the rules, but now that I helped you and you have no further need for me, I've got to hitchhike back to Austin." I complained. I wasn't really expecting the chopper to take me back, but then I was helpful in saving the University $1.3 billion. But Tom was a bureaucrat, constrained by University politics, and what had I done for him lately, like in the last five minutes?

"I'll get you a car with a driver to take you back," Dr. Tom said.

I nodded. For a bureaucrat, Tom was okay, but he wasn't his old man. Then again I had a big debt to Tom Sr., and I'd do anything to help one of his kids, including take a boring hour and a half car ride from Waco to Austin.

"JR, in all sincerity, I can't thank you enough for helping me," Tom said.

"Glad to help out," I said.

"I'd be glad to hook you up with some Baylor paraphernalia. I think we've got some Baylor ball caps in the closet," Tom offered.

"I wouldn't be caught dead in a Baylor hat. If you insult me like that again, next time I'll help the hackers," I said.

Forty Seven
Bali, Indonesia
Nitup Resort

"I don't know anything about Bitcoin, other than having heard the name. And seeing that it trades somehow. Some of the detectives in New York were buying it, but it was the crazy guys, the guys who were always trying to make a fast buck," Sierra Quinn said.

"Bitcoin is a cryptocurrency. It is designed to replace national currencies, like the dollar, the euro, the yen. It is a currency that knows no international borders," Turgenev explained.

"No disrespect intended, but that sounds like gibberish to me. What does that mean?" Quinn said.

Oleg considered his next statement for a long moment. "To be quite candid, I don't know. I do know that my boss is very interested in Bitcoin. There is one particular area about which he is very concerned about getting the details." Turgenev answered, then he smiled at Quinn.

Quinn considered Turgenev's smile. It wasn't friendly, she thought that his grin might well have been the last gesture many people saw before they were put into a 55 gallon oil drum.

"What particular area is he, er, are you, interested in?" Quinn asked.

"Bitcoin was launched in 2009, by an identity known as Satoshi Nakamoto. No one knows if this is a person, a group of people, some form of Artificial Intelligence. It has been unhackable, unable to be penetrated by even the world's best computer experts. No one knows who Nakamoto is. What

145

makes Bitcoin different than all the national currencies is that there is a finite amount of Bitcoin, that Nakamoto had said there will never be more than 21 million bitcoins in circulation. That is in contrast to the U.S. government for example, that creates more than $20 million per second out of thin air. All the other countries do the same thing," Turgenev said.

"You mean there isn't some gold in Fort Knox, or some other assets backing up the dollar?' Quinn asked.

"No, it hasn't been that way for over 50 years. And all the other countries are the same way. So national currencies devalue over time. A dollar now is worth about what 10 cents was worth in 1968," Turgenev said.

"Okay, so where do I come in?" Quinn asked.

"We need to talk to Nakamoto, if he is a person. Or somehow get assurances that Bitcoin will stick with their vow to never issue more than 21 million Bitcoins," Oleg said.

"And?" Quinn asked.

"There are two reporters from the New York Times who claim they are on the trail of Nakamoto, that they have had some sort of preliminary discussion with him that will lead to an interview. If they are successful they will become famous, rich, the next Woodward and Bernstein. We need you to get close to these reporters, to find out what they know," Turgenev said.

"Why me," asked Quinn.

"The team is a man and a woman. They are said to be kinky in their sexuality. We think that you can lure them." Turgenev said.

Forty Eight
Chicago, IL
Waldorf Astoria
Margeaux Brasserie

"We're so screwed!" Charles Phillips said, "I never should have let you talk me into this."

"Buck up Charles," Leslie Chandler replied. "Or just have another drink."

The two reporters sat at the bar in mid-afternoon. The place was almost empty.

"When I got the job at the Times my parents were so proud. I thought I'd be doing great things," Charles said.

Leslie laughed. "We are doing great things. We're going to be rich and famous after this. Our book will sell millions of copies."

"That's assuming that we get away with this scam," he said.

Forty Nine
Over the Pacific Ocean

Sierra Quinn had been given her instructions by Turgenev. She flew from Jakarta to Tokyo and then on to Chicago, using her very convincing fake passport and other identities as Patricia Sizemore. The only people who looked twice at her were people who were looking for attractive women, she wouldn't be anyone the authorities noticed, for Patricia did not fit the profile of a terrorist or other person of interest.

On the trans-Pacific flight some creepy baggy eyed businessman who sat next to her in First Class tried to start a conversation.

"So are you traveling on business or pleasure?," he asked.

"Neither" she replied.

"Oh, what then?" he asked.

"I was at a clinic in India, looking to cure a particularly virulent form of sexually transmitted disease. It might have worked, but I still have an open sore in my mouth. In fact, I noticed some empty seats here in First Class. You might be more comfortable moving away from me. It's up to you. I won't take any offense." He moved. She wasn't going to shoot him, so this was as much fun as she would have on the flight.

When she got to Chicago, Patricia Sizemore would be checking into the Waldorf Astoria. One of Turgenev's associates would be assisting her.

Fifty
Chicago, IL
Waldorf Astoria

Charles Phillips woke up. His mouth tasted like vomit. Leslie
was sitting up in bed next to him reading a newspaper.

"Newspapers are dead. We need to have a big score on this
project, then we can retire, write our memoirs," Leslie said.

"What time is it?" Phillips asked.

"Eight o'clock," Leslie answered.

"PM?" he asked.

"Yeah."

Phillips looked over at Leslie. He hated her. But he hated
himself more. How had he let himself get dragged into this
situation? At first this had been a wild adventure. Leslie had
enticed him into her realm of booze, drugs and three way sex.
She liked to have Charles and another woman. Leslie Chandler
looked as prim as the Boston Brahmin she projected to the
world. She was attractive, thin, and as flat chested as his
girlfriend in eight-grade. But she knew how to attract women
into her sexual schemes and they had no shortage of partners.
He couldn't help but smile when he wondered how many other
men would sign up to take his place, but he was burned out,
tired of Leslie's demands and kinkiness.

Charles found himself wishing that their venture would end
successfully, and he'd extricate himself to a regular life. He'd
find a normal woman, get married, have a front porch, a dog.

"Get cleaned up, we're going back down to the bar," Leslie startled Charles out of his reverie.

They had gotten wasted at the bar by late afternoon, and having no prospective partners in sight, Leslie had decided that they would go up to their room and sleep it off for a few hours.

"Let's go Charles, I'm feeling really horny. I'm in the mood to wear my high heels and dominate a couple willing subjects. There's bound to be a crowd at the bar tonight," Leslie said.

"Can't we just…you know… the two of us.. just stay here and have sex?" he asked.

"Get serious. Charles, you're in this deal. Stop farting around, brush your teeth and let's go," Leslie said.

When they walked into the Margeaux Brasserie there was a decent crowd of people, but most of them as couples. There were a few single men, but Leslie almost immediately fixed her sights on an attractive woman sitting by herself at the bar.

The woman was deeply tanned and dressed expensively. She wore a camel hair blazer over a white sweater, and the jacket was opened just enough to show off her splendid figure. Her skirt was modest length, but not so long as to hide her tan and shapely legs.

"Are these seats taken?" Leslie asked the woman, pointing to the two seats.

"No, please sit down," the woman gestured, and offered to shake hands with Leslie. "My name is Patricia."

Fifty One
Chicago, IL
Waldorf Astoria

Sierra quickly sized up the situation. She didn't want to seem too eager. Leslie, the woman was the Alpha dog, Charles was her pathetic underling. Within minutes the three of them were alone on the elevator, headed to Leslie and Charles' room. Leslie grabbed Sierra and kissed her, and bit her lip. Sierra went along with it. It was tolerable, better than being kissed by the wimp who accompanied them. He spent the elevator ride with his hands in his pockets. The elevator stopped, the bell rang, and the three of them got out.

Leslie fumbled for the keycard to the door. "I'm very anxious to get started," she said.

"Me too," Sierra said.

They entered a spacious room equipped with a king-sized bed. As soon as the door closed Leslie began to unbutton her blouse. Sierra turned and bolted the door and latched the chain.

"Hold on for a minute," Quinn said.

A man walked out of the bathroom. He was about five foot six, build like a fireplug. His name was Lev. In his hand was a large pistol. He pointed the gun at Charles. Leslie buttoned up her blouse and crossed her arms across her chest.

"What is this, a robbery?" Charles said.

"This man is named Lev. He does not carry business cards, but if he did it could say: *Professional Torturer. Specializing in Severing Body Parts,*" Quinn said.

"What the hell is going on?" Leslie demanded.

"Shut up and both of you sit down on the bed," Sierra said. "We're going to have a talk. If you cooperate you can both live." Quinn drew her Glock from her handbag.

"Why should we talk to you?" Leslie asked.

Sierra raised her gun. "Well there's this," she said. "And we have other ways of persuading you. Quinn looked at the man and used her empty hand to point to Leslie.

The man walked in front of Leslie and with his free hand punched her in the stomach. It was the punch of a professional, and he did not hold back. Leslie fell frontward off the bed, onto her hands and knees and vomited. She gasped violently, trying to catch her breath. The man grabbed her by the shoulders and tossed her back on the bed. She sat bent over with her hands on her knees.

"We need to know everything you know about Satoshi Nakamoto," Sierra said.

Leslie managed to eke out between gasps, "we don't divulge our sources."

Quinn was quiet for a moment. "That's quite brave of you. Do you really want to get punched again?

Leslie said nothing but the fear on her face was evident. "You do realize that we're not from the Washington Post, or some government regulator, right?" Sierra said.

"You're from Nakamoto, and you're here to keep us quiet?" Charles blurted.

Sierra looked at Lev, and gestured with her head at Charles. The man punched Charles in the stomach, just as he had punched Leslie. Charles fell off the side of the bed and screamed.

"Sit back on the bed or he'll punch you again," Sierra said.

With great difficulty Charles managed to sit back next to Leslie.

"Look. In the next several minutes you're going to tell us everything you know about Nakamoto, including where he is. If I feel that you have told us everything, I'll let you live. If I think you're holding back, we'll kill you." Quinn said.

"We don't know anything…. Nothing…we just made everything up," Leslie said.

"I don't believe you," Quinn said.

"We don't know anything," Leslie repeated.

Quinn stepped back and gestured for the man to come closer to her. Softly in his ear she said, "Which one do you think will talk?"

The man grunted and pointed to Charles. Quinn nodded and raised the gun at Leslie. Quinn pulled the trigger and shot Leslie Chandler in the heart. She slumped back violently, dying. Quinn had shot her in the chest rather than the head so it would take a while for her to bleed out and Charles could watch. Leslie moaned and foamy blood oozed out of her mouth, but she could not speak. The Glock was equipped with a silencer so the shot had produced a loud thump, but not loud enough to attract attention from anyone who happened to be walking down the hallway.

"You should realize now that we're serious. You seem to be the more reasonable person, Charles. That's why we're giving you the opportunity to talk. If you tell us everything, I'll let you live." Quinn said.

"Alright, alright… is she dead?" Charles said.

"Yeah, just about. It will probably take a couple more minutes before she stops breathing," Quinn said. "Start talking."

"We don't know anything. We made everything up. We've never talked to Nakamoto, don't even know who or what he is. We have no idea of his location," Charles said.

"That's hard to believe. Do I need to have my friend persuade you with his fist again? Or perhaps use his knife?" Lev produced a large knife from beneath his coat. "Lev is a man who enjoys his work. I'm told he has a collection of pickled penises in jars," Quinn said.

"No, no, no, please," Charles held his hand up. "We were lying all the time to our editor, claiming to have leads, sources. We claimed that Nakamoto was planning to use us as a conduit to divulge some important information to the public."

"Doesn't an editor want names, more than one source, some kind of proof, things like that?" Quinn asked.

"Yes, but in a situation like this all we needed to do was convince the editor that we were telling the truth. We were concocting a fanciful story, making sure that the details couldn't be checked. It wouldn't hurt anybody, and we'd win a Pulitzer. Leslie is a great liar, very manipulative." Charles said.

"No so much now," Quinn said.

Charles looked over at the lifeless Leslie. He was crying, blubbering, snot running out of his nose. "That's the truth, really. We just made up a line of bullshit. We thought we'd get away with it, that we could make up some story and get rich and famous."

Quinn looked over at the man. "Do you believe him, Lev?" she asked.

He nodded, and finally spoke in Russian accented English, "Yes, he's not brave enough to lie."

"That's disappointing Charles," Quinn said as she raised her gun and shot him dead.

Once Leslie and Charles had left the bar with Quinn their fates had been determined, no matter what they had said. This was not a situation from which any live witnesses would be allowed to emerge.

Fifty Two
Fort Meade, MD
Windowless Room

Yesterday had been a triumph for the Group of Six who met in
this room, but none of them were jubilant. They were involved
in an endless war. It was hard to even imagine a final victory.
There would be no VE Day, no signing of a peace treaty. One
situation just morphed into the next situation, and yesterday
had the feeling of a hollow victory. One side or another was
always coming up with a new technology, and a new more
insidious program. They all had enough experience to sense
another attack was coming.

"Cyber warfare has gone from nothing in the 1990's to an out
of control escalation now," Laudano said. "We employ a
futurist who gives us new scenarios all the time. As soon as the
scenarios are printed, they're out of date."

"So you have excellent job security," Sokolov said.

Toni Anne Laudano sat with Yuri Sokolov. It was just the two
of them. "The others will be joining us in fifteen minutes,"
Toni Anne said. "Cyber warriors have to balance when to
launch an attack, and when to play defense."

"Just like chess," Sokolov said.

 "In a way, yes, and in a way, no," she said. "Cyber is as
though you are simultaneously playing multiple opponents, and
each one of them has thousands of pieces."

Sokolov stroked his chin, lost in thought. Finally he said, "I
have two thoughts. First, in the short term the way to defend
yourself is carefully planned offensive thrusts. You must keep

156

your opponent off balance. Second, why play your opponent's game? Invent a new game. Play by your rules."

Toni Anne smiled, "I knew you were a pretty smart guy," she said.

"I'm a fast learner. And this assignment is very interesting, a new challenge," he said.

"If I'm right, it's gonna get a lot more challenging soon. And I'm always right," Toni Anne said.

"At the risk of mixing my metaphors, we do have an ace up our sleeve," Sokolov said.

Fifty Three
Austin, TX

Even though Gab was gone I had not resumed working in the casita. I wouldn't let myself admit why.

Life seemed humdrum since Gabrielle left and the Baylor ransomware situation had been resolved. I was bored with the stock market, and my clients were bored with me. I didn't have any new ideas.

One morning my phone rang, the private line on my iPhone, not the line my clients called on. I saw on caller ID that it was Dr. Tom Good. I decided to let it go to voicemail. I recommend this technique to people, but they always pick up their cell phones like trained chimps, a bad idea.

I listened to the message. "JR, this is Dr. Tom. I know I promised not to ask, but we have a very important fund raiser coming up and I was hoping that you'd play in our Charity Golf tournament. I'm counting on you, buddy. Give me a call, will you?"

The nerve of this guy! I was part of an effort that saved his University $1.3 billion. He would be out on the street, or making calls as the doctor on an Indian Reservation if it wasn't for me. It would be a while before I returned the call. Maybe after the tournament.

I absent-mindedly watched CNBC and my computer, looking for some investment idea. I toyed with the thought of fooling around in my own account, maybe doubling up on Bitcoin. For sure Bitcoin wasn't boring, it moved up or down at least 5% on an average day. I was ahead so far. What made Bitcoin fun was the action. I had bought and sold ten times so far. It was another world from my long term investing. I was even more afraid now. Bitcoin was getting to be like a drug.

A couple hours went by. My private line rang again, this time it was Barbara Jean Parker. After a brief pause I picked up.

"Hi JR, it's me, Barbara Jean," she said.

"Hey. You as beautiful as ever? Maybe we could make it one of those picture calls," I said.

"Of course I'm as beautiful as ever. Not that you'd care," she said.

"Barbara Jean, I'm a secret admirer of you," I answered.

"Yeah, Top Secret," she said. The background was noisy. "JR, could I ask you a major favor?"

"Sure."

"I'm stuck at the airport. Can you come and give me a ride home?" she said.

"That depends. What airport, it's not Laguardia, is it?" I asked.

"You're so witty. I'm stuck here in Austin. Can you come get me?" she said.

"Okay," I said. We made arrangements on where to meet. On the drive over I wondered just what was going on here. She had the cab fare to get home. Hell, she could afford to charter a helicopter to fly her home. Was this some ploy to snare me in her spider web? I began to think this might be a cozy spider web to get snared in. Barbara Jean did use a nice scent of perfume. Gabrielle certainly hadn't called me lately.

Fifty Four
Chicago, IL

Turgenev had made arrangements to meet Sierra Quinn the morning after her interrogation of the New York Times reporters. They met in a diner near the elevated train tracks in a shabby neighborhood.

Sierra was dressed much differently than the night before, wearing a black overcoat and a scarf covering her head. Nobody gave her a passing glance. Turgenev was seated at a booth when she came in, and she walked over and sat down.

"I've talked to Lev. He's not joining us." Turgenev stared at Quinn. "You look very plain today. You have the ability to change your appearance. That is useful in your line of work," he said.

"You should see me in my blue bikini," Quinn said.

"That is not something I would do," Turgenev said. He picked up the salt-shaker from the table and fiddled with the top. Then he stared right into her eyes for what seemed like an hour.

Quinn had seen a lot of tough hombres in New York, but Turgenev's stare was colder than she'd ever experienced. She had always thought she wasn't afraid of dying, but she was afraid of what Turgenev might do.

Turgenev was silent, choosing his words carefully. "You're a very attractive woman. I never mix business with pleasure. That's particularly important in our relationship. I wouldn't want to lose my objectivity. Depending on your performance, I might have to terminate your employment sometime in the future."

"Would there be an exit interview, where you'd review my benefits, my 401k plan?" Quinn said.

"Probably not," Turgenev answered.

Fifty Five
Austin, TX

I picked up Barbara Jean at the airport. She gave me a big hug, like she was returning from a two year deployment in Afghanistan. There was definitely some mutual pelvic touching. I thought of asking her why she couldn't just take a taxi home, but said nothing.

"JR, it's so good to see you," she said.

"You too," I answered.

After I left the airport I wasn't going 80 miles an hour or running the red lights, so Barb said, "why are you driving like my grandmother?"

"I'm taking my time. I'm nervous that you might accost me when we get to your house," I answered.

"You're a good judge of character," she said.

"Barb, you have lots of men chasing you around. Why are you after me?" I said.

"I like you, JR. I think we'd make a good couple," she said. "what are you waiting for?"

"I told you Barbara Jean, I need some time to think," I said.

She reached over and rubbed the inside of my thigh. "What are you thinking about now?" she asked.

Fifty Six
Chicago, IL

"As I said, I spoke to Lev about your conversation with the New York Times reporters. Lev's been with me since I was a boy. Lev used to break people's legs for me. He's progressed. Lev's one of the few people in the world that I trust," Oleg said.

"And?" Quinn asked.

"Tell me from your point of view. Then I'll tell you my conclusions," Turgenev said. "When we're done here I fly to Moscow to update my boss on the situation. Would you care to join me?"

"No," Quinn answered.

"Yeah, Moscow can be bleak this time of year. Bleaker if my boss is displeased," Oleg said.

Sierra Quinn started by describing the scene at the bar, and told Oleg in detail everything that had happened. She omitted nothing and did not try to color the story in any way. Her training as a detective was evident, she gave an excellent point by point summary of the action.

"So, do you think the reporters were telling you the truth? You think they were just making up a story for their editors?" Turgenev asked.

"Yes. The woman was braver, she might have lied, but once she was dead the man was a coward. A worthless little puke. I've interrogated a lot of people. He would have told us if there was any substance to their story, to try to save his life," Quinn said.

"You don't think he knew that you would kill him no matter what?" Turgenev asked.

"He might have suspected that, but he was a coward. I could see it in his eyes. He held out hope that we would let him go, even after he told us the whole thing was a fabrication," Quinn said.

"I see," Turgenev said. "Lev agrees with you. He's had a lot of experience in these sorts of interrogations. I'll have to go tell my boss this was a dead end. Meanwhile, you are to fly to Austin, Texas. Our computer experts are seeing some unusual activity in computer servers in that area that might lead to the location of Satoshi Nakamoto. Patricia Sizemore has a reservation in a very nice extended stay executive hotel. When you get there, stay in your room until further instructed. Order room service. Don't try to meet any Mr. Lidinski's. Texas isn't Indonesia, it's harder to make a mistake disappear." He handed Quinn a plane ticket.

As Quinn got up to leave Turgenev said, "we won't be blamed for this by my boss. We were just following the lead we were given. That might not always be the case."

Fifty Seven
Spicewood, TX

Barbara Jean put her hand on my thigh when we turned off the two lane blacktop into her ranch. She had done this several times during our ride from the airport. Barb giggled. I liked it.

"I figured out why you had to call me," I said. "You pulled this move on the taxi driver at the airport and he threw you out of the cab."

She pulled her hand away. "You're so clever," she said. "What do I have to do, take off my clothes and lay down on the floor?"

"Not in the truck. That would be uncomfortable," I said.

"I meant that as a figure of speech," Barb said.

What was the matter with me? Barbara Jean and I had been intimate before, back when Lola was alive. Lola and I were apart for months, sometimes over a year at a time, and I hadn't thought twice about having it being bad to have sex with Barbara Jean. It was great. Why was I being faithful to the unattainable Gabrielle? Or was I afraid of a commitment to the very real Barbara Jean?

"You're going to play hard to get for too long, and I'm going to find some fat, bald accountant who will appreciate me." She looked at me. "You wouldn't want that to happen, would you?"

'I want whatever would make you happy, Barbara Jean, my dear," I said.

"What a fuckin' jerk you are," she said.

165

"I've been told that before," I said.

"You ought to get a bumper sticker: Fuckin' Jerk," she said. Barb held her hands out as though holding up the proposed bumper sticker.

"I thought that was implied just by having Texas license plates on a pickup truck," I said.

"You're not real Texan. You're just an eastern elite snob, posing as a Texan," she sneered.

"Hey that's enough! You're starting to hurt my feelings," I said.

We were still going up the long driveway to her hacienda. She sat back against the passenger side door. "Hey, do you want to come in and have a---," she stopped herself in mid-sentence, "never mind, I can't take anymore rejection. In fact, you're not invited in the house."

"But what if I have to pee?" I asked.

"Go over by the tree," she suggested. "Watch out for the rattlesnakes."

We had arrived at the house. Surprising me, she sat in her seat until I came around and opened the truck door for her. She allowed me to take her bag to the front doors, and extended her hand for an exaggerated handshake. "I'll say good day to you sir, and thank you for the ride."

"You're welcome, ma'am," I said as I turned to walk back to the truck.

"Fuckin' Jerk" she said.

166

I thought she was right. I bet if I went on the internet I could find a bumper sticker that said just that, in a variety of colors.

Fifty Eight
Moscow
The Lider's Apartment

The Lider listened impassively to Turgenev's explanation of the situation involving the New York Times Reporters.

"Very well," The Lider said. "That whole thing sounded too easy. I knew we would have to work harder to discover the identity of Satoshi Nakamoto. The good news is we have a source inside the U.S. government with access to the highest levels and they have been working to unmask Nakamoto, but they seem no closer to than we are."

"The reporters were foolish to try to pull off their stunt," Turgenev said.

"Who cares?" The Lider replied. "These young punks have no idea of what they're getting involved with when they stand in the way of trillions of dollars. This is serious, and my plan to be the first trillionaire is going fine. We're about to start Phase Two. I would be more assured if we can identify Nakamoto, but as long as the U.S. doesn't know anything about him…" The Lider shrugged. "And Phase Two involves meddling in the upcoming Presidential Election. We have a multi-level attack planned. It should keep our adversaries diverted while we await putting Phase Three in place."

"What are my responsibilities in the new phase," Turgenev asked.

"I thought I had made that clear," The Lider said, "I need you to keep pursuing Nakamoto. We would very much like to have a chat with him before this deal is consummated. We could make a deal that is mutually beneficial…or kill him. Either way would work."

Turgenev nodded.

"As you were notified last week, there has been an abnormal amount of Bitcoin activity associated with a server in the Austin, Texas area. This is the best information our technical people have been able to generate, but it is just ether for now. I have told the technical people that I expect better results in the near future,' The Lider said.

"I have our asset, Quinn in place," Oleg said.

"Yes, the resort in Bali seems to be running fine without her," The Lider laughed.

"This Austin thing might be nothing. We'll see. You may go now," The Lider said.

Turgenev rose to leave. The Lider said, "I expect results from you, Oleg. You are not getting paid $6 billion to murder a couple of reporters. I need to know about Nakamoto."

Turgenev understood The Lider.

Fifty Nine
Fort Meade, MD
Cyber Command
Office of General Goldstein

Colleen Powers had been called to visit General Goldstein in his lead-lined conference room. The lining was installed to prevent any eaves-dropping, high tech or otherwise. Powers had been ordered to bring Toni Anne Laudano and Gabrielle McHugh.

Powers spoke, "Gabrielle the purpose of this meeting is to bring you up to speed on the situation here."

"The two New York Times Reporters were found shot to death in a Chicago hotel room yesterday," Goldstein began, "they were the reporters who had been hinting they had some connection with Satoshi Nakamoto."

"This may be a situation we can exploit," Powers said. "Toni Anne, want to continue?"

"We are seeing heavy Russian activity, trying all sorts of attacks, queries, backdoor attempts to find out whatever they can on Bitcoin and Satoshi Nakamoto. We know they haven't gotten anywhere. We also a have human intelligence situation." She directly addressed Gabrielle, "Murder Bitch, this is where you get involved. The three of us met yesterday," Laudano pointed to the two Generals, "and have decided to read you into the situation."

"Okay," Gabrielle said.

The other three spent fifteen minutes explaining what was happening. They told her about Sokolov, and that she would be attending some of the meetings in the windowless room from now on. They had other plans as well.

Sixty
Austin, TX

Another boring day. Nothing going on.
My iPhone rang. Caller ID said Gabrielle, so I picked right up.

"JR, I have a serious issue to discuss with you," she said.

"Oh, you want to pick a wedding date?" I said. I get nervous
when people get all serious on me.

"No," she said.

"Well, I'm always an optimist. What's so serious?" I asked.

"This is a chance to serve your country. Have you ever thought
of paying back the country that's been so good to you?" she
said.

"I always buy Girl Scout Cookies," I said.

"God damn it JR! This is probably the most important phone
call you've ever gotten in your life, and remember that my
organization did get the Baylor University ransomware
situation fixed for you! And all you do is act like a clown." She
sounded like she was ready to kick my ass, and I was sure that
she could.

"Alright Gabrielle, I'm listening," I said.

We need you to fly up tonight, to be at a meeting here at Fort
Meade tomorrow at 10 am," she said.

"I told you that I'm not interested in being the golf pro at an
Army base," I said.

Complete silence from Gabrielle. Finally, I could hear a deep breath. "JR, this is very serious. I have, well, volunteered you for a special, uh, let's call it a mission," she said.

"You're not kidding?" I asked.

"Do I sound like I'm kidding?" she said.

"No Captain McHugh," I said.

"That's Major," she said.

"Yeah, sorry. Major. So what's the deal? Give me some details," I said.

"We can't discuss it on the phone. JR, I did save your life. We got Baylor off the hook, and made you look like the hero. You owe it to me to come here tomorrow and hear our proposal," Gabrielle said.

"Wow, you're calling in all your chips. Your organization saved Baylor, you personally saved my life. I do owe you. Yeah, what the hell. It's a good excuse to not play in a charity golf tournament," I said.

"You can't tell anybody!" Gab said sharply.

"I'll just say I have to travel on business. Okay, I'll be there," I said. Gabrielle gave me the details, time, place, things like that.

"How should I dress?" I asked.

"A business suit would be a good idea," she said.

What would be wrong with just going to hear the details of the proposal? Then again, one of my favorite Willie Nelson songs goes: I know just what I would change if I went back in time somehow, but there's nothing I can do about it now.

173

Sixty One
Fort Meade, MD
Cyber Command

I got to the building thirty minutes early for my appointment.
I'm habitually early anyhow, and this was the U.S. Army, so I
wanted to be even earlier than usual. There were armed guards.
The armed receptionist gave me a visitor badge to clip to my
lapel. The lobby was well furnished. It wasn't some fancy New
York investment banking headquarters, but it wasn't a bunch of
olive drab metal folding chairs at the local armory either.

Right on the dot of 10 am I was met in the lobby. I was
expecting that it would be Gabrielle coming out to greet me,
but it was a redheaded woman in an Army Uniform with a
single star on her epaulettes. Even I know that's a General.

"JR Johnson?" she asked.

I stood up. "Yes…General," I answered. I almost said 'sir'
before I caught myself.

"I'm General Powers," she said, shaking my hand with a firm,
but not aggressive grip.

Gabrielle's description of Powers was accurate. The General
was beautiful. She had shortish but still feminine red hair and
green eyes, very striking. Her lightly freckled complexion was
perfect and she was tall, but not in the Gab range, maybe
5'10". She did not seem like a barrel of laughs.

"Follow me," she said. I guess Generals don't say 'please',
except to Generals with more stars than them, or the President.
They probably also say 'please and thank you' to congressmen
when they're looking for funding.

Even though I had passed through a metal detector on the way in, I had to go through another metal detector to get into the next hallway. The General was let through, but I was wanded by an enlisted man.

"Go ahead, sir," he said.

That was better. Somebody called me 'sir'. Maybe they'd make me a Commander. James Bond was a Commander.

General Powers began walking fast, and I followed her to the end of the hallway. She made no attempt to talk to me. After I took one glance at her shapely rear end, she turned around and looked at me. Was she a mind reader? Then again, I don't have the hardest mind to read. I decided I better not do that again. I was sure they had cameras watching my every move.

'Eyes front, Commander! Above waist level!' I ordered myself.

At the end of the hallway General Powers stopped at a doorway on the right. Above the door were two lights, one red, one green. The green light was on. She gestured for me to go in.

As I passed her Powers said, "This is a secure room. When I close the door the red light will come on. No one will enter then."

Big deal, just like the lav in an airliner. I decided to keep that to myself.

There were three other people standing at a conference table. This was a room for the top brass, well appointed. There was a man in an Army uniform with four stars, Gabrielle, also in uniform and a woman in civilian clothing. The civilian was dressed in a green jumper with a white blouse. Her brown hair was in a pixie cut. She was pretty, and was the only one who smiled at me. She looked sweet.

The sweet woman in the jumper said, "Sit down. We don't have all day to fuck around."

So Gabrielle's description had been right. The foul mouthed Mary Poppins introduced herself as Toni Anne Laudano, and introduced General Goldstein. "You already know the Murder Bitch."

I said nothing and sat down after General Goldstein had gestured for me to do so. The four of them were on one side of the conference table, me on the other.

I have been interrogated as a murder suspect by New York City detectives. The four people facing me were much more intimidating than the detectives.

"You know what? I'm not that crazy about the atmosphere here. You're acting like I did something wrong. What's going on?" I said.

I looked at Gabrielle, and tried to picture her in her damp underwear by my pool. It didn't work. She didn't seem like the same person. Maybe Murder Bitch was an accurate description.

The four were quiet, and finally the Four Star spoke. "We are trying to impress upon you the seriousness of this situation."

"Okay, I'm suitably impressed. What situation?" I said.

Sixty Two
Fort Meade, MD
Cyber Command
Commanding Officer's Conference Room

The female General spoke. "We've already had an extensive look at your background."

"What do you mean? You can just pry into a private citizen's life whenever you want?" I said.

"Of course. Don't be naïve," Gabrielle said, "They started to investigate you after you were involved in the Baylor ransomware situation."

Were you investigating me when you sat on my lap?

"Do you know what a Security Clearance is?" Toni Anne asked.

"Vaguely," I said.

"Can you think of any reason you wouldn't get one?" Toni Anne asked.

I thought for a minute. I was pretty sure that my experience with the two cheerleaders from SMU wouldn't be held against me, and that was a long time ago anyhow. "No, I've never done anything disloyal, or radical. Never been arrested. Don't do any illegal substances. Is that the kind of thing you mean?" I asked.

"Yeah," Toni Anne said, "any political activity?"

"I'm an unaffiliated voter. I make small contributions to both sides of the fence when I feel it's in my best interest," I said.

"We know a lot about you. Anybody who's looked at your college transcript will know that you didn't work that hard," Toni Anne said.

"Well, I ain't that crazy about you or the horse you rode in on either, right now," I said. "I didn't fly up here on my own nickel to hear this shit." I was about ready to leave. I put my hands on the arms of my chair.

General Goldstein held up his hand, a gesture intended for Toni Anne to shut up. "Toni Anne has her own peculiar style of diplomacy. But you're safer as an American having her work here."

"A better way of expressing my last statement might be to say that if the Russians look at your educational background they'll know that you're not capable of supplying us with any technical knowledge," Toni Anne said.

"Yeah, so?" I said. "Why would the Russians be looking at my background?"

General Goldstein made eye contact with the other three people on his side of the table. Then he looked at me. "Would you be willing to commit to a project of ours? It is intended to be a diversionary tactic. It would involve some of your time. It shouldn't be dangerous."

"Probably," Toni Anne said.

Sixty Three
Moscow

The Russian Cyber Warfare system is a department of the FSB, or Federal Security Service. Most Americans still think of this organization as the KGB. From the time of the Czars the name of this arm of the government changed from the Secret Police, under the Soviets to the Cheka, then KGB, and now it was called the FSB.

Their main purpose has always been to use any means necessary to keep whatever current regime in power. Human rights have never been a factor. Suspects are guilty until proven innocent, and nobody tries to prove them innocent. In earlier days this simply meant kicking down doors in the middle of the night, hauling suspected subversives to the basement of a jail, and killing them, or after repeated beatings sending them off to a Siberian labor camp.

There was never any shortage of applicants to work for the Secret Police. The money was not good, but the sense power was great, and the Russian educational system profiled candidates beginning at age ten. To be identified by the system as a smart bully at an early age was the way to get the attention of FSB recruiters for this unit.

The FSB and its predecessors also had an arm that trained and ran spies in foreign countries. These people were much brighter than the shit kicking goons who worked internally in Russia and were skilled at languages. The Lider spent most of his KGB career in this arm.

To be sure, the FSB still participated in these sorts of activities, but technology had advanced to the point that the mission of the FSB had been enlarged. The emergence of Cyber Warfare created new possibilities and Russia and The Lider were quick to jump on the opportunities. There were two new groups within Cyber Warfare at the FSB, The Information Technical Group, or ITG, and the Psychological Group. ITG was responsible for offensive hacking, subverting, and disrupting foreign computer networks and creating defenses against foreign attacks, while the Psychological Group's purpose was to spread misinformation.

Russia and The Lider were proud of their Cyber capabilities. The profile for ideal candidate to serve in the Cyber arm of the FSB was different. The FSB looked for children, male and female, who were savants at Chess. The very best would as always, be cultivated to be Grand Masters, to compete at the highest level for World Championships, but the next level down was recruited by the FSB.

The U.S. saw the success of the Russian Cyber Warfare operations and had organized in much the same structure as the Russians. Russia had the advantage that there were no competing organizations to the FSB. The U.S. had the CIA, FBI, and each branch of the armed forces had their own cyber operations. This caused bureaucratic infighting and competition for Congressional funding, thus making the American efforts less streamlined than the Russians. But U.S. Cyber Command was the top dog, and tried to ignore the other agencies except when necessary.

The Lider had called in the head of the Psychological Group of the FSB. The man stood rigidly in front of his desk. He looked nervous, and that was fine with The Lider.

"Tell me about your plans to disrupt the American Presidential Election," The Lider said.

"Sir, as you instructed we are commencing multiple strategies to create as much havoc in the U.S. as possible, without necessarily influencing who wins," the Psych Group head said.

"That's right. I couldn't care less who wins," The Lider laughed. "The best result would be if they can't decide who won for a year or two. We want both sides to be at each other's throats, for them to lose focus on other important issues."

"Then this is the opportunity of a lifetime for our group!" the Group Head said.

"I like the way you chose to express that," The Lider said with a deadpan expression on his face.

Sixty Four
Fort Meade, MD
Cyber Command
Conference Room of Commanding General

"Probably not dangerous?" I said.

General Goldstein smiled at me. This did not have the intended effect of putting me at ease. "It's unlikely the Russians would do anything to you."

"Russians?" I asked.

"Mr. Johnson. I have to ask you now if you're committed. Will you do the job for us? I can't tell you anymore until you've agreed to work for us." Goldstein said.

"I'm hearing: probably not dangerous, Russians. I'm sitting here in Top Secret-ville, what the hell is going on?" I said.

Gabrielle looked uncomfortable. She wasn't used to people speaking to four star Generals in that tone of voice.

Nobody in the room spoke. Finally Gab said, "JR, I suggested you for this role. You're perfect. You should trust me and just go ahead and volunteer."

"Besides, the Russians already know that you're here. They'll be watching you whether or not you volunteer," Toni Anne said.

"What?" I said.

Toni Anne continued, "the Russians know who goes in and out of this building. They watch, and there's really nothing we can do about it. And to be blunt, we're going to let it leak that we called you in here today to interrogate you about a certain subject, and that you were uncooperative."

I was definitely out of my element. I addressed General Goldstein. "You all are trying to tell me that I'm screwed whether or not I volunteer?"

"Pretty much," Goldstein said, "Yes."

"In that case, I volunteer," I said.

"I told them that you'd do the right thing JR," Gabrielle said.

I glared at her. "Alright, so I'm in. So where do I sign?"

General Powers said, "There's nothing for you to sign. We have your commitment, and we have measures to ascertain your loyalty."

That sounded ominous. I decided not to pursue that train of thought.

"Alright. Now explain to me what's going on," I said.

"Have you ever heard the term 'Useful Idiot'?" Toni Anne asked.

"Yeah," I said.

"The Russians use that term a lot. That's what you're going to be for us, a Useful Idiot---no offense," Toni Anne said.

"None taken," I said. I didn't mean it. "Why ever would I be offended?"

All four of them smiled tolerantly at me. It was the smile a researcher would aim at a lab rat.

Sixty Five
Austin, TX
Extended Stay Hotel

Sierra Quinn had phoned Turgenev. "I've got to at least be able to go to the health center and work out. I can't just sit on my ass and eat room service all day long," she said.

"Alright, you can go. Dress modestly. And don't make any friends. Just go there and to your room. Alone. Do you understand?" Turgenev said.

"Yeah," Quinn said. "Any idea of how long until I get some action?"

"We're watching something interesting right now. There might be something for you to do soon. Keep your phone with you," he said.

"C'mon, who do you think you're talking to, some novice?" Quinn said.

There was a long silence on Oleg's part. Finally he said, "did you talk like this to your superiors when you were a detective?"

"No, I wasn't this polite," Quinn answered.

Sixty Six
Fort Meade, MD
Cyber Command

"Okay, you're in now, understand?" General Goldstein asked.

"No, not really," I answered.

He kept a neutral expression. "You'll understand more before you leave today. I have to excuse myself…I have an important meeting. The three here will brief you. They'll tell you all that you're authorized to know." He stood, walked around the table, shook my hand and left.

I wanted to say, 'you mean *this* meeting isn't important?' but I kept my mouth shut. It was important to *me*.

I wondered if he had another meeting, or whether he was leaving so he could later deny being present for something the three remaining people were about to tell me. Maybe I had seen too many movies. This reminded me of one of Lola's movies where she played the U.S. Ambassador to Sweden.

Except this wasn't a movie. I was smart enough to know that when they told me I probably wasn't in any danger, that meant that I was in danger, and Gabrielle had signed me up for this mission without even asking me. I'd have to talk to her about this in the future. If I had a future.

I looked across the table at the three women and the thought occurred to me that they were all good looking enough to actually be in the movies. I forced that thought out of my mind and looked at each one of them individually. I came to the conclusion that old Sewer Mouth, Toni Anne Laudano was likely to be the most trustworthy.

I thought about Gabrielle. What a waste it had been for her to be a bodyguard. This was where she belonged, but her personality had changed. She never lacked self-confidence but in this environment she radiated confidence. I was wondering why she had ever left…

"Johnson…Johnson, we need your undivided attention," General Powers said to me.

So that was my title now "Johnson". I guess I hadn't been promoted to Commander yet.

"Okay," I said.

Powers shot me a withering look, and Gabrielle joined in. I guess "okay" was not the approved mode for a 'Johnson' to address a General. *Screw that, what were they going to do, shoot me? Well, then again…*

"Tony Anne is going to take over the briefing," Powers said.

I braced myself for an attack by Mary Poppins, but she proceeded calmly. "Do you know much about Bitcoin?"

"I'll be honest. I probably know more than most people, and I've done a lot of reading on it, but I still don't understand it. I have bought and sold some in my own account. Just screwing around. Right now it's just an experiment in mass psychology," I said.

"Yeah, honest is what we're looking for," Toni Anne said. "We're not going to ask you to write a Doctoral Thesis, but it's time for you to get more interested. There are a lot of people smarter than you who are writing opinions forecasting the price of Bitcoin. The range of the predictions go from Zero to $1 million per Bitcoin."

"Yeah, that's why I haven't bought much," I said.

"Does the name Satoshi Nakamoto mean anything to you?" Laudano asked.

"I'm not real stupid," I said.

"So then, tell me the significance of Satoshi Nakamoto," Toni Anne said.

I hesitated for a moment. I didn't like being treated like an idiot, but here I was, and I'd play along. "Satoshi Nakamoto is the supposed creator of Bitcoin. Nobody knows who he is, or even if it's one person, or a committee, or a robot."

"Exactly," Laudano said. Powers and Gabrielle stared at me.

"Do you know who Nakamoto is?" I asked.

"That's not something you need to know," Toni Anne said. None of their expressions changed, it looked like they had prepared themselves for that question. "You shouldn't read anything into that answer, it just not a compartment that you need to investigate."

"So what compartment am I in?" I asked.

"We're seeing a lot of interest from one major player in finding out who and where Nakamoto is: The Fuckin' Commies! The Lider!" Toni Anne said.

"So where do I come in?" I asked.

"First step. You're going to become a major trader in Bitcoin for your own account. We've gone over all your accounts and know that you're squeaky clean and not aggressive. Get this: I'm giving you some inside information," Laudano said.

"I'm pretty sure inside information is illegal," I said.

"Think about this: Bitcoin is unregulated. There's no ruling government agency nobody to catch you, and it's not a crime if you did get caught," Toni Anne said.

"True," I said. "Bitcoin is very volatile, it has wild swings. I'm not much of a trader, I'm more of a long term guy."

"That's perfect, the Russians are going to know that too," Laudano said. For the first time, both Powers and Gabrielle smiled.

"The Russians!" I said.

"Look, stupid, the Russians can hack into every trade you've ever done in every account in about five seconds," Laudano said. "I'm not talking about some low life hacker in Uzbekistan, I mean the FSB, their equivalent of us, of Cyber Command. Hell, we've already looked at everywhere you've ever been on the internet. You should be more careful about some of the websites you've visited."

"I didn't mean it. My finger must have slipped!" I said.

"Don't worry about it, you're fine. You should see some of the shit we have on people, Senators, Congressmen---"

"Toni Anne, don't you think that's enough on that topic?" Powers said.

"Okay," Toni Anne said to the General. Looking back at me Laudano said, "I'm telling you the Bitcoin is going up---a lot. Unless you're the worst trader in the world you ought to be able to handle that. We want you to be the Big Swingin' Dick Trader in Bitcoin. Buy and sell a lot, a shitload. Every time it goes down, it's going back up. You have my assurances. I wish I had this part of your job. It's going to be fun, and you can keep the money you make."

"Hmmm. So you wish you had that part of my job. Which part of my new job do you *not* want?" I asked.

Sixty Seven
Moscow
The Lider's Apartment

The Lider had called in the Russian Finance Minister. The minister had been educated at the London School of Economics and The Wharton School at The University of Pennsylvania. He projected the perfect sophisticated moderate global operator to the outside world, but inside he was as loyal a stooge to The Lider as anyone in Russia.

"Yes Mr. President," the Finance Minister said with a nod of his head that could be interpreted as a slight bow. As usual for this type of meeting, it was just the two men.

"How much of a position do we have in the national account in Bitcoin?" The Lider asked.

"We've just begun buying, on your orders." The Minister started fumbling through papers in his briefcase, but The Lider raised his hand.

"The exact position right now is not important. What is important is that we become a major buyer, starting now," The Lider said.

"How major, sir?" the banker asked.

"Up to 100% of our total assets, more if you like," The Lider answered.

That was a stunning amount. "Sir, at today's prices, we'd own more than all the Bitcoin in the world," the Minister explained.

"Bitcoin is going to rise a lot, and there's going to be another group of buyers who need to own it. They'll have to buy it from us." The Lider said.

"I don't understand, sir," the Finance Minister said.

"Of course, we must buy it in different puppet accounts, scattered all around the world, they can't know that we own it," The Lider said.

"Yes sir," the banker said. He was completely confused, but he loved his job, and he wished to stay alive.

"The beauty of the situation is that the parties that buy the Bitcoin from us will be forced to *give* it back to us. It will be the biggest financial windfall in the history of the world, and you'll be part of it. You'll share in our glory, and our profits of course." The Lider said.

"Sir, I don't understand. Do you wish to explain it to me?" the minister asked.

"You'll have to know eventually, so very well," The Lider said. He raised the index finger of his left hand. "Just a moment." He stood and reach for an object behind his ornate curtains. He walked back and gently placed the object on his desk. It was the pickled head of the Oligarch who had tried to cheat him years ago in a transaction. The Finance Minister had heard stories of the jar, but even so, he felt cold, nauseated, and most of all, terrified.

"I enjoy my work, as I'm certain that you do as well. Sometimes I must take drastic action to insure that my commands get carried out exactly as I specify. You are not to repeat anything I tell you tonight, to anyone. Your wife, your mistress, your other mistress, your most trusted subordinate. Have I made myself clear?" The Lider asked.

"Yes sir, no one is more loyal to you than I am!" the Finance Minister said.

The Lider smiled, and pointed at the jar. "Oddly enough, this man made roughly the same comment to me!"

The Finance Minister opened his mouth, but no sound came out. He looked at the jar, and when he realized that his expression looked just like the embalmed Oligarch he closed his mouth.

"I cannot overstate how important it is that you remain quiet about our plan. I'm certain that you will. It is necessary for you to understand the nature of the transactions I am specifying," The Lider said.

The Minister nodded vigorously.

The Lider began to explain the plan. It took several minutes.

Sixty Eight
Fort Meade, MD
Cyber Command
Conference Room of Commanding General

Nobody answered my question, so I asked it again.

"So, what part of my new assignment would you not want to do?" I looked at Toni Anne, then at Gabrielle.

"We're going to have you busy visiting Tech companies, some in Austin. Maybe some in Silicon Valley. a couple in Salt Lake area," Toni Anne finally answered. "That could be awfully boring. Or not."

"Why am I going to do that?" I asked.

"It's a diversionary tactic. We want to make the Russians think that you know something. Maybe about Satoshi Nakamoto. We want to take their eyes off the ball, to think they have a solid lead when they actually have nothing," Toni Anne said.

"Why are the Russians all the sudden so interested in Bitcoin?" I asked.

"We can't tell you about that." Laudano said. All three women sat with their hands folded identically in front of them. It reminded me of the tribunal I had faced when in Fifth grade I got caught flushing an entire roll of toilet paper down a toilet. The stakes were higher here, but the atmosphere was the same. It's a matter of perspective.

"It's time to be candid with you," Laudano said.

"Okay. You haven't been candid so far?" I asked.

"That's an excellent question. You're proving to be smarter than I thought," Toni Anne said.

"I'm under the impression that you thought I was just a little smarter than a rock, so that's not much of a compliment," I replied.

General Powers spoke, "That's a good compliment considering the source. Toni Anne might be the smartest person in the world."

"Yeah, and she has such a winning personality, too," I said.

Toni Anne didn't seem to take any offense. She smiled at me. I was momentarily charmed, then she said, "enough of this bullshit, I've got to show you something."

She picked up a remote control and aimed it at a big screen on the wall to my right. "This is a replay of news that was on CNN this morning."

The screen showed two separate photos that looked to be taken from employment IDs. A man and a woman, both looking to be in their late twenties. The caption below said: Two New York Times Reporters Murdered in Chicago. A news anchor off screen was saying 'Authorities are investigating...' Tony Anne froze the picture.

"CNN doesn't know anything, and the Chicago Police don't know anything, and we're telling them through back channels that they're not ever going to know anything, and make the investigation look good, but you're not going to solve this one." Laudano said. "It was a top level professional hit, there's no evidence they can find."

"You're not telling me that the government did this!" I said.

"We don't do things like this, despite what you might have heard," Laudano said. "But we think *a* government was behind it---The Russians."

"What does this have to do with me?" I asked.

The tribunal of women was quiet again. General Powers stroked her chin. Gabrielle looked at me without giving away any emotion.

"These reporters had published a couple stories, hinting that they were on the trail of Satoshi Nakamoto. They were implying that they were working on interviewing him." Toni Anne said.

"Is there any chance they were telling the truth?" I asked.

"Zero chance. They were bullshitting. I can't tell you why we know, but they were completely bluffing. It's happened before, to the Times, the Washington Post, Wall Street Journal. Reporters got caught making up shit, hoping for glory and money. Lots of times, and that's just the ones who got caught. Who knows how many times reporters have gotten away with stuff like this," Laudano said.

I've never been hit with a ton of bricks, but that instant was what it must feel like. It was my turn to sit quietly with my hands folded in front of me. Now I knew why the four star general left the meeting early.

I spoke softly, "So you're setting me up to be their replacement?"

"Yes and No. The most important difference is that you are under 24 hour protection from our best operatives," Toni Anne said. "Those reporters were just freelancing. We were going to warn them off the story, but they got killed before we contacted them."

"So when does this protection begin?" I asked.

"It has already begun. It started when you landed at Reagan National." General Powers said. "You haven't noticed anybody tailing you?"

"No," I said.

"That shows you how good they are," Powers said.

"So, you're in….some… danger, but you're being protected by our best people, and they're very good. The good news is even *you* can't fuck up making maybe a billion dollars trading Bitcoin in the next week," the charming Toni Anne explained. "You'll make a fortune!"

"I have a fortune," I said.

"You'll have a bigger fortune. Start a charity or something," Laudano said.

The biggest surprise in this morning of surprises happened next.

Sixty Nine
Fort Meade, MD
Cyber Command

General Powers and Major Gabrielle McHugh stood up. The General said, "Toni Anne wants an opportunity to speak to you one-on-one. Then she'll give you a brief tour of our facility."

Powers shook hands with me, then Gab shook my hand as though I was someone she had met just this morning. The two uniformed officers left. When the door closed Toni Anne gestured for me to follow her.

"Just follow me to my office. Don't talk on the way."

I followed Toni Anne. She had a nice rear end too. I'm so shallow. *What if they have Artificial Intelligence monitoring my eye movement?* When we got to her office she closed the door and motioned for me to sit down.

"I'm the brains of this operation," Toni Anne said.

"Yeah, I figured that out," I said.

"I'd like to tell you a little of my background. I dropped out of MIT when a supposedly expert professor told me the Encryption Algorithm I was developing wouldn't work. I figured 'why do I need these assholes?' So I started my own company. Sold it five years later for $300 million, then I came to work for the government.," Toni Anne said.

"I know that. I was on the conference call at Baylor, remember?" I said.

"Yeah, sure. By the way, this conversation is not being recorded. The recording stopped when those two left the room.

I insisted on that. You have my word, and I'll always tell you the truth. They, even General Goldstein, will not screw with me." Toni Anne looked me in the eyes and I believed her. "The President has told me that I can pick up the phone and call him whenever I want, and he told me that in front of the Generals. I don't know how much you know about the Chain of Command, but that's never done."

"Yeah," I said.

"You know why the President told me that? Because I'm the best, and they need me," Toni Anne said.

"I believe that too," I said.

"I've got to be really blunt about something. Okay?" Toni Anne said.

'Go ahead," I said. *What could be next?*

"Don't sit around pining for the Murder Bitch. You'd be pulling your pud for the rest of your life," Laudano said.

"Don't beat around the bush. Tell me what you really think," I couldn't help but laugh.

"Major McHugh wants to be a General. I've seen the look, the way they act," Laudano said.

"So why are you sharing this with me?," I asked.

"You seem like a nice guy. I'm going to do my best to get you through this," she said, "not everybody around here cares about the collateral damage. Anybody who helps me, I help them. Besides, you're a good looking guy. You got a much better shot with me."

"I see you're wearing a wedding ring," I noted.

"It's my second husband. You might meet him on our little tour. I'm sure he'll notice you. I may be shopping around for a replacement in a short while. And I've always wanted to date a billionaire," Toni Anne said.

I'm a pig. I tried to imagine what Toni Anne would look like getting out of my pool in her wet undies. "I'm not a billionaire yet," I said.

"Listen stupid, just start buying Bitcoin—big. Use options, straddles, hedges, stuff like that. Big-just keep plowing it back in. Whenever it goes down, buy more. I'll give you my number, you can call me once in a while. I'll help you. This is a pooch that can't be screwed. Just don't lose your nerve," she said.

"Yeah, but these things usually end bad. How will I know when to get out?" I asked.

"Good question, but I've got a better answer. Trust me, getting out will be easy. I can't explain any more right now. Somebody will take you out. You have to trust me, okay?" Toni Anne said.

"By 'take you out' you mean out of Bitcoin, or that somebody will shoot me?" I asked.

"Ha. I meant Bitcoin. We're going to protect you. For one thing tomorrow you'll be hiring a husband and wife team as ostensibly a housekeeper and a gardener. In reality they're the best kick ass bodyguards in the world. And there'll be some others in place that you'll probably never be aware of. I told you I'd take care of you. I'm making them pull out all the stops." Toni Anne said.

"I already have a part-time housekeeper. She needs the money," I said.

"Why don't you give your housekeeper a weeks' paid vacation. Explain to her that these two people are just coming on for a special project for a week, then she can come back."

"So you think I'll make a billion in Bitcoin in a week?" I asked.

"How many fuckin' times do I have to tell you? If you're stupid you'll make a billion. If you don't have your head up your ass, you'll make two billion," Toni Anne said.

"That'll be a good head start on a Foundation. I'll fund some hospitals---the ones my siblings work at, but in my name, with a big sign. That should really piss them off. You know, my brothers and sister---"

"I know all about you. You don't have to tell me about your family," Toni Anne paused. "Look, I'm not done being blunt. I've got to tell you the whole story. Since your ass is on the line, you deserve to know."

What else was she going to tell me? I wasn't sure I wanted to know any more. "Okay, lay it on me," I said.

"General Powers, then Colonel Powers, was having an affair with Gabrielle. Powers told her husband, a congressman, about it. He went apeshit, and part of the deal he made with Powers was that she'd ditch Gabrielle, then he'd give her a divorce. It was just a sham marriage. The congressman didn't care about his wife, he wants to run for President someday, he just cared about appearances. So Powers threw Gabrielle McHugh under the bus to save her own career. Gabrielle overreacted and quit the Army," Toni Anne said.

"Slow down, I'm having a hard time processing this," I said.

200

"By the way, this congressman is a total dipshit. You've got a better chance of being President. But Washington is filled with these assholes, all ambition, no brains," Toni Anne said.

"You should be on the Sunday morning political talk shows," I told Toni Anne.

Toni Anne laughed. "Yeah, that would be fun. Listen, our country is all screwed up. The political backstabbing that goes on here makes Wall Street look like the kiddie pool. But we're still the best country in the world. That's why I do this," she said.

"Yeah, And you get to show everybody how smart you are," I said.

She shrugged. "I gotta finish telling you. This might be a little tough to hear."

I exhaled. "Go ahead."

"When Gabrielle was out of the Army, wasting her time as a friggin' bodyguard, she realized she wanted to get back in. So she started talking to Powers," Toni Anne said.

"So?" I said.

"So, the idea of having a Useful Idiot came up. Gabrielle told Powers she had the perfect candidate. The whole time Gabrielle McHugh was in Texas she was setting you up," Toni Anne told me.

Seventy
Fort Meade, MD
Cyber Command

Man, did I feel stupid. Toni Anne put her hand on mine.

"In a couple months, maybe I can help you forget about all this," she said. "I'm sure I can comfort you," she laughed. She slowly pulled her hand away.

"I know about disappointment. I was a good wife until I found out my first husband was banging two of the Washington Redskins cheerleaders. At the same time! My second husband, well, we'll see. I don't think it's going to last much longer," Toni Anne said.

"It's not that I don't find you attractive Toni Anne. It's just that the last hour has been a bit of an overload. 'Well JR, you're going to volunteer for a mission that you're stuck doing whether you want to or not. You're going to make a couple billion, but the Russians might kill you before you can spend it. By the way, the woman you are pining over is a manipulative bitch who doesn't care about you, she set you up for all this, so she can get to be a General' And now this other beautiful, but married, woman Super Genius wants to get you in the sack. Does that sort of sum it up?" I asked.

"Good synopsis. I like beautiful. I like 'Super Genius'," Toni Anne said. "I have to tell you some more."

"Sure, why not?" I said.

"I'll tell you what's going to happen, assuming that we pull off this mission. I mean my mission, which you are only a small part of. Gabrielle McHugh is smarter than Powers. Powers is at her level of incompetence, even she's beginning to realize it.

General Goldstein realizes it, he just promoted her for Equal Opportunity purposes. When this is a success, Powers will get forced into retirement. Gabrielle McHugh will get promoted to Colonel, with the promise of being a general in a couple years if she doesn't screw up," Laudano said.

"Why should I give a shit?" I asked.

"You shouldn't. I'm the only one here that you can trust. Don't call Gabrielle again. I'll give you my number," she said.

"Okay," I said.

"Keep one thing in mind. McHugh has the motive of revenge. She's going to get Powers for throwing her under the bus. Gabrielle is making nice now, she has to. Powers is her CO. If I'm judging Gabrielle McHugh right, she'll put the knife in Powers' back, and Powers won't figure it out until she's retired, if ever," Toni Anne said. "I'm sorry to put it this way, but McHugh doesn't care about you, you're just a pawn."

"Jeez," I said.

"Don't worry. I've got access to a lot better chess players than Gabrielle McHugh," Laudano said.

I sat in my chair. I felt like I weighed one million pounds.

"One more thing. The Russians don't want to kill you. Right away. They want to torture you until you tell them what you know about Bitcoin and Satoshi Nakamoto. Then they want to kill you. I hope it doesn't come to this, but the longer you don't talk while being tortured, the longer you'll be alive, and we have a chance of saving you."

"Oh, that's reassuring," I said.

Seventy One
Austin, TX
Extended stay hotel

Sierra Quinn was on the treadmill. She was wearing a bulky
old fashioned grey sweatsuit and had a towel wrapped around
her neck. Quinn had resolved to stay on the treadmill as long as
she could take it. She had to stay in shape in her line of work,
you never knew when you'd have to chase somebody, or run
away yourself. She did know that she could never run away
from the Russians if they became displeased with her.

Her phone rang. It could be only one person. She got off the
treadmill to answer it.

"Yes," she said, breathing heavily.

"What are you doing, that you are breathing like that?"
Turgenev asked.

"I was on the freakin' treadmill. What did you think, I was
screwing?" Quinn said. A man on the treadmill next looked
over. She didn't care.

No reply from Turgenev, so Quinn said, "If I was screwing I
wouldn't have answered. And I know how to follow orders."

"Alright," Turgenev said. "We need to have a face to face
meeting. I can't be there until tomorrow. We'll have lunch in
the hotel restaurant where you're staying. Noon. Be there."

"Where else would I be?" Quinn asked.

Seventy Two
Fort Meade, MD
Cyber Command

I sat in Toni Anne's office. The thought occurred to me that I might have been better off all those years ago going to Medical School. I knew from observing my father that being a doctor could be a pain in the ass, but it did not involve the very real potential of being tortured by the Russians.

"Hey, I'm not looking for another husband. I think I'm done with that route. It's just that you and I could have a pretty good time for a while. I'm still married, and it wouldn't be appropriate for us to do anything until this mission gets resolved, anyhow. Whichever comes first, you know?" she said.

When I said nothing she continued.

"I've studied the human brain for research in Artificial Intelligence, and came to the conclusion that people have gifts in different areas. In the extreme, look at the guys who can't tie their own shoelaces but can sit at a piano and play a Beethoven sonata after listening to it once. Me, I was given special gifts at Math, Logic, and sex. I excel at all three," Laudano said.

"I've always said that sex is like golf. You can have a lot of fun at both, even if you're not good at them," I said.

"Hey, just think about it, okay?" Toni Anne said.

"I'm a guy. I'm already thinking about it," I said.

"Great. Now, go back to Texas, start buying Bitcoin. Buy your ass off. Hedge a little, so when it goes down cover the hedge and buy more. Use leverage, be a big player. We want you to be so big that you move markets. Don't worry, the Russians will notice you. Just know, Bitcoin is going up an amount that you can't imagine, in the next few days. I wish I could trade Bitcoin for the week instead of what I've got to do." Laudano said.

"You telling me that there's another player, somebody who has to own Bitcoin in a big way," I asked.

Laudano nodded. "Yeah, the Fuckin' Commies! How dense are you. And they've got to own it," Toni Anne said. "And remember that tomorrow you're getting a new housekeeper and a gardener. They'll come by in the morning. You'd never guess by looking at them what kickass people they are. They'll be there at 8:30. Their names are Eric and Bonnie."

"Are those their real names?" I asked.

"Real enough," Toni Anne replied.

"Okay. What, do I leave now?" I asked.

"No. I'm taking you on a quick tour of the facilities. It's not for your benefit. We know about a mole, so the purpose of the tour is so the mole will see you," Toni Anne explained. "You know what a mole is, right?"

"Hey, I watch The Americans," I said.

"The mole will tell the Russians that you were here, but they already know that. That's how we use the mole, we feed him with stale or useless, but true information, so the Russians believe what he tells them. When the time is right, we'll use him once for disinformation. I can't tell you anything more," Laudano said.

"You know, I'm a simple guy. The other day I was thinking about getting a bumper sticker for my truck. This stuff today is a big load to process---"

"Hey, you were class valedictorian in prep school. Deep down you're a smart guy, just lazy," Toni Anne said.

"That's a big compliment coming from you," I said.

"Don't get a big head, you're not remotely in my league, but you're smart, okay. Let me explain what's going to happen over the next 20 minutes," she said. She took a few moments to explain. These people were not just geniuses at Cyber Warfare, they were World Class in deviousness. I guess that's a subset of Cyber Warfare.

She concluded her remarks with, "When you get back to Texas, and you get a break from making a few billion on Bitcoin, have some fun with that blonde with the Corvette. I wouldn't be holding out your love for the Murder Bitch any longer."

"How do you know about the blonde---"

"We know everything, don't be stupid," Toni Anne said.

I felt stupid.

Seventy Three
Fort Meade, MD
Cyber Command

Toni Anne took me on a tour of Cyber Command. Since I had
already seen a lot of the building we focused on the Control
Room. It looked like Mission Control at NASA, or the Sports
Book at a Las Vegas casino. It was packed with very
impressive and showy technology, lots of giant color computer
displays that cover huge sections of walls. In the center of the
room was the Cyber Command Logo, designed to impress and
make people feel safe. It features an eagle flying over an
electronic world and lightning bolts and a key. It does make
you feel safe.

There were about 50 people sitting at workstations, each station
with multiple computer screens. There were a few bigger
workstations, that looked to be the realm of supervisor types,
and officers walked around the room having serious
conversations with the drones sitting at the workstations. It
looked like everybody was watching the store. As far as I could
tell nobody was shopping online at Amazon or playing Fantasy
Football.

Quietly Toni Anne said to me, "The people staffing this room
are very bright, much brighter than the average Joe, and they
do useful work. But realize that this room is also designed for
show. We bring visiting politicians here. We need them to give
us the money, instead of funding another four lane bridge to
nowhere in their home district. Congressmen are like children;
the colorful blinking lights make them think we're doing
something."

In another part of the huge room Major Gabrielle McHugh was
escorting three men on a tour. "Let's go over," Toni Anne said.

When we got there Laudano said, "Excuse me, Major McHugh. I wanted to just say hello to the Congressmen."

So much for diversity, the Congressmen were three white guys in blue suits. I think they were all named Jim. Toni Anne greeted them each by name, and they seemed pleased.

One of the politicians said, "Ms. Laudano, we hear very good things about your work."

"Right back at you Congressman Fasi," Toni Anne said. "Don't forget to exit through the Gift Shop."

They all laughed. Neither Laudano nor Gabrielle made any attempt to introduce me, but the Congressmen all checked me out. As we walked away I heard Congressman Fasi ask Gabrielle, "who was that man with Ms. Laudano?"

"I can't say," answered Major McHugh.

Laudano and I walked away from the tour and over to an entrance of the room. "McHugh's going to be a General. You watch. Those guys all want to nail her."

"You mean members of Congress aren't all high-minded men of dignity?" I asked.

"Mostly scumbags," Toni Anne said.

"She's pretty good at manipulating men," I said.

"Women too. Yeah, she's got it all. Don't forget that she's the Murder Bitch, you saw that first-hand. It's not just that. Old Gab can switch back and forth from shooting somebody to being the perfect bureaucrat. She was born to be in the military. Some people don't function in the outside world. She belongs, and she knows how to operate. She's working on getting rid of Powers right now, and Powers is just starting to get the message." Toni Anne said.

"*You* were quite the politician back there," I said.

"Yeah, I can turn on the phony charm. It works better than when I say to the Congressmen, 'Hey shithead, just vote for our budget if you want the friggin' ATMs to work'."

I looked around the Control Center. "Who designed this room, Walt Disney?" I said.

"How did you know that?" she said.

"I was kidding," I said.

"Well, Walt's been dead for a while, but it was designed with the help of Walt Disney Studios. Kind of looks like a movie set, doesn't it?" she said.

"Yeah," I said, "how about the rest of the tour?"

We walked into the lobby. She pointed at another wing. "We won't bother going there. That's where the real smart people work. It's as drab as the Control Room is showy. There's a bunch of geniuses in cubicles with four or five screens on their desks. They're the ones who keep you safe. But there's nothing to see."

A man in blue coveralls with a patch that read Mid Atlantic Vending and a Washington Nationals baseball cap asked Toni Anne, "Excuse me miss, can you direct me to the second floor vending machine service area. I'm a little lost."

Toni Anne was uncharacteristically patient with the workman, and looked at his name embroidered above his right shirt pocket. "Yes…Gary, it's right up those stairs."

The workman thanked her and took a look at me. A long look. Then he walked away, toolbox and all.

"So where do the super geniuses work?" I asked.

"In a room you'll never see. And most of the people in this building will never see," Laudano said. "It's time for you to leave."

Before she escorted me out of the building she smiled at me and said, "I like you. Let's have some fun when this thing is over. And believe me, you'll know when it's over."

"Would we be doing Math and Logic?" I asked.

She winked at me. Not many people wink anymore. It's a lost art. We left the building.

My car was parked in a visitor's spot close to the entrance. When we got to the vehicle we repeated the lines that we had rehearsed in her office.

"I'm not sure that you were completely candid with us today," she said.

"I told you, I don't know the answers to the questions you asked. You seem to think I know a lot more than I do," I said.

"Call me if your memory improves," she said, handing me her business card.

"Sure," I said. Then I got into the rental car.

That conversation was just in case the Russians were listening with long distance parabolic microphones.

Seventy Four
In the air

On the flight back to Austin the First Class cabin was almost
empty, including the widow seat next to me. Mandy, the very
attractive flight attendant got a little flirty with me, but I wasn't
in the mood. I'd had enough with women in uniform that day.
Maybe Mandy was a Russian spy. Even if she wasn't I didn't
feel like talking to her.

Mandy made a frowny face at me. "Tough day? How about a
cocktail to cheer you up?"

"I'll just have a club soda please," I said. I never drink on
planes anymore.

As she served me the club soda Mandy said something to me,
but I wasn't paying attention. From the inflection of her voice
it was apparent that she had asked me a question.

"Huh?," I said. "I'm sorry, I was thinking about something
else."

"Evidently," she said. "Never mind."

I've been told 'never mind' lots of times by women. It's not a
sign of affection. It's frequently accompanied by them folding
their arms across their chest.

Mandy's attention was taken away when a man on the other
side of the aisle, one row back said, "Hey missy, can I get a
couple more scotches?" I glanced over. It was a red nosed
Congressman from Waco. I'd been stuck playing golf with him
once at a tournament for Baylor. I put my hand up by the side
of my face, trying to hide, but it wasn't necessary. The
Honorable Gentleman from Waco was busy unscrewing the

tops from a couple mini bottles of scotch, and he wasn't the kind of guy who had the brain power to multi-task.

I always flew First Class. Why not, I had the money. A month from now I'd have the money to buy my own plane if I wanted to. If I was alive.

So when Gabrielle had been sitting on my lap, running her fingers through my hair, she was setting me up. I was going to be the 'Useful Idiot' who'd help her on her quest to be a General. Maybe the Russians would torture me, and then kill me. Gabrielle knew this. When she was sitting on my lap.

Seventy Five
Austin, TX
Extended Stay Hotel

Sierra Quinn was back in her room. She was just out of the shower, and felt the best she had in days. Quinn resolved to get in a vigorous workout every day, except if she had to shoot somebody that day.

Her cell phone rang. It was Turgenev.

"Yes," Quinn said.

"Change in plans. We're not meeting for lunch. It's too early for you to be in Austin. We're flying you out to San Francisco. Lev will meet you there. It's probably just a surveillance mission. You two will be watching a few people in Silicon Valley we suspect may have some knowledge of the party we're interested in," Turgenev said. "We'll continue electronic and internet surveillance in Austin. You may be coming back."

"Okay," Quinn said. Turgenev told her she'd be receiving travel instructions via text message, then he hung up.

Quinn thought this Silicon Valley thing sounded like a wild goose chase, but it would be better than just sitting around in a hotel room in Austin. At least she'd get to drive and walk around, perhaps meet one of the targets in a bar or something. Sex was probably impossible but maybe she'd get to shoot somebody.
After all, that was her job.

Seventy Six
Moscow
The Lider's Apartment

The Lider had called Turgenev, so Oleg flew from New York
to Moscow. This was not a request, not something that
Turgenev would allow himself to show the slightest
resentment. Oleg stood to make $6 billion, but if it had been $6
he would have come with the same sense of urgency. The Lider
didn't handle disappointment well from his subordinates.

The Russian President didn't sleep much, and he didn't expect
his minions to do so either.

When Oleg was seated The Lider began speaking. "Oleg, we
are initiating Phase Two of our Plan. Phase Three will begin
shortly after. It's not necessary for you to understand the
technicalities, but I do need you to understand why it is so vital
for you to carry out your responsibilities. Are you following
me?"

"Yes sir." Turgenev said.

"I've never asked you. Are you much of a chess player?" The
Lider asked.

Turgenev knew that The Lider never asked a question he didn't
know the answer to. Russian schools had rigid standardized
tests, students' chess skills were measured every year, and the
results were recorded on their permanent records. The Russian
President was so thorough that he'd never let anyone get close
to him without knowing every detail of their lives. Therefore,
since The Lider knew the answer, Oleg assumed that the
question was a test of truthfulness, so Turgenev told the truth.

"Sir, I showed little promise as a youth. When the other boys in my village were concentrating on chess, I was learning how to break people's fingers to collect debts. There's a trick to breaking people's fingers you know." Turgenev said.

The Lider nodded. Oleg realized the Russian President knew the trick. The Lider had spent time interrogating suspected subversives in East Germany early in his KGB career.

The Lider smiled. "It's a sign of intelligence to know your weaknesses and cultivate your strengths. Your chosen path has rewarded you. I don't think any of the other boys in your village have become Billionaires."

Turgenev nodded. He knew that even The Lider wouldn't make someone fly from New York to Moscow to discuss their boyhood chess ratings. Oleg had enough experience to know that The Lider would now get down to business.

"Phase Two of our plan is to use the Psychological Division of FSB to disrupt the upcoming American Presidential Election. We are launching an all-out disinformation campaign. What we have done in previous elections will pale in comparison to what we have planned. What makes this particularly effective is that we will be simultaneously helping and subverting both sides. Initially both sides will blame their opponents, but we will leave just enough digital footprints that they will soon tie the responsibility back to us. We want that. Are you with me so far?" The Lider asked.

Turgenev nodded yes.

"Just when the Americans are concentrating all their resources to stopping the disinformation, then we use Information Technology Group to launch Phase Three," The Lider said.

Turgenev nodded again. A history of nodding to The Lider had made him a Billionaire.

"Phase Three is what I've referred to before as the biggest financial windfall in history," The Lider said. "We feel very confident, but to completely assure this windfall, you need to find Satoshi Nakamoto."

Seventy Seven
Austin, TX

It had been a long day by the time I got back to the compound in Austin. Not just physically, but I felt mentally 500 years older. I wasn't sure I wanted all this sophisticated knowledge, and I knew I didn't want to know that Gabrielle, the beautiful Warrior Princess, was just a cold hearted schemer who didn't care about me.

I thought I'd go right off to sleep, but it took a while, and when I did sleep I dreamed of Gabrielle, not good adolescent dreams of her emerging in her wet underwear from the swimming pool, but disturbing dreams. Gab would shoot me, then I'd wake up.

Not exactly what I'm looking for in a girlfriend.

The next morning I decided to take action on Toni Anne Laudano's advice. I would call Barbara Jean Parker and invite myself over. I would wait to make the call until a decent hour, even though I knew Barb still kept farm girl hours and probably would have been awake since sunrise.

But the first thing I had to do was get ready to be the Biggest Swingin' Dick in the Bitcoin Universe. Because Bitcoin isn't a stock you don't have to wait for trading hours to buy. It trades 24 hours a day, seven days a week. I'd be drinking a lot of coffee in the next week.

About the phrase: Big Swingin' Dick is a Wall Street term. It is used by the really aggressive traders to describe themselves. "I'm the Big Swingin' Dick" they say. It is said without irony. The people who say it are assholes. The women they marry are assholes, and their kids are assholes. It's hereditary. If you don't believe me, just go to any country club in Greenwich, Connecticut.

I didn't want to be them, I just wanted to play the role of Big Swingin' Dick in the Bitcoin world for the next month. After that I'd just to go back to being me. Or dead.

I had trading accounts at several firms, and had signed and been approved for all sorts of trading including buying stocks, bonds, options and futures, for cash and using borrowed money, also called margin. Because of the size of the assets I held with the trading firms I got to speak to a real person when I called, and I called all of them to make sure I knew exactly how to trade Bitcoin for cash, and on margin, and buy options and futures on Bitcoin. It is complicated, but the options and futures let you hedge your bets, so when you're ahead on a Bitcoin position you can make a short term bet that Bitcoin will go down. Then if it goes down you cover your hedge, and use your gains to buy more Bitcoin. You can also use options and futures to make straight bets that Bitcoin will go up in a certain period of time, a day, a week, a month, six months.

I had the tremendous advantage of knowing there was another major player who had to own a huge position in Bitcoin in a week. This is like betting on a horse race when you know the winner. But I didn't have enough money to just buy Bitcoin and watch it go up. I had to use borrowed money and the leverage of options and futures to create so much demand that I made Bitcoin go up all by myself, as I competed with this other huge player to corner the market.

I had to use just my personal money. I could not commingle client money in this project. My clients had conservative accounts and I would never even dream of getting them involved in this thing.

When I understood how to handle all the Bitcoin transactions by myself on my computer I went in and bought large positions for cash in accounts I had at four separate investment houses. I had to use all of them to have enough leverage to do all the necessary trading. Bitcoin started going up by thousands of dollars in each trade. It started at 8 am Texas time at $32,000 per Bitcoin, and by noon was over $42,000. I used my gains to double up my position, and a two o'clock I was up over $4 million for the day with Bitcoin trading at $49,400. I put a hedge on, effectively neutralizing my position, but I would not participate in any gains if it kept rising. It was like taking a time out. Bitcoin traded down below $40,000, so I sold the hedge and used the profits to buy more Bitcoin. It went back over $42,000, so I was up over $7 million. This was all in less than a few hours.

I told myself a little joke: And just think, it takes some Big Swingin' Dicks over a week of hard work for make $7 million!

The price of anything, a pound of sugar, a house in Beverly Hills, an ounce of gold, or a share of GE stock depends on one factor: supply and demand. That's it, everything else is bullshit. If there is lots of demand and little supply, the price goes up. There were just 21 million Bitcoins. Satoshi Nakamoto said that when he created them. There would never be any more. So with two buyers with huge resources who looked for all the world like they intended to completely corner the market, and no real sellers, how high would the price go?

Market trend followers would see the action and also be buying. Wise guys who somehow bet against Bitcoin would get their brains kicked in, and create even more demand for Bitcoin when they scrambled to buy back their short positions as Bitcoin went up.

Inadvertently I had discovered how I would create time for sleep and what I hoped were several visits to see Barbara Jean Parker in the next two weeks. When I fully hedged against my Bitcoin position I effectively took a time out, and couldn't win or lose at all until I took the hedge position off. By using the hedge strategy I could take some time off and not have to sit at my computer 24/7.

I looked out the window. Eric the gardener was mowing the lawn by the pool. I think it was the second time that day he had mowed that particular patch of grass. My yard was going to look real shipshape for the next week.

During one of the periods I had the hedge position in place I used the pause in the battle to call Barbara Jean Parker. She picked up right away.

"Hi JR, you calling because you want to come over for some shooting practice?" she said.

"No. No shooting practice, but I do want to come over. I want to ratchet up our relationship… you know." Jeez, could I be any more awkward?

"You mean you want to have sex?" she said.

"Well now that you put it that way…Yeah," I said.

"Is this some kind of joke, or trick, or something?" she asked.

"Nope. Straight up truth," I said.

"Well come right over then," she said.

"I can't, but I can be there at around 5:30. Is that okay?" I asked.

"You want to stay over?" she asked.

What is it with women and staying over? "Barb, I can't…I'm involved with some really intricate business stuff right now," I explained.

"And you have to do this in the middle of the night?" she said.

"I'll explain when I get there," I said. "I just wanted to tell you upfront."

"Oh. So it's 'seven or eight quick ones, then off with the boys to boast and brag' huh?" she said.

I was surprised that she said that. It's a direct quote from a Mel Brooks classic. Madeline Kahn's character says it to the monster. It's one of my favorite movies.

"Wow. It's a quote from Young Frankenstein," I said.

"I know that, silly. It's one of my favorites," Barb said. "I love old movies."

"Do you like *Dr. Strangelove*?" I asked.

"Are you kidding? I've watched that with my father at least 20 times," she said.

"We might just have more in common that I knew," I said.

"So after we get married, we can watch movies together when we're not having sex or target shooting?" she said.

"Hey, I have a lot of stamina, but even I need to rest up once in a while," I said. I decided to let the marriage comment pass. Since I might be alive for just a few more days, I figured that I would have my relationship with Barbara Jean and see what the consequences were later. She'd understand, right?

Seventy Eight
Spicewood, TX

"You son of a bitch!" she said, as she was throwing a whiskey glass at me.

Barbara Jean Parker was stark naked, while I fully clothed was trying to leave her house through the front door.

She had a good arm, and threw in the proper manner, holding the glass in her right hand as she stepped forward with her left foot, like a quarterback. Although Barbara Jean had a perfect body, especially for someone her age, the throwing motion made her less attractive.

The thrown glass was a little high and inside and hit the wall of stone by the door. The glass shattered. Having thrown the glass Barb stood still with her hands on her hips. Now she looked great.

"Wow, you look great," I said. I am charming.

The act of chucking the glass had apparently let her blow off some steam and she seemed calmer. Barb said, "Why can't you stay over?"

"Barbara Jean, I told you on the phone, and I told you as soon as I got here that I couldn't stay over. I've got to go. I'm working on a deal that involves an unbelievable amount of money."

"So you have to work in the middle of the night?" she asked.

"Yes. This is an international thing. It trades 24 hours a day, seven days a week," I said.

"Oh, so you just came up here for a little sex break?" she said.

She had me there. I considered my potential replies, but decided to say nothing. We just stood looking at each other, but I had an advantage. I got to look at a beautiful naked woman. That's a nice thing. A wild thought occurred to me. I decided to change the tempo of the conversation. I got down on one knee.

"Barbara Jean, when this thing is over, would you marry me?" I heard myself say.

"When is it going to be over?" she asked.

"A week tops." I said.

"You promise?" she asked.

"Yeah. I've been promised that it will just last a week," I said.

"Do you trust the person who told you it would just be a week?" she asked.

That was a good question. "Barb I can't tell you how much money this involves, but it's an unbelievable amount. I couldn't walk away from this opportunity," I decided to share my charity plan. "It's so much that I'm not even going to take it. I'm going to set up a charitable foundation to help sick people, to fund hospitals."

"You're not going to keep some of it?" she said.

"Nah, I've got enough. You've got enough. But I do have an ulterior motive," I said.

"What's that?"

"I'm going to give huge donations to the hospitals where my brothers and sister work. And I'm going to do it with great fanfare, so they know about it. I'll demand big signs: The JR Johnson so and so Wing." I smiled.

"What a good idea. You are good at revenge," she said.

"So, we're engaged?" I asked.

"Sure sweetie," she said. "Where's my ring?"

I picked up a shard of broken glass from the floor and held it to her ring finger. "Why don't we have a ring made of this?" I asked.

She squinted her eyes at me, then flipped the shard off her finger, back near the rest of the glass on the floor. "You're getting me a ring."

There didn't seem to be any room for compromise in that statement. I also didn't think that expressing my opinion that a fortyish year old woman on her second marriage didn't need an engagement ring would go over well. Time to take the initiative.

"Okay, let's get you an engagement ring that will make every woman at the Austin Country Club jealous. What's your favorite jewelry store?" I asked.

The computers at Cyber Command could not have been faster. It took Barbara Jean one nanosecond to answer. "Franzetti on Kirbey Lane."

"Let's meet there tomorrow at 11:30 and buy you a diamond ring that's so big that you have to work out with weights so you can lift up your hand, so big that your first husband will have to buy his current wife a new ring because she's so jealous." I suggested. I do have a way with words. Barb looked pleased. This is Texas.

"That's a fine idea, JR."

"Do you think I could have a conjugal visit tomorrow night?" I asked.

"Sure," Barbara Jean said as she wrapped her arms around my neck. "How about a conjugal visit right now?"

I decided the Bitcoin marketplace could wait a while.

Seventy Nine
Moscow
The Lider's apartment

"Oleg, I want to make sure that you know the importance of your part of the mission," The Lider said.

"Yes sir."

"Only a Russian chess master could have come up with this plan! It is an easy way to more than double our windfall profits." The Lider paused. "Right now I have instructed our central bank to start buying all the Bitcoin in the world if they can. These purchases are being made through offshore banks in corrupt countries, like Panama, Indonesia, The Cayman Islands, Cypress. No one in the West will know it is us accumulating all the Bitcoin. These purchases will, of course make the price skyrocket. Today each Bitcoin is trading at around $40,000. In a few days the price might be $200,000 per Bitcoin, maybe $400,000. We'll have to pay more and more for each purchase of Bitcoin, but in a week we'll control the Bitcoin market."

"Mr. President, I am not a financial man, but isn't there a danger in trying to corner a market? In the end don't we have to sell, and won't that drive the prices down?" Turgenev asked.

"Ahh, who says you're not a financial man? That's an excellent question, Oleg." The Lider was enjoying himself, and Turgenev prepared for one of The Lider's lectures, but this one had the promise of being quite interesting, since with a bit of quick calculation Oleg realized that The Lider was talking about trillions of dollars. Soon Oleg's billions would look pitiful next to The Lider's pile.

"There's a difference this time. We have a Malware attack, which we will aim at the U.S. Financial System. They have no defense for this Malware. For five minutes nothing will work in the U.S. Financial System. At that time, I will call the President of the United States and take full responsibility for the attack. We will then turn off our attack and let the American financial system run normally. The ransom will be payable in two days, or we will then permanently cripple the American economy, along with key utilities, like the power grid. Any attempt to launch an attack on us will end the two day cease fire, and we'll immediately turn on our Malware," The Lider said.

"I'm not following. What does have to do with Bitcoin?" Turgenev asked.

"The ransom demand is not in dollars, or euros or gold---it is in Bitcoin. We will demand a certain number of Bitcoins from every large U.S. financial company, then the assets are to be pooled at the U.S. Treasury. They will be forced to go out into the open market and buy from all of our phony banks. They will be bidding against each other, and we estimate will drive the Bitcoin price to double again in two days, to at least $400,000 per Bitcoin, maybe more."

Turgenev shrugged. It was too much for him to figure out.

"Don't you see Oleg? We will force the U.S. institutions to buy it from us, and perhaps make double what we paid for the Bitcoin. Maybe make $2 or $3 trillion in profit in two days," The Lider explained.

"And then?" Turgenev asked.

"That's the beautiful part! We play chess! We play chess! No American could have devised this. Then we force the U.S. institutions to give us the Bitcoin for free! It's their ransom payment for getting relief from the Malware," The Lider said. 'We profit twice. We make more than twice as much profit!"

"So, the U.S. institutions have to buy the Bitcoin from our puppet banks, which we sell them at huge profits. Then they have to turn around and give us the Bitcoin back for free?" Oleg asked.

"Exactly," The Lider said.

"That sounds good," Turgenev said.

"You share my gift for understatement, my friend," The Lider said.

Turgenev knew that The Lider didn't have any friends, but he got the point. "Then what happens to the Bitcoin?" Oleg asked.

"Do you know what the Gross Domestic Product of Russia was in 2019?" The Lider asked. Turgenev shook his head, no.

"The GDP of Russia in 2019 was about $2 trillion," The Lider said, "keep that in mind."

"Yes sir," Oleg said.

"We estimate the Bitcoin will be worth around at least $4 trillion at that when we complete the deal with the U.S, perhaps more. Each Russian citizen will get a voucher for a fractional share of Bitcoin, signed by me. At that level each voucher should be worth around $12,000. We are preparing the checks now. Those checks should keep them quiet. And, as I mentioned before, I will keep a Finder's Fee."

"May I ask again how much is the Finder's Fee?' Turgenev said.

"Two trillion dollars, minimum," The Lider said. Both men laughed.

Eighty
On the road to Austin, TX

As I drove home from Barbara Jean's I did a new mental status check. In the last couple days I'd found out that the woman I pined for was an ice cold ambitious manipulative sociopath, who set me up to be a Useful Idiot for the U.S. government, that I was somehow given the green light to go into the Bitcoin market and make probably one billion or two billion dollars in profits in a week, but at the same time I would be watched by the Russians who were being led to believe that I knew more than I did about Bitcoin, and that they might torture me for information I didn't know, and then kill me. Check.

I had live-in bodyguards named Eric and Bonnie to protect me. Bonnie carried around an Uzi slung under her smock.

I also just got engaged to be married to Barbara Jean Parker. There had been a lot of men who were jealous of my relationship with Lola Madison, but that's because they didn't know Barbara Jean. She was a real woman, and she was a fan of Dr. Strangelove and Young Frankenstein. Barb could ride a horse as well as any cowboy, and she was a deadly shot with pistol, shotgun and rifle. And she cooked huevos rancheros and did one hell of a conjugal visit. A fellow couldn't ask for much more. Well, she was a good dancer, too.

Then a thought popped into my head. I sure hope I don't drag Barbara Jean into this mess.
Ah, it's only a few more days.

Eighty One
Austin, TX

When I got home I checked Bitcoin trading. It hadn't changed much, but I made some money on my hedge, so I covered that position and bought more. Bitcoin went up 10% in an hour. I was up about $20 million this first day. It's fun betting on a rigged horse race. I needed some sleep, so I put a hedge— remember it's like taking a time out-and went to sleep for a few hours.

I got up 4 am Texas time, so it was 5 am New York time. A few months ago when Bitcoin was at the tail end of getting slammed from around $50,000 to $4,000 CNBC never talked about it, but now with Bitcoin going wild it took about 50% of the airtime. You can't blame CNBC because they're in the game to make money, and the way they do that is have more people watch, so their ratings go up and they can charge more for each advertising minute.

I took the hedge off and used my $20 million to buy more Bitcoin, this time on margin. I had thought about buying slowly, but then *screw it, I'm supposed to be the Big Swingin' Dick,* and I bought around $40 million of Bitcoin in one shot. After that it took off, and by 10 am Bitcoin was trading at $56,000 per coin. I was up $100 million dollars, and I hadn't been trading Bitcoin for even one full day. This could be an interesting week.

CNBC trotted out just about anybody who had an opinion on Bitcoin. It was funny for me to listen to the theories being proposed, because none of them, whether they were positive or negative about Bitcoin prices had any idea of what was causing the price movement, but that didn't stop them from making up shit. Two guests with opposing views got into a heated discussion on whether the price movement was caused by Modern Monetary Theory or by Darwinian Capitalism.

Years ago my Texas investment mentor, Tom Good Sr, had told me once when he heard some economists arguing the obscure points of investing, "JR, just keep in mind—Up is good, and Down is bad."

"Got it chief," I had answered. That philosophy had serve me well.

CNBC anchors kept saying things like, "At 9:15 investors sold into the marketplace, but then investors bought at 9:20, causing Bitcoin to jump another $10,000." They were calling guys who were paying $50,000 for something that had been trading at $20,000 the day before "Investors." And none of these "Investors" had any idea of what a Bitcoin was really worth. That was like calling the guys who bet on the coin toss at the Super Bowl "Investors."

At around 9 am my fiancé, Barbara Jean Parker had called me, and suggested that she stop at my house so we could go together to the jewelry store rather than go in separate pickup trucks. I agreed, so she was coming over at 10:30. I explained to my new housekeeper/machine gun toting bodyguard Bonnie that it would be best if she worked in the casita that morning so I wouldn't have to explain anything to Barb.

So when Barbara Jean walked in at 10:30 she came right up to me at the computer. I was just about to hit the ENTER key to execute the hedge order that would give me a timeout to visit the jewelry store.

"Hi, sweetie, I just wanted to show you something," Barb said. She peeled off her knit top to expose a diamond studded bra beneath. It was an ultra-pushup model with little diamonds somehow sewn into strategic areas. Barbara Jean strutted around the room, shaking her shoulders. I was overcome with lust.

"What do you think?," she asked.

"Very nice," I said.

"That's all you can say, 'Very Nice'?" she teased me.

"Uhh," I said.

"I just wanted to show you how good I look in diamonds, before we go to the jeweler," Barb said.

"Well, mission accomplished," I said. She put her knit top back on.

I turned back to my keyboard. I looked at the screen. This couldn't be! In the maybe one minute respite I had taken to watch Barb's exhibition, the account had gone down around $19 million. I quickly hit the ENTER key. Well, I knew it was volatile. I couldn't say anything to Barb. She was just having some fun; it was my fault. So it would turn out to be a more expensive engagement ring than I had anticipated. I'd have to remember to hit ENTER in the future, no matter what exotic outfit Barbara Jean showed up in.

As we drove to the jewelers Barb couldn't stop talking. "Oh, JR this is so great. I'm going to have a big old diamond ring, and we're engaged! I can't wait to wave it in the face of the women at the Austin Country Club!"

"And we're in love, and getting married?" I asked.

"Yeah, that too," Barbara Jean answered. "Look, I want to get a BIG diamond. If you like we can split the bill."

"No way," I said. "I'll be a sport."

Franzetti Jewelers was in a cottage-like building with a couple big shade trees in front. The outside was decorated with strings of white lights, making the whole operation look quaint. On closer inspection the windows were reinforced glass, maybe two inches thick, and looked like they could stop frontal assault by rocket propelled grenades. There was a no nonsense armed guard right inside the front door.

The realization hit me; I had never bought anything in a jewelry store in my life. I had no idea what things should cost. It made me more nervous than placing an order for $100 million worth of Bitcoin.

There wasn't a lot of merchandise on display, but the items featured were in museum quality glass cases. Didn't Walmart sell engagement rings? Too late.

A handsome dark-skinned man in a well-tailored dark suit and a crisp white shirt and silk tie came around the corner and greeted us.

"Barbara Jean, so nice to see you! I'm glad you called ahead, so I could prepare to show you our very best," He looked at me. "And you are the lucky gentleman?"

I didn't feel lucky right then.

"Oh, let me introduce you two! JR Johnson, this is my friend Miguel," Barbara Jean said.

Great. They were friends. They'd work together to set me up on the shakedown that was coming in the next few minutes. Miguel escorted us to a room down a hallway from the main showroom. We went in. The room just said money, and the air conditioning was cranked up so it was cold. I was sure that as soon as we got settled in and started to look at the choices in rings the a/c would be turned off so within five minutes it would be 100 degrees in there, and I'd agree to anything just to get out.

We sat around a small circular table, the chairs arranged so Barb and I sat together facing Miguel on the other side. In front of him was a velvet box, which he held in close to him, like he was protecting the Presidential nuclear launch codes.

"I've selected a few rings that I thought would be appropriate after our discussion," Miguel said. He opened the box just a bit and took out one ring. It was big. Barb put it on her finger and held it up for me.

"What do you think, sweetie?" she asked.

"It's nice," I said.

"I think so too," Barb said, "but Miguel, do you have anything bigger?"

Miguel placed that ring back in the velvet box and pulled out a bigger one. We went through the same little skit. Barb asked to see the biggest diamond, and Miguel pulled that one out. It looked like the rings I had seen on the fingers of the wives of the Wall Street hotshots. Only bigger.

Barbara Jean beamed. "Oh this is perfect. I'll take this one! Ok JR?"

"Sure," I heard myself say.

I was out of my element. "Is it okay to ask the price?"

Miguel looked at me. Barbara Jean looked at me. It was quiet.

"This is a four carat diamond. A mediocre diamond in this category is priced at around $200,000," Miguel said.

Gulp.

"But this diamond is flawless,"

Bigger gulp.

Miguel offered me a jewelers eyepiece so I could inspect the perfect diamond. I passed.

Then he said some letters and numbers that didn't mean anything to me, but the way he said alphanumeric gobbledygook implied that the diamond was expensive, "so this diamond, one of the world's finest, together with the ring would be $980,000."

Oh.

"Plus, of course the applicable 6.25% Texas sales tax," Miguel said.

Of course.

"Oh JR, it's perfect," Barb said. Then, addressing Miguel she said, "Do you think I could get it sized so I could wear it home?"

"Certainly, Barbara Jean. What an excellent choice," Miguel said.

Miguel grinned, and it turned into a big smile. He began to laugh, and Barbara Jean joined in. She gave me a big slap on the back.

They were laughing hysterically.

"We had you going there, JR!" Barb said. I was confused. She held up the ring. "It's Cubic Zirconium."

"Huh?"

"It's a fake. What does this thing cost, Miguel?" Barb asked.

"A couple hundred bucks," he said. "I think that was a test for you JR."

"And you passed," Barb said. "I don't need a ring. Why don't you get me a Purdey Over and Under for our wedding present?"

"Sure," I said. "What is that?"

"It's an expensive shotgun. Maybe $200,000," Barbara Jean said.

"Sounds reasonable," I said. It felt like I'd just saved $800,000. Maybe that was the plan all along.

Eighty Two
Silicon Valley, CA

Sierra Quinn spent the afternoon in the rental car as the
passenger while Lev drove. Quinn thought of Lev as a statue
who sometimes spoke. His main form of self-expression was
violence, but even during his violence he was calm. Sierra
noted that Lev didn't once give her a glance. This was different
than when she was a New York City Cop. In those days when
she drove around with a male partner they gave her a poorly
disguised mental undressing every couple of minutes.

They had a tip on some tech company guy, Lennie Beck, who
was shooting his mouth off about Bitcoin and Satoshi
Nakamoto in bars. He was probably just trying to impress
women, but they wanted to be sure. Lev took Quinn to a motel.
They got a room, which Lev stayed in while Quinn followed
Beck from his workplace to a local bar frequented by the Tech
types. If Beck seemed like he knew something, he'd be lured to
the room by Quinn and then get to meet Lev. Sierra wore a
blonde wig and sunglasses.

Lennie Beck was standing by himself at the bar working on his
first beer when Quinn stood next to him.

"Is your name Lennie?" she asked.

"Yeah, do I know you?" he asked.

Quinn sized him up. He might as well have been wearing a
sign that said 'Jerk'. "You were talking to my friend Sarah and
me last night for a few minutes."

Lennie didn't remember, but he did get wasted last night, and
had tried to chat up several women.

Quinn got over closer to Lennie, which he liked. Quietly she said, "You mentioned that you knew about Bitcoin. I'd like to make some money trading Bitcoin. I wanted to come back myself. If you help me, we can be more than friends. You know what I mean?"

Sierra could sense that Lennie hadn't been this close to a woman as good looking as herself...ever. "Does that sound good, Lennie?"

"Ummm, yeah, let's talk," Lennie said.

"How could you help me, you know, give me some inside information?" Quinn asked.

Lennie leaned in close so he could whisper to Quinn. "I went to school with THE GUY. The guy who invented Bitcoin. He gives me a tip once in a while. But I gotta tell you, it can be weeks between conversations."

"You went to school together. College?" Quinn asked.

"Yeah, Caltech. We were roommates. We're very tight, still." Lennie said.

"What was they guy's name again," Quinn asked.

Lennie froze. It was plain he couldn't remember. He cupped his hand in front of his mouth. "It's a Japanese name. Satoshi.....Yamamoto."

"Yamamoto?" Quinn said.

"Yeah. Keep it quiet, I think some people are listening." Lennie said.

This guy didn't know anything. Lennie was just bullshitting to try to pick up women. He wasn't worth wasting a bullet on.

One of her former NYC detective partners would have described Lennie as a guy who couldn't get laid if he drove up to a whorehouse in a Brinks truck.

"Lennie, I'm sorry, but I need to use the ladies room. But stay here. I'll be right back," Quinn said. "Okay, stay right here. I'm all ears."

"Sure," Lennie said as he ordered another beer.

Quinn went to a ladies room stall and removed her blonde wig and sunglasses. Then she left the bar and went to her car. She called Lev on her way to the motel. He was waiting in the parking lot when she arrived.

"That guy doesn't know shit," Quinn told Lev. He made his usual comment. Nothing.

Eighty Three
Fort Meade, MD
Cyber Command
Windowless Room

"Let's talk about the Russian virus. Sheldon, tell us about how they have the main virus that contains thousands of encapsulated micro viruses," Toni Anne said.

The Group of Six had convened, including new member/vending machine repairman Yuri Sokolov. Sheldon, who had advanced degrees in Computer Science and Virology, gathered his thoughts. He simplified his explanation for the benefit of Sokolov, who while brilliant was still learning about Cyber Warfare. The other people in the meeting realized this, and were tolerant because it was important to have the mind of Sokolov involved in their strategizing.

"We've been analyzing the Ransomware attack on Baylor. To refresh your memories, the main virus, which came in through a poorly protected password in the Art Department, carried thousands of encapsulated micro viruses," Sheldon said.

Toni Anne asked, "What was the password at the Art Department?"

"Art123," Sheldon answered. "At least they capitalized the 'A'", Sheldon said.

"Morons like this guarantee full employment in our field. I wonder if they had a committee meeting to decide on the password," Toni Anne said.

"Baylor had password requirements of at least six characters, with one capital letter and one number. We've since advised the IT Department there to go with a random prime number generated system that---"

"Okay Sheldon, they have better passwords now. Let's talk about the encrypted micro viruses," Toni Anne said. Sheldon could go off on tangents unless directed to focus.

"Yeah. So the Baylor attack had encapsulated micro viruses—"

"Sheldon, for the benefit of everyone here, could you explain that a bit?" Toni Anne said.

"Sure. When the main virus got in the system it contained other smaller viruses that had software protection around them. That's what we call the 'capsule', so even when we kill the main virus that's when the micro viruses are activated and then begin to continue the malware attack. The micro viruses aren't killed by our fix for the main virus. The concept comes from the real world of viruses, like the flu. The mutations of the flu keep happening, that's why we need new flu vaccines every year. Everybody with me on that?" Sheldon said, looking at Sokolov.

Yuri nodded. "Makes sense," he said.

"Five years ago the Russians took three of their top virologists out of the National Health Ministry and moved them to the Cyber Warfare Division of the FSB. We already had Sheldon and another guy in place," Toni Anne said.

"Cyber is a lot more fun than Virology," Sheldon said.

"We're glad you're happy Sheldon. Now explain what you think about micro viruses," Toni Anne said.

"The Baylor attack only had one micro virus type. There were thousands of the embedded micro viruses, but they were all identical," Sheldon said.

"So killing one of them killed them all?" Sokolov asked.

'Exactly," Toni Anne said. "Yuri, you probably already know this, but I want to emphasize: A specific attack only works once. After you've used it your enemy creates defenses against it. So the Baylor episode was a sacrificial thing—"

"They sacrificed a pawn. Their first Gambit, they sacrificed a minor piece to give us a false sense of superiority. A clever move, really," Sokolov said. "They may launch another Gambit, before they show their real intentions."

"That's why we have you Yuri," Toni Anne said. "That, and you have some interesting friends."

Toni Anne and Sokolov laughed. The others in the room didn't understand.

Eighty Four
Austin, TX

On the third day of trading Bitcoin I got a call for Toni Anne Laudano. I wasn't expecting her to call me at all.

"Hey, you're doing a good job of trading. The Russians have noticed you." she said.

"How do you know that?" I asked.

"C'mon JR, you're being stupid again," Toni Anne said.

"One of my strong points," I said.

"That move where you lost $19 million in about a minute was clever. A good head fake," she said.

I didn't bother telling her that the $19 million loss was caused by being distracted by Barbara Jean's diamond studded bra. Tom Good Sr. had taught me to always answer a compliment by just saying thanks.

"Thanks," I said.

"You should lay low for a few hours. This program is working great, and we don't want you pushing up the price too much so soon. So slow down the trading some, do some hedging. We don't want to spook the Russians just yet." she said.

"Maybe I'll reduce my position some, take some profits," I said. Maybe take an hour or two off."

"Okay," Toni Anne said. "That was some bra your girlfriend was wearing. I have nothing like that in the wardrobe, but I've got a few things I could model for you when this project is over."

What! They were watching me? The U.S. Government was spying on me in my own house! My stomach turned over. I had signed up to work for Big Brother.

When I didn't say anything, Toni Anne continued. "Relax, we're just watching you through your computer. Nowhere else. Just when you're sitting at the computer."

"I'm not sure that I believe you," I said.

"Tough shit," Toni Anne said, "Hey we're letting you make a billion or two. Besides, you're fine. You don't pick your nose that often compared to most guys."

Eighty Five
Fort Meade, MD
Cyber Command

The Russians launched their disinformation campaign. To be
sure, there was always some disinformation being fed to
Americans through Facebook, Twitter, and the like, but this
was a whole new level.

Americans for Freedom, Americans for the Second
Amendment, Progressives for Justice, Towards of Socialist
Country, Vaccine Freedom Fighters and scores of other groups
were pumped into the social media platforms, and algorithms
fed more and more of a frenzy. All of these groups and many
others had something in common, they were creations of the
Psychology Division of the FSB, of Moscow, Russia, and not
headquartered in Peoria, Illinois or Fort Worth, Texas or
Anywhere, USA as they claimed, and run by someone named
Boris, or Igor, or Svetlana. When some American clicked on
one of these sites, the algos kept feeding them more of the
same kind of disinformation, and the gullible kept "liking' and
forwarding this stuff.

Gullible Americans became Faccbook friends with Russian
bots, that claimed they had gone to the same High School as
their brother. This phenomenon is what is called the Echo
Chamber, and the more people clicked on whatever they were
already inclined to believe, the more they got back, always
slanted toward a bit more radical than the last. The Russians
were very skilled at taking someone who was moderate but
leaning one way and within two weeks filling them full of
radical left or right wing beliefs.

Pavlov, after all, was a Russian psychologist, and the Russians
knew how to reward the people who came to their phony
political sites. The psychic reward of hearing back what you

247

are already inclined to think produces an emotion in people that is much the same as watching your favorite team win a game. People get the sense of belonging to a pack, and the pack reinforces and expands a sense of purpose. Within days mild mannered accountants were wearing Camo and flak jackets, and carrying unloaded AR-15s to rally at state capitals where some liberal legislator had been bold enough to try to restrict the size of clips on semi-automatic rifles after a school shooting. Nobody was going to take away my Second Amendment rights, Man! The Mainstream Media wants to take away our guns so they can force my kids to be vaccinated!

School teachers were joining rioting and looting mobs who were sacking downtown areas after police shootings of minorities.

There were vast portions of the American Public who believed that Joe Scarborough of MSNBC was a serial killer who had multiple affairs with secretaries, then murdered them. About the same number of people, but a completely different subset, thought it was credible that Fox's Chris Wallace was financing Q-Anon death squads, armed with military hardware, who were gunning for supposed Liberal child molesters. Believers in these fables could not be moved by logic or evidence, because the Russians who had conditioned them had done such a good job that it just felt good to believe, and they didn't want the good feelings to end. It was like rooting for a team that never lost. Waking up every morning to a new revelation about something bad regarding people you hated made life worthwhile. It was an easy path to follow, a lot easier than thinking.

Facebook and Twitter share prices hit new highs. The CEOs of those companies told the media that those sites were just conduits for information, and there was nothing that they could do about it, any changes would be an infringement on Freedom of Speech.

Then the Russians turned up the heat on American politicians in the social media. Within two days 85% of Republicans believed that the last Presidential election that was won by a Democrat was stolen by rigged voting machines. 85% of Democrats believed that the last Presidential election won by a Republican was stolen by rigged voting machines.

General Goldstein called General Powers and Toni Anne Laudano into his office. "An unofficial bi-partisan committee of both the Senate and the House want to meet secretly with us. Here."

"Why here, sir?" Powers asked.

"Well, these are the potty trained members who want to get something done about the Russian meddling into our political system. They're afraid if we go to Congress their esteemed room temperature IQ colleagues will spend all day making speeches denouncing one another just playing to their bases and we'll get nothing accomplished. And they don't want all this stuff to be public," Goldstein said. "They're pretty apeshit right now, concerned with the potential of complete destabilization of the political system. They're afraid of violence in the upcoming elections," Goldstein said. "Things are so toxic that they're coming over in separate vehicles. Republicans don't want to be seen riding with Democrats, and vice versa."

"This situation is of grave concern, General," Powers said to Goldstein.

Toni Anne thought *Powers is making a lot of statements like this lately. She can sense her hold on power slipping away, but can't figure out what's really going on, She's helpless, so she makes meaningless statements that she hopes will make her sound smart.*

Toni Anne wasn't going to show her hand to Powers. Only the President, General Goldstein, Yuri Sokolov, and she knew how the U.S. government was going to handle the next few days. Nobody else could be trusted in on the secret. Powers would share in the glory of the outcome, if it worked, and then she'd retire.

Toni Anne addressed Goldstein, "Sir, the disinformation traffic coming out of Russia has been ten times normal. As you know, Congress could shut this down if they'd just change the laws to make social media companies have the same liabilities as newspapers or TV news organizations. All this crap could get shut down, just like that." Laudano snapped her fingers.

Toni Anne knew that would never happen. It wasn't that the Congress was getting paid off by the social media companies. Both sides considered social media the cudgel they could use to beat down the opposition. Both Democrats and Republicans thought they were better at disinformation than their opponents, and they didn't want to give up the weapon of social media. So they made cynical speeches about First Amendment rights of Freedom of Speech, but what they really thought is they could lie better about their opponents than their opponents could lie about them. But now Russia was making both sides look like amateurs.

Eighty Six
Fort Meade, MD
Cyber Command

The meeting with the Senators and Congressmen took place in General Goldstein's conference room, and since it was informal there wasn't the parliamentary crap that accompanied a Capitol Hill hearing. But that didn't stop one Senator from repeatedly threatening to drastically cut funding for Cyber Command if they didn't start doing a better job.

After a few such threats, Toni Anne, who had been silent, had enough. "Senator, why don't you cut our funding? Then when the fuckin' ATMs in your state don't work, your constituents can just call you!"

Normally General Goldstein would not tolerate this kind of outburst to a Senator, even from Toni Anne, but in this case he let it go unchallenged. It was quiet in the conference room.

Toni Anne continued, "Look, we all know you could stop this shit in ten minutes if you'd change the regulations under which the social media companies operate. But you don't have the balls to do it, and then you come crying over here wanting us to help after you've tied our hands behind our backs."

Bi-partisan Congressional delegations who are visiting institutions that are dependent upon them for funding are not used to being spoken to like Toni Anne had just spoken to them. But they all knew she was right.

General Goldstein spoke, "As you are well aware, under the present rules for social media we are virtually powerless to stop this sort of disinformation. The only thing we can do is to launch a disinformation attack on the Russians. Only the

President can order that. We can also closely monitor the Russian situation."

The Senate Majority leader spoke. "Nevertheless, we insist that you deploy every possible resource to stopping the current Russian campaign of disinformation. Monitor them stringently. If this includes diverting personnel from other less urgent projects, so be it."

Toni Anne wanted to say; *That's like ordering us to piss in the Pacific Ocean to make the tide rise.*

General Goldstein didn't get to be a four star without knowing how to handle politicians. "Yes Senator, I think that's an excellent solution in the current situation. I'll order Ms. Laudano to make any personnel changes to reflect our new priorities."

That was perfect. She could make some superficial changes and it would look good to the politicians. And she'd make sure the mole knew that Cyber Command was focusing on the Russian meddling in the upcoming American elections. Perfect.

Toni Anne noted that Powers hadn't said one word during the meeting. But her uniform was immaculate, and the single star on each shoulder was especially shiny.

The meeting concluded soon after. As they broke up the Senate Majority leader made a point of coming over to Toni Anne and shaking hands with her. "I can always count on you for a candid opinion," he said, smiling.

Smiling back, Toni Anne said. "Thank you Senator." They hated each other.

Eighty Seven
Austin, TX

After a day of moderate trading I was ready to get aggressive again, so the first thing I did in the morning was to take off any hedges and buy my ass off. Be Long or Be Wrong! Bitcoin started jumping, wild even for Bitcoin, and it didn't go down in the usual air pockets, it just went up. I turned on CNBC.

Robin Hood, the app platform for small investors, after being threatened by pending lawsuits started by their own customers, had taken off all restrictions on trading Bitcoin. Knowledge had become public that several Hedge Funds were shorting Bitcoin in a big way, meaning betting that Bitcoin would go lower. The small Robin Hood investors had banded together in online chatrooms and decided to teach the Hedge Funds a lesson and keep buying Bitcoin to make it rise and give the Hedge Fund boys multiple billion dollar losses. There was no regulatory gatekeeper, nobody to tell the Merry Men of Robin Hood World that they were crazy. Bitcoin was going up, nobody could tell them not to buy, and not only did they think they'd get rich, but they would punish the Fat Cat Hedge Fund boys along the way.

And why buy Bitcoin for cash, say $10,000? In that case if Bitcoin doubled you'd make a $10,000 profit. Why do that when you could buy options? That way if you had $10,000 to put in you could control say, $100,000 worth of Bitcoin, and make ten times your money. All it had to do is go up. If it went down at all, you'd lose your $10,000. But it would never go down, right? Theoretically you could keep selling lower targeted options and buying higher targeted ones, and keep rolling over your gains.

The even crazier speculators bought what are called futures contracts on Bitcoin. A simple explanation of futures is that they are even more leveraged than options, vastly multiplying any move in either direction. Normal people should not trade futures for the simple reason that you could lose much more than you put in. A $10,000 futures contract could easily throw off a $100,000 loss, in minutes. It happened all the time. People who had no idea what they were doing were buying futures contracts. The masses had demanded that they be given equal access to capital markets! Nobody was stopping them. But all the little guys were just betting on UP, and Bitcoin just kept going up. There was no natural seller, unlike say, in the Oil markets, where if the price became ridiculous, Saudi Arabia would sell. They produced the oil, and if somebody wanted to pay them a fantastic price, they'd take it.

CNBC, Fox Business, Bloomberg TV, and the BBC kept referring to these unhinged Bitcoin buyers as "Investors." Didn't they have a dictionary?

When I attended the University of Texas School of Business we had to know that the price of a stock over the long term was the market's consensus of the discounted future value of the underlying company's earnings. That means investors are willing to pay for future profit growth. Not two people in every thousand could tell you that.

But Bitcoin is not a stock. It is a Cryptocurrency. Strip away "Crypto" for a minute, and it's a currency, like a Dollar, or a Euro, or a Yen, or a Pound. Normally regular folks don't trade currencies, they're too dull. It's a big deal if the U.S. dollar loses 4% of its value versus the Euro over the course of six months.

Currencies have an extra layer of weirdness. When people in the U.S. talk about a stock, they might say it "went up two points", meaning that the stock price rose by two U.S. dollars. But currency prices are quoted only in relation to other currencies, so when the Dollar goes up it might mean that it rose in value compared to the Euro.

Infrequently, for example, it might happen that in a given day the Dollar rises in value to the Euro, but goes down in relation to the British Pound. Foreign currency trading is a market dominated by multi-national companies, especially banks. A foreign airline may purchase a jet from Boeing, and to pay for the transaction, the airline might have to go to their bank and convert their national currency to U.S. dollars, so they have to buy U.S. dollars, and if there are more buyers than sellers, the price goes up.

But Bitcoin had the magic of "Crypto" in front of "currency." Currency was meaningless. Bitcoin was something that was going up, forever. You had to get in. Part of the attraction was a kind of Populism. Little guys could beat the rich guys. Elitist Fat Cat Hedge Funds were betting that Bitcoin would go down, and by forcing the prices up, the Robin Hood boys were inflicting billions of dollars in losses to the Hedge Funds. People seemed to be willing to pay anything for the pixie dust of Crypto. Unlike every national government that just kept creating more and more of their own currencies out of thin air, Bitcoin would only ever have 21 million Bitcoins issued. Satoshi Nakamoto had promised that, remember him?

So Bitcoin, that had started the week at $20,000 per coin traded that morning at $230,000 per coin. After a couple hours I was up week-to-date over $220 million. I wanted to call Toni Anne and ask her if I could just sell everything and stop, but I knew my job was to keep buying. I had to be the Big Swingin' Dick so I'd get the attention of the Russians.

I would be rewarded a billion or two in gains assuming that I was alive. Toni Anne had hired me to wave the red cape in front of the Russian bull. "Look at me!" was my job, a way to cause a diversion to the Russians while Toni Anne Laudano worked whatever plan it was that I could not be privy to. The Russians were serious, they had already killed those two New York Times reporters who had claimed knowledge of Bitcoin and Nakamoto. But I did have the heavily armed Bonnie and Eric guarding me when I was home, and a couple of undercover bodyguards following me when I left the premises. And I didn't know anything. Was that good, or would it just make the Russians torture me longer before killing me? But they couldn't get ahold of me, right?

I decided to focus on the positive. I was winning the rigged horse race, and it was fun. My logical brain told me to sell some of my position, but I decided to let it ride. Why only make $1 billion when I could make $2 billion? It would let me make bigger donations to the hospitals, and thus make my siblings even more furious. In my experience when people talk about what motivates them to make charitable donations, they're pretty much not telling the truth. But as long as they make the donations, so what if they're really just resolving some decades old grudge they have against their sister and brothers, or just proving that they are the Genuine Big Swingin' Dick, after all?

I had zoned out mentally and was just watching my computer instantaneously calculate my net gains. It was like watching a pinball machine, and the number kept going higher. I thought of myself as The Pinball Wizard. And I didn't even have to flip the levers. Then I snapped back into reality and began paying attention to the competing guests on CNBC.

Cable TV News likes to put everybody in boxes on the screen, like the opening of the Brady Bunch. The particular argument I was watching about Bitcoin featured just two contestants, who happened to be very fat guys, so their faces took up the whole box that was their designated half of the screen. It looked like Jabba the Hutt arguing with his twin brother. They we going at it, big time. It's too bad they were not in the studio together; they could have had a sumo wrestling match.

CNBC host: So (Jabba #1) what is your firm's short term price target on Bitcoin?

Jabba # 1: One million dollars, maybe an extended price of up to four million.
CNBC host: and (Jabba #2) How about your price target?
Jabba #2: Zero.

The experts discussed how since Bitcoin was a Cryptocurrency it operated outside the realm of any national government. The guy who thought the short term price target was $1 million considered that good, the Zero price target guy considered that bad. At the end the Zero price target guy had to disclose that his firm was short Bitcoin, and the Million dollar guy had to disclose that his firm was long.

Both men had charts and graphs to defend their positions. They both had multiple degrees from prestigious schools, and awards and other street cred. Institutional investors paid them for their opinions. But they couldn't both be right, now could they?

Eighty Eight
Fort Meade, MD
Cyber Command
Windowless Room

Toni Anne was again meeting privately with Yuri Sokolov
before the other members would be joining the session.
Sokolov did not come to Cyber Command every day, there was
no need for him to do so, and he continued to act out his cover
role sitting on the boards of a few international committees for
political freedom and the like. He also maintained an office
where he went on the days he was not required to meet with the
international groups. Every day he left his townhouse dressed
in a suit, but on the days he went to Cyber Command he went
first to his office in a professional building, changed into his
blue coveralls, and left in the Mid Atlantic Vending panel
truck. Before he went home the order was reversed. Toni Anne
was sure that the Russians had not caught on to this ruse, it
only had to hold up for a few more days, and nobody at Cyber
Command looked twice at the vending machine repairman.

"Bitcoin trading is going crazy, just as we thought it would. To
give the Russians something more to think about, I've arranged
for JR Johnson to visit a couple of Tech firms in Austin today.
When he gets home from the visits he's going to double up on
his positions," Toni Anne told Sokolov.

Sokolov asked, "Are the Russians buying Bitcoin as we
thought they would?"

"Yes, the Fuckin' Commies are buying through offshore
intermediaries. I'm not sure they think they're fooling us, or
they just don't care if we know. But every time the price blips
down their stooge banks are buying big time. They've started
using futures, real aggressive stuff. The Russians are acting

like they want to own all the Bitcoin in the world," Toni Anne said.

"And are they going to succeed?" Sokolov asked.

"That's not realistic even in a stable environment. But some of the Robin Hood boys pledge they'll never sell Bitcoin, at any price. Of course that's not true, everybody has a price at which they'll sell, but it's driving the price up. A couple of Hedge Funds who are short are going belly up today unless they can do a capital raise. We'll see how they do after JR Johnson jumps in with both feet." Toni Anne said.

Laudano then called in the other three members of the team. Sheldon was responsible for monitoring social media. He liked doing it.

Sheldon said, "Disinformation is going wild. Today's news: 81% of Americans, regardless of political affiliation, believe that Gwyneth Paltrow is marketing a candle that smells like her pubic…. Oh what a minute… that's one's true!" There was laughter in the room.

"Oh that Gwyneth! She's a pistol. I'm thinking of getting one of those candles as a stocking stuffer for someone I know," Laudano said. "Now Sheldon, no more screwing around, get down to business."

Sheldon continued, "There's a small but adamant right wing group that's convinced that Hillary Clinton is selling baby's blood mixed with V-8 Juice to liberal elites, and that the proceeds are going to buy absentee ballots in Battleground states, so much so that it will assure the Democratic presidential candidate victory. A supposed splinter group of Antifa, really the Russians, is calling for the assassination of at least 12 Republican congressional candidates on the eve of the election, putting their elections in limbo. The idea is getting a lot of traction on the dark web," Sheldon said.

"Perfect," Laudano said.

Eighty Nine
Fort Meade, MD

Laudano's husband, John Driscoll was a genius. You had to be genius level to work as a manager in the Cyber Command Control room. Genius is defined as someone being within the top two percent of IQ. That means there were 6 million geniuses in the US. But he knew that he was not in the same league with Toni Anne; there was a lot of room between being barely in the top two percent and being THE TOP. He had been told many time that many people considered Toni Anne the smartest person in the world. It depended on how you measured. He was tired of hearing that.

She had explained to him before they got married that she would not be taking his name. "That will make it easier for me when I kick your ass out, and I don't have to change my name back on all the forms and accounts."

Driscoll had laughed, and he also signed the Pre-Nuptial agreement. Toni Anne had sold her Data Encryption business for $300 million before coming to work for the government, and Driscoll did not stand to get a nickel of her money when they inevitably divorced. But he had other satisfactions.

After her meeting with Sokolov and the other three Toni Anne had stopped in the Control Room at Cyber Command to have a brief word with her husband. They rode to work in separate cars, because Toni Anne worked about twice as many hours as Driscoll. She worked seven days a week. She was a driven patriot; he was a Civil Servant.

"Hey John, I'm leaving at 5 o'clock today. Let's go straight home," Laudano said.

"Oh, you want to stop for dinner on the way home?" Driscoll asked.

Without lowering her voice in the crowded room she said, "No, I want to go straight home and have sex, Then maybe dinner. I have to come back in here later tonight. Conference call with some people in Asia."

Ninety
Austin, TX

I had appointments that morning to see the CEOs of two of the scores of high tech companies that had sprung up around Austin in recent years. Most of them were transplants, companies that had fled Silicon Valley in California. Not only is there no personal state income tax in Texas, unlike the 11% tax in the Golden State, but Texas was business friendly. California had become a tangled bureaucracy that made it almost impossible for businesses to expand, and then looked at companies as villains to be shaken down for the purposes of budget balancing. California: Government run amok. Texans believed in letting Companies run amok, without much government intervention. The different approaches of the states were an important lesson in Federalism.

Before I left my house Bonnie and Eric had a talk with me. Bonnie had established herself as the lead spokesperson. Eric filled in details.

"We have the security vehicle following you. You won't see them, they're very good at what they do," Bonnie said. "No one will be able to kidnap you."

Gulp

"The worse thing the bad guys could do would be to take out your truck with something like an anti-tank weapon," Eric said.

What!

Bonnie gave Eric a dirty look. "But they won't do that. They don't want to kill you."

"They want to take you alive," Eric said.

263

"So they could…. persuade… you to give them information," Bonnie explained. "It's highly unlikely they'd go after you in one of the corporate buildings. We'd have to have a shoot-out with them, and we have a lot more firepower."

"In that unlikely event, get down on the ground," Eric suggested.

I had heard advice like that before.

"You're most vulnerable walking from your car into one of the buildings," Bonnie said. "But we have extra personnel in place doing maintenance at both companies. You're as safe as you could be under the circumstances."

"Jeez, this is worse than working on Wall Street!" I said.

As I drove to the first appointment my arms felt like they weighed a thousand pound each. *Loosen up, JR! It's unlikely they'll blow up the truck.* It was hard to be casual. What would an anti-tank weapon headed toward my truck look like, anyhow?

These CEOs had been among the people who had called me to open Money Management accounts and I had avoided them up until now. I couldn't care less if they opened accounts, it was just that Toni Anne had thought I should visit a couple high tech businesses, to make it look interesting to the Russians. Maybe they'd think I was getting information about Satoshi Nakamoto from these CEOs! Maybe one of them was Satoshi Nakamoto!

The companies were near each other, so I lined up one hour appointments one right after the other. I didn't bother wearing a tie, but it was High Tech Austin, not Wall Street. I carried a briefcase with nothing in it but a ring bound notebook, but turned off my cellphone. It's very rude to have your cellphone ring in someone else's office, even when you're not interested in them, just using them to trick the Russians, and are eager to get home to manage trading $100 million chunks of Bitcoin every few minutes.

The first appointment was with a man who had been second in command at a big company who had left to form a start-up. The start-up was wildly successful. His name was Steve.

Steve was very enthusiastic about everything. The chairs in his office were great! It was great being bald! The sparkling water he served was great! I was great!

He knew everything about me, including the method I used for managing money, and he knew my track record. I interrupted.

"Steve you're a brilliant guy. What do you need me for?" I asked.

"That's what I like about you—you're honest. That's great!" he said. "Let's start out with $40 million. It will be our Beta Test!"

"Okay," I said.

"Now, what do you think about trading Bitcoin?" he asked.

"I don't have any opinion on that," I said. "I'd never trade Bitcoin for one of my clients."

"That was a test, and you passed!" Steve said. He came around his desk and slapped me on the back. "You're great!"

Who was I to argue? He was wildly successful, so he must be an excellent judge of character. He gave me his accountant's contact information, and I'd call and set up the account.

As I began to leave his office I stopped and asked, "Hey Steve, can I just bring you around with me? You can make the pitch, and we'll split the business."

"Ha-ha! Yeah, I'll do that if I ever want to make less money!" Steve said. "Hey, try not to shoot any more Hedge Fund guys!"

I didn't want to explain to Steve that in the next couple of days I was much more likely to be the shoot-ee than the shoot-er.

I walked out of the building toward my car. This is where I was the most vulnerable according to Bonnie. There was a maintenance man with a huge wrench, but no huge bolt in sight for him to turn. I assumed that he was one of my protectors, but then again he could be a Russian agent looking to hit me on the head with the wrench. I made it out to my car without incident.

The next appointment was a five minute drive away. This guy was the direct opposite of Steve. His name was Paul Glass.

Paul was wearing a suit and a tie cinched up so tight I thought it might strangle him. After a couple minutes I hoped it would strangle him.

He was the kind of guy who examined the hidden meaning of everything you said to him, including, "Good morning." After getting my balls busted every time I opened my mouth I wanted to get out of there, but I kept the conversation going for appearances sake to the Russians who were supposed to be watching me.

To ensure I'd be there for another ten minutes I asked the question guaranteed to set off a speech. "How did you become so successful?"

If I had threatened him with a gun it still might not have stopped him from talking for the next ten minutes. I stopped paying attention, I just didn't care. It was clear that he was very impressed with his own wonderfulness, but I couldn't recall any of the details even five minutes after our discussion.

At about the ten minute mark he paused. "Well that's enough about me," Paul said.

No shit

"So, I've had my eye on trading Bitcoin," Paul said. "What's your opinion on that?"

"No opinion," I said. "It's not something I would ever trade for my clients."

He raised his eyebrows and looked at me like I was dangerously stupid. "You wouldn't want your clients to profit on something that's so obviously going to change the world?"

"I'm a Value Investor. Value goes in and out of style. Right now it's out of style, but I'm not going to change," I said. "It's virtually impossible for me to determine what the fair value of Bitcoin is."

"Well, I want an investment advisor who's flexible, who will take advantage of major trends. I do most of my business with Todd Smith. What do you think of him?" Glass said.

I knew Todd Smith from my days at the Major Investment Firm. He was a well-dressed moron who retained his clients by treating them to lavish dinners and golf outings and the like.

"I never heard of him," I said. That's always a good reply when some dope is trying to impress you with the name of his investment advisor.

"Well, he one of the most important investment people in Austin, in the United States. He's on Barron's Top One Hundred Advisors list," Paul said.

"Oh. Well I don't pay much attention to other advisors. I kind of march to my own drummer," I said. I had been there long enough, it was time to get out, to walk the gauntlet back to the car and return to the pinball machine of trading Bitcoin.

"Well, aren't you going to pitch for my account? For at least some of my business?" Paul asked.

"With all due respect, no. I don't think we're compatible. I've been doing this long enough to know when to walk away. It's for our mutual benefit." I said. *Especially mine.*

"That's certainly not what I expected you to say. You're an odd duck," Paul said.

"That's… a good description. Thank you for your time, I know it's valuable, and I wouldn't want to waste any more of it," I said.

As Paul shook hands with me he said, "By 'valuable' do you mean 'invaluable' or do you really mean worthless? Why would you value my time, yet supposedly not want to do business with me? Are you playing mind games?"

"I'm leaving now," I said. As I walked out of the building I saw a few employees scurrying around hallways and the lobby. They looked depressed, but maybe I was letting my opinion of what it must me like working for Paul cloud my judgment.

Ninety One
Austin, TX

Sierra Quinn was in the car with Lev. He always insisted on driving. He was a clumsy, slow driver and he got plenty of middle finger salutes from Austin natives for his cautious driving style.

If those people only knew what Lev could do to them. But Lev was a professional and even he wouldn't kill somebody for just giving him the finger. Probably. Maybe. The quiet ones you have to watch out for.

"Let's see where Johnson goes now," Quinn said to Lev. They had been tailing him all morning from quite a distance. Both of them had identified Johnson's escorting bodyguards. "These guys protecting Johnson are good, but not great," she said. Lev grunted. Lev had maybe 20 different grunts and managed to communicate well using them.

Quinn decided to call Turgenev, who she thought was in New York, but it didn't matter. He wasn't the kind of boss you'd ask where he was, and how was the weather. He could get the information that Quinn wanted no matter where he was.

When Turgenev picked up Quinn gave a report. "Johnson visited the CEOs at Clipper Tech and Innodyne. We're following him now, he's probably on the way home. Do you want us to try to take him now?"

Turgenev was silent for a minute. "No, I have another idea. Try to stick on his tail, but it's important that his bodyguards don't make you. I'll call you back."

Ninety Two
Austin, TX

I was anxious to get home. After years of being Mr.
Conservative Value and hardly trading stocks at all, I was
getting hooked on the action of trading Bitcoin. As I passed a
convenience store on my right I got a sudden hankering for a
big bottle of Dr. Pepper, so after a quick look I cut across three
lanes and bumped over the curb into the parking lot of the
store.

I know soda is bad for you, they call it pop in Texas, and I
don't keep any in the house, but once in a while I crave a Dr.
Pepper. It's a habit I picked up when I got to the University of
Texas. That beverage was not big in Maryland, where I grew
up, but the Texas college boys drank it in the mornings when
even for them it was too early to have a beer.

Dr. Pepper was invented in Waco, and it is said to be named
after the father of a girl who jilted the creator. Maybe I'd
invent a soft drink called "Gabrielle" someday. It would have a
bitter after taste. Or maybe I'd come up with an Energy Drink
called "Murder Bitch." That would have an edgy appeal to the
millennials who drink that kind of crap.

I was so pleased with my witty thoughts as I took a long pull
out of the plastic bottle. Then it occurred to me that the sudden
maneuver of pulling across three lanes might have created a
problem for the bodyguard car that was following me. Oh well,
I was almost home.

As I screwed the top back on the bottle I looked at a car that
was stopped at the light in front on the convenience store. In
the passenger side of the car, I was sure it was Sierra Quinn.
She looked right at me. I waved slowly to her. She hesitated

and waved back. We looked each other right in the eyes. Her car drove off when the light changed.

Ninety Three
Austin, TX

I drove home at Ford F-150 Pickup Truck Warp Speed and
hurried into the house. Bonnie was there to greet me.

"Bonnie, I have a problem!" I said.

"Explain it to me." Bonnie was calm, but as I told her what
happened she frowned more and more. When I finished she got
on her little walkie talkie microphone thing and called Eric in
from the yard. He had been mowing the same spot of grass by
the pool again.

Bonnie and Eric had a discussion in front of me as though I
wasn't there. When Bonnie finished explaining things to Eric
he looked at me and said, "What an idiot."

She said she would call her control officer and that I should get
on my computer and do whatever it was that I did. Bonnie
would report back to me.

I got on the computer and things didn't look right. Bitcoin had
doubled while I was gone. My account went up way more than
it should have under any kind of normal circumstances. Simply
put, my underlying Bitcoin position was way up, but the hedge
I put on to protect myself while I was gone should have gone
way down, and it didn't. The hedge position was virtually
unchanged. This didn't make any sense, even for wacko
Bitcoin traders. My computerized Pinball Machine showed my
net gain at over $800 million. The first thing I did was close
out the hedge position, and my account kept going up.

So I was going to see the $1 billion dollar gain soon. But I had
also seen Sierra Quinn. What did she have to do with the
Russians?

272

Bitcoin didn't have news like a stock. Apple could announce unexpectedly high iPhone sales numbers and that would make the stock go up. But Bitcoin was just a commodity, a currency. Bitcoin didn't have earnings or losses, or report sales numbers or executives being hired or fired or sued. What could make it jump like this?

I turned on CNBC, There was a still photo of The CEO of Tesla. That CEO had a burning hatred of Hedge Funds that tried to gang up and create artificial air pockets in short positions. Again, that means the Hedge Funds are betting a stock, or commodity will go down. These bullies had tried to get Tesla a few years ago, and it almost ruined that CEO. He did everything he could to get revenge on the Hedge boys. And those bullies had been betting against Bitcoin.

That morning the Tesla CEO announced that the only currency that would be accepted for the purchase of a Tesla was Bitcoin. So in the U.S. if you wanted to buy a Tesla, you'd have to take your dollars and buy Bitcoin, then use the Cryptocurrency to go pay for your Tesla. It was simple. Teslas were no longer priced in Dollars, or Euros, or Yuan. At the same time the CEO announced Tesla Credit Corp would be financing purchases solely in Bitcoin. The customers would borrow Bitcoins, and repayment was acceptable in Bitcoins only.

CNBC reported that there were rumors that other, more establishment companies, were going to accept payment in Bitcoin also. Nothing was firm.

No wonder the price of Bitcoin was going crazy. The Hedge Fund boys who had bet against it when it was $20,000 per coin a week before were wiped out when the Bitcoin price blew through $400,000 that morning.

The Hedge fund boys who had shorted, or bet against Bitcoin when it was $20,000 per coin had lost at least 20 times their money, more if they had used borrowed money. So if they had put in $1 billion, they had lost at least $20 billion.

The frenzy explained why the prices of the hedges, or options that bet on Bitcoin going down, hadn't changed. The desperate people who had shorted Bitcoin a week ago, and still had any money, were using the options and futures market to bet once more that Bitcoin would go down. So, without going too deep in the weeds, futures contracts that would be worthless unless Bitcoin went down 50% in a month, and normally might trade for $1 per contract, were trading at $20,000 per contract.

If Bitcoin was a stock, some regulator, like the New York Stock Exchange, or the SEC would have stepped in at this point and halted trading temporarily, or could raise margin requirements, meaning speculators had to put up more money for each trade.

But Bitcoin lives outside regulators. It doesn't even have a country. And there are no physical coins. It's all just electrons. Nobody could halt trading or regulate it, and it traded 24 hours a day, seven days a week.

Bonnie came into my office. "I just got off the phone with my control officer. We're okay for now. He says for you to call Toni Anne Laudano."

Ninety Four
Austin, TX

I called Toni Anne.

"Oh, if it isn't James Fuckin' Bond! How many times did you ever see James Bond stop for a Dr. Pepper on the way home?" Despite her words, Toni Anne seemed in good spirits.

"Screw you, Toni Anne," I said.

"Oh. I like when you talk that way," she said.

"Besides, James Bond had better training than me. You took about five minutes to tell me half of what I need to know, and then you said not to worry because nothing was probably going to happen," I said.

"You have a good point there," Laudano said.

"Did you hear about me seeing Sierra Quinn? Do you know who she is?" I asked.

'Yeah. Now we're putting two and two together and we think it might have been her and a Russian guy who killed the New York Times reporters," she said. "There was a guy driving the car she was in?"

"I didn't get a good look at him, but it was a guy. I was sort of focusing on Quinn. She was the one who killed Lola and a friend of mine. And shot Gabrielle," I said.

"We know that. You should call McHugh and tell her you saw Quinn," Toni Anne said. "But that's all. Don't mention anything about Bitcoin. Only a few people in this building know what's really going on, and McHugh is definitely not one of them."

I didn't want to, but I asked Toni Anne if she could transfer me.

"No, it's not that kind of phone. You'll have to call her back," she said. "In the meantime, just keep doing what you're doing. We really didn't expect this sudden a rise in the price of Bitcoin. That might create a problem for the Russians. We're analyzing that now. Hey, JR---"

"Yeah?"

"Bonnie and Eric are the best. Nothing will happen to you while you're in your little compound."

"I'm getting a little nervous," I said.

"Only a little? What are you, stupid?, Tony Anne laughed, "Did you talk to Paul at InnoDyne about Bitcoin?"

"He asked about it. I told him I had no opinion." I said.

"Did you two get along?" she asked.

"No. We each thought the other one was a jerk. I was right." I said.

"Interesting. Because as soon as you left, he called The Tesla CEO. Those two are buddies. When that call was over he placed an order on his computer to buy $5 million of Bitcoin, on margin." She said.

"You think the Tesla guy told him something?" I asked.

"Probably. It's not illegal, because Bitcoin isn't regulated. But guess what. If we know that he bought, the Russians also know that he bought. They probably know he talked to the Tesla guy. They must think you told him something, or that he told you. Maybe they think he's Nakamoto, or that the Tesla guy is Nakamoto. Of course, as soon as you got home, you bought, so maybe they think you're in on the loop. But we're sure that they don't think that you're Nakamoto,' Toni Anne said.

"Why is that?" I asked.

"Because you're not smart enough," she answered.

Great

Ninety Five
Austin, TX

I never wanted to talk to Gabrielle again, but thought it was my duty to tell her that I had seen Sierra Quinn. I called Gabrielle, but her phone went immediately to voice mail.

"Hey Gabrielle, pick up. I'm not calling to chit chat. This is urgent. Pick up the phone---"

"Major McHugh," she said.

"Yeah, no kidding. I knew who I was calling," I said. Her greeting set the tone. I guess we weren't going to talk about her volleyball career. "I've got to tell you something," I said.

"What is it?" she asked.

"I saw Sierra Quinn today," I said.

"You sure?" Gabrielle asked.

"Yeah." I told her the circumstances. "I just got off the phone with Toni Anne. She wanted me to tell you."

"Alright. Now you've told me. Quinn must be working for the Russians. I'm not in that end of the business anymore," she said.

The implication of Gabrielle's comment was: I'm safe, but you're in Austin. Sierra Quinn's in Austin. Quinn thinks you know something.

"Your level of concern is touching," I said.

"You have bodyguards. You should be okay," Gabrielle said.

"Thanks." I hung up.

Ninety Six
Moscow
The Lider's Apartment

The Russian Finance minister stood in front of The Lider's desk.

"Mr. President, the price of Bitcoin has exceeded our expectations," he said.

"Why is that?" The Lider asked.

"There seem to be all buyers and no large sellers. Then yesterday The Tesla CEO came out and said that Teslas would be priced in Bitcoin, no matter where in the world they were sold," the Minister said.

"Does he know something? Do you think he's Nakamoto?" The Lider asked.

"The Tesla CEO likes to be a troublemaker, and his hatred for short sellers is well known. They tried to gang up on him a few years ago, and almost put Tesla out of business. So his actions have caused great pain for the Hedge Funds who are betting against the price of Bitcoin. And unlike a pure speculator, Tesla wants to take delivery of the Bitcoin, as payment for the cars. As far as whether he's Nakamoto, I have no opinion," the Finance Minister replied.

"Hmmm, well maybe when this project is complete, I'll buy myself a Tesla. They are attractive automobiles." The Lider laughed.

The Finance Minister, not knowing whether he too was expected to laugh, just smiled and nodded.

"So what's the problem," The Lider asked. "I can tell you think there's a problem."

"It's not so much a problem as it is a two edged sword. On one hand the sizable initial purchases we made through the shell accounts in the offshore banks are wildly profitable," the Minister said, "but on the other hand any further purchases will cost a lot more than anticipated. Maybe we should hold off on further purchases for the time being."

"No!" The Lider barked. He saw the look of terror in the Finance Minister's face and decided to temper his remarks. He rose from his chair and went around his desk, putting his arm around the banker.

"There's a reason why I am in this office and you are Finance Minister. I am here because I made bold actions during my career, and you are Finance Minister because you are cautious." The Lider slapped the man on the back.

The Lider returned to his chair. "I appreciate your thorough report, but no, we will not pause our purchases. We will boldly and aggressively keep buying, because we know in the end the American financial institutions will be forced to buy from us at higher prices in order to pay our ransom demands. And then they have to give us the Bitcoin for nothing! Maybe instead of making $4 trillion, we'll make $6 trillion, $10 trillion," he paused, "maybe I'll purchase two Teslas. Do you happen to know if they come in red?"

Ninety Seven
Austin, TX

Sierra Quinn's phone rang.

Turgenev spoke. "We think Johnson's visit with Steve at Clipper Tech was a decoy. His real mission was to visit with Paul Glass. As soon as he left, Glass called the Tesla CEO, then Glass purchased $5 million of Bitcoin. Soon after Tesla announced that they would only accept Bitcoin as payment for purchase of a Tesla. The Tesla CEO could be Nakamoto. Are you following me?" he said to Quinn.

"Sort of, where are we going with this?. Do you want us to go after The Tesla guy?" she asked.

"No. His security it too good, you'd never get near him, and he's currently in California," Turgenev said. "I want you to kidnap Paul Glass and find out what he knows."

"Do you want me to come on to him in a bar or something?" Quinn asked.

"Not a good idea. He's gay…and I don't think Lev's his type," Turgenev said. "No time for subtlety, just chloroform him in company parking lot when he leaves work tonight, and throw him in the back of the van. Put Lev on the phone."

Lev took the phone and grunted. It was his 'hello' grunt.

"Lev, do you have any 55 gallon oil drums in the van?" Turgenev asked.

"Yes," Lev said.

"How many?" Turgenev asked.

"Two."

"That should be enough," Turgenev said. "Give the phone back to Quinn. She picked up.

"Glass might be the best source we've had so far. He's going to end up in an oil drum, so don't hold anything back. We've got to know what he knows. It's alright if he's dead when he goes in the oil drum, I've got nothing personal against him," Turgenev said.

Ninety Eight
Austin, TX

Paul Glass finished work at six, and headed out to his
"Reserved for the CEO" parking spot. Before he could reach
his Porsche Turbo Carrera an unmarked white van pulled up
behind his car.

Sierra Quinn was driving, which allowed Lev to hop out of the
panel truck's sliding door with surprising agility for a man of
his bulk. He came up behind Glass and put a chloroform
soaked rag over his face and threw him in the cargo area in one
swift motion. No one at InnoDyne noticed as the van drove off
at a reasonable speed.

Lev put zip ties on the wrists of the unconscious Glass after
having rolled him face down, then did the same to his ankles.
Quinn drove out toward the Hill Country, 20 miles from
Austin. They had found an abandoned quarry that would be
perfect for their purposes.

Texas has many fine characteristics, beautiful alpine lakes not
being among them and this pit, really just a glorified, but deep,
mud hole was dismal even in that league. The water looked so
polluted with sludgy oil that you might walk across it. Nobody
ever went there, even the stupidest drunkest kid would never
try to get his girlfriend to skinny dip in this awful place, but it
was big and deep enough to hold as many 55 gallon oil drums
as you would like to dump there, that would never be found,
and it had a steep embankment right on the dirt road that made
it easy to roll the barrel right into the deeper water.

When Quinn pulled up next to the embankment Glass was
stirring, waking up. Lev opened the sliding door and carried
Glass out leaning him up against a big boulder. With his hands
and legs bound Glass couldn't move. Lev took an ammonia

capsule out of his jacket, broke the capsule and held it under Glass' nose. He seemed to be fully awake now.

Paul Glass' eyes bulged as Quinn approached him. Lev stood to the side.

"Do you know why you're here?" Quinn asked.

"I suppose it's some kidnapping attempt. You want my company to pay a ransom. Let's be civilized about this. I'm sure we can work something out," Glass said.

'Wrong, shit for brains," Quinn said. "Lev, roll over one of the oil drums, and bring the pliers that we use to close the top."

Lev opened the back of the van and rolled an oil drum in front of Glass, then went back for the huge industrial pliers, and grabbed a crowbar as well. He walked over and stood next to the drum.

"First of all, we don't want money. You can keep that $5 million worth of Bitcoin you bought today," Quinn said.

Glass nodded, but looked confused.

"We know a lot, but we want information from you. If I'm satisfied that you told us everything, you can walk out of here. If not," Quinn took out her Glock with silencer and shot two holes in the oil drum, "we'll be putting you in the oil drum and rolling you into the lake. I shot holes in it so it would sink. It's a shitty way to go. You with me so far?"

"Yes," Glass said.

"Lev, take the top off the drum." Quinn said.

Lev took the pliers and pried several metal tabs on the top of the drum open, enough of them so he could pull the top off, which he then placed on the ground. He picked up the crowbar in his free hand.

"Those pliers can be used to reseal the top after you're in the barrel, but they also come in handy for pulling out your teeth, cutting off your cock, removing fingernails. The crowbar is more of a blunt force instrument. But we don't want to kill you. We don't even want to hurt you. But you have to start talking now," Quinn said.

"What do you want to know?" Glass said.

"Everything you know about Bitcoin. Who is Satoshi Nakamoto. Are there ever going to be more Bitcoins issued? What did your contact at Tesla tell you today? Is he Nakamoto? Stuff like that," Quinn said.

"How do you know I talked to Tesla today?" Glass asked.

Quinn gestured to Lev with her head. Lev paused for a second seeming to decide between the pliers and the crowbar. He chose the crowbar and walked to Glass. Lev smashed him on the right side of his ribcage, but Lev was a professional, and only caused severe pain, not enough to make Glass unconscious.

"Did you ever see in the movies where they have good cop, bad cop? Forget it, we're both bad cop, and we don't have time to screw around with you. You don't have the right to remain silent. So, either start telling us everything you know, or after spending the worst fifteen minutes of your life, it will be capped off by putting you in the oil drum, sealing the top, and a roll down the hill into the water. No one will ever find your body," Quinn said. "We do it all the time."

Quinn was accurate. It was without question the worst fifteen minutes of Glass' life. Between beatings he told them that he was friends with The Tesla CEO, didn't know JR Johnson until today, that the CEO had told him that he was going to make the announcement about Tesla, that's why he bought Bitcoin. But he didn't know anything about the structure of Bitcoin, didn't know who Nakamoto was, he had never discussed it with anybody.

Quinn stepped away from Glass and motioned for Lev to join her. "I think he's telling the truth. You think so Lev?" He nodded.

She walked over to face Glass. "I think you're telling the truth, so I'm going to do you a favor. See that road over there?" She pointed to her right and Glass turned his head to look, and in that instant she shot him twice in the forehead.

"Okay, Lev let's get him in the barrel and seal it up. Hey, do me a favor, two of his teeth are over on the ground. Let's make sure they go in the barrel. Let's not get sloppy and leave evidence around that might identify Glass." Quinn said. She picked up her shell casings.

When Glass was sealed in the barrel Lev shoved it down the incline into the lake but it got stuck ten feet from shore.

"There must be some underwater rock. Lev, go in there and get the barrel out to deep water, will you?" Quinn asked.

Lev waded into the industrial waste and struggled to roll the barrel over the underwater obstacle. It slowly sank, and within seconds the oily ooze had sealed up the hole the barrel had made while sinking, and there was no sign of anything other than the oil slick.

Ninety Nine
Austin, TX

After I got off the phone with Toni Anne and had doubled up on my Bitcoin position, I called Barbara Jean. I didn't want to ignore my fiancé, and just in case Sierra Quinn was going to kill me soon, I figured another conjugal visit with Barb would be nice.

"I was wondering if you'd ever call me again," Barbara Jean said.

I considered telling her that I had been busy, but I thought that was a lame response. I went with, "I've been working. Made about $1 billion so far on this project."

"Yeah, sure," Barbara Jean said, "if I thought that was true I'd take you back to the jewelry store and ask for the real thing." She laughed. "Starting our relationship off on a foundation of lies makes me worry about you."

"Barbara Jean, I always tell you the truth…. Pretty much… About the important things," I said.

"So what did you call me for? Just to practice your lying?" she asked.

"Well, my dearest fiancé, I called to invite you over for a little cookout tonight," I said.

"I'll only come if I can sleep over tonight," Barb said.

I hesitated, picturing her staying over for endless days. That was not something I was ready for. I'd have to ease my way into that sort of living arrangement.

As if reading my mind, Barb said, "Don't worry, I have to leave in the morning. Tommy, the ranch hand had to go in the hospital for surgery, and his wife Alice and I have to take care of the livestock for a while."

"Well, that's fine," I said, "and to show you how even-tempered I am, I promise not to throw a whiskey glass at you when you try to walk out the door."

"Ha-ha," she said.

One Hundred
Washington, DC

Toni Anne lived in a brick townhouse in Georgetown. The neighborhood was populated with diplomats, retired politicians who had sold out to become lobbyists, and trust fund dilettantes. It was not the kind of place a government bureaucrat lived, even high ranking ones. But Toni Anne was now worth around $500 million, having invested the proceeds from the sale of her business wisely. Hubby John Driscoll knew he was living way above his status, and knew that the marriage with volatile Ms. Laudano wouldn't last, but he had motivations that were more important in his mind than money.

When Driscoll walked in the front door Toni Anne called from the upstairs bedroom. "Hey, what took you so long! Get your ass up here."

Toni Anne wasn't interested in preliminaries, she told Driscoll to take off his clothes and they got into bed and screwed. She was the aggressor.

"That wasn't so bad, now was it?" Toni Anne asked.

"It was great, as always. I do feel like you're using me," Driscoll said.

"I am using you," she said. Toni Anne wasn't a post coital cuddler, so she rolled over to the right side of the bed to have some space of her own. With her head on the pillow she pulled the blanket up to armpit level, not out of modesty, which she had none in this setting, but to avoid a chill in the overly air-conditioned room.

Driscoll adopted a similar pose on the left side of the bed. "So what's going on at work? What's with the middle of the night conference call?" he asked.

"Well," Toni Anne said, "The Russians, as you know have gone way past any previous levels of messing with our political system. The disinformation is ten times what it was for the last Presidential campaign. And now we're seeing real threats to voting machines and absentee ballot infrastructure. The more responsible politicians are going apeshit, and they're afraid that the election will be declared invalid by whoever loses and that determining the winner will go to the Supreme Court and take years during which time the country will be ungovernable." "It's that bad?" asked Driscoll.

"Yeah. And the politicians are putting major heat on General Goldstein. So we're diverting all possible resources away from other areas. There's not much going on in the Threat Board anyhow," Toni Anne said.

"Doesn't that make us vulnerable to other attacks?" Driscoll asked.

"Theoretically yes, of course. But we live in the real world. If Congress thinks we screwed up and they cut our funding we're out of business. So we have to hope to put out this fire right away, and then get back to normal operations. The top level committee that we pretend doesn't exist is all getting put on the Protect the Election Task Force. Nobody said this was going to be easy," she said.

'So what's with the middle of the night conference call?" he asked.

"Different subject. I shouldn't tell you this, but the President wants to know the identity of Satoshi Nakamoto, you know the Bitcoin guy? We've got some assets from around the world, and they have contacts. We're almost positive about Bitcoin. It looks like the Bitcoin thing is for real. For one thing no more Bitcoins are going to be issued." Toni Anne said.

"How do you know that?" Driscoll asked.

"We've got a very good source. I really can't tell you anything more. Just forget I told you that much, okay?" Laudano said.

Toni Anne got out of bed, went to her closet and got a change of clothes. She put on a plaid jumper with a white blouse, which made her look even more like Mary Poppins than before. "I'm leaving now. See you when I see you," she said.

"Why do you dress like that? Driscoll asked.

"Because I like it," she said.

"Well it's early. I'm going down to the pub for a while," he said.

One Hundred One
Washington, DC

Driscoll waited for Toni Anne to leave, then put on his clothes. He went downstairs to his briefcase and took out a phone, not his usual iPhone. This was a cheap burner flip phone. He hit some buttons.

"Hey Tommy. I'm going down to the pub. Want to play some darts?" he said. "I'll be there in half an hour."

Normally when Driscoll had information that could wait he went to what was called a Dead Drop. He took a walk in a nearby park and left a coded note under a specific rock. There had never been any problem with this procedure, but the conversation with Toni Anne gave him urgent information that he had to get to his Russian handler. So 'want to play some darts?' was the signal for his contact to meet him at the pub. He was tired of this bitch, and maybe this information motherlode would get them to finally get him out of the country. The Russians had promised to relocate him in Cuba, and he hoped to drink rum and live with a more pliable Cuban woman, one who wasn't so much smarter than him.

There were cozy pubs in Georgetown, one a block and a half from Toni Anne's townhouse. When Driscoll arrived the place was relatively empty, and Tommy was already at the dartboard, John walked up to the bar and ordered a Guinness.

"Hey pal, want to play some darts?" Tommy asked.

"Sure," Driscoll answered, and he walked over carrying his stout.

The two went through the motions of having a couple games, accompanied by good-natured needling and congratulations for good shots. As the players passed each other it was easy for Driscoll to tell Tommy the information Toni Anne had let slip while they were in bed.

"Very good job," Tommy said.

"Get me out," Driscoll said quietly.

"I'm sure after tonight that you helped yourself," Tommy said.

The bartender didn't pay any attention to them, except to ask them if they wanted another drink.

When they were done with a couple games of darts both men approached the bar. "Can you give me two fives for a ten? Tommy asked the bartender, "it seems my new friend here beat me out of five bucks."

Tommy slapped the five on the bar. Driscoll said, "hey stick around. I'll buy you a beer."

"Can't do it, man. Got a crack of dawn flight to the coast to catch," Tommy said.

"Nice to meet you," Driscoll said.

John Driscoll stayed at the pub for two more Guinnesses. He settled up with the bartender, giving him the five he had won in darts as a tip.

On the walk home a woman came out of an alley. "Oh thank god you're here. My dog, my poodle has his leg caught in a drain. Can you please help me?"

Driscoll walked a long distance down the alley, but saw no dog. "Oh my god, look what's happened!" she said. When Driscoll turned to face her she shot him in the heart with a pistol from point blank range. He fell to the ground. The woman checked him, made sure he was dead, then dragged his body behind some garbage cans. She took his wallet, watch and the money in his pocket. She had used a .25 caliber gun, the Saturday Night Special that a street punk would carry, and it took good aim to get Driscoll in the heart. This murder would look like a mugging gone bad. The cops would think it was just the case of a guy in the wrong place at the wrong time.

One Hundred Two
Washington, DC

Tommy, really Dimitri, hung up his phone at the Russian consulate. He went down the hall and knocked on the door of his superior, the FSB agent in charge. He was motioned to come in.

"Driscoll is taken care of. He won't be bothering us with his whining about going to Cuba anymore," Dimitri said.

"Very well done," his boss said. "It's best to put this behind us and go on to other cases."

Dimitri nodded.

One Hundred Three
Fort Meade, MD
Cyber Command
Office of the Commanding General

It was 1:30 am. Cyber Command was staffed 24 hours a day, 365 days a year, but this night there was more than just a skeleton crew. The place was full.

General Goldstein had summoned Toni Anne into his office. "Have a seat, Toni Anne," Goldstein said.

'I have some…news," he hesitated. "Umm… John Driscoll was found dead in a Georgetown alley about half an hour ago."

"Yeah, well fuck him," Toni Anne said. "That fuckin' Commie rat! Are you sure it's him?"

"We followed him from your townhouse to the pub. He met with his handler, and on the way home got lured into an alley by a woman, a Russian operative. She shot him. Made it look like a robbery," the General said.

"Now what?" Toni Anne asked.

"We notified the police. He didn't have any ID so it would have taken them awhile to figure out who he was, and we didn't want them going around asking too many questions. Fixed it on high at the police department, just said it's National Security. And we told them to hold off releasing his identity, pending notification of the next of kin," Goldstein answered.

"Good. That's good. Now I don't have to take any time off from work to pretending to be the grieving widow. I've got to—"

"Toni Anne don't you have any mixed---"

"Screw that. Look, we knew he was a mole. He thought he was using me, and we used him. I was a bit of a Patriotic whore. So what? He passed on the fake intel to the Russians, and they did us a favor by getting rid of him. Hey, can we ask the cops to just John Doe this guy? I'm sure as hell not going to any funeral, and his parents are dead," Toni Anne said.

"That's a good idea," Goldstein said.

"General, do you have a bottle of booze in your desk. I hear Generals always have a bottle of something in their desk," Toni Anne said.

"I happen to have a bottle of bourbon," the General answered. He got the bottle and a couple plastic glasses, and poured a shot for each of them.

"I'd like to propose at toast. To my late husband. Rot in Hell, you Commie Rat asshole!" Toni Anne said. "Thanks for helping us!"

"I'll drink to that," Goldstein said.

One Hundred Four
Moscow
The Lider's Apartment

The Director of the FSB stood in front of The Lider's desk. The Lider gestured for him to have a seat.

"Mr. President, the Americans have taken the bait. They have concentrated most of their assets on trying to fight the disinformation campaign. It's time to launch Phase Three," the director said. "And they believe that Nakamoto will not ever create any more than 21 million Bitcoins."

"Excellent," The Lider said. "Let's go over the timeline."

"With your approval, at noon Washington D.C. time, 9 am California time, we will shut down the American financial system. The stocks will not trade. The cash machines will not work. Any online interfaces will not function. Doors on bank vaults will not open. After five minutes, we'll turn the system back on, as though nothing happened," the director said.

"Then I will place the call to the U.S. President?" The Lider asked.

"Yes sir."

"At that time I will tell him that we were responsible for the shutdown of the Financial System, and that I will be calling him back within an hour to discuss the situation further."

The director nodded.

"I have the greatest job in the world!" The Lider said. "We have set the stage for Russia's greatest victory, and we will not have to fire a single shot."

One Hundred Five
Austin, TX

Barbara Jean showed up around five. She drove the Corvette
with the top down and spun up some pebbles in the driveway.
My fiancé!

I went out to greet her as she took a six pack of Pearl Beer out
of the passenger seat. "I wouldn't want to show up empty
handed, especially for the guy who bought me the million
dollar diamond." She laughed. Man, she looked beautiful.
`

"Oh and I brought you another gift. It's in the trunk." She
opened the trunk of her Corvette. Wrapped in a blanket was a
pistol. "It's for your protection while you still live here. Before
you move out to the ranch after we're married."

We hadn't discussed living arrangements yet. I hadn't thought
out that we'd actually have to live in the same location after
marriage, but then again, I'd been preoccupied making a billion
or so dollars in the last few days. I guessed that we would live
together. There were some things I'd have to get used to.

"It's a SIG Sauer M 17. My favorite handgun. It's the one
carried by U.S. military officers. All the best technology. It
even has a GPS chip in case it ever gets stolen. I'll teach you
how to shoot it. Maybe you can come out to the ranch in the
next couple days," Barb said.

She gave me a big hug. She smelled great, she looked great,
she felt great. It was great. I had lost all perspective on reality
because as of the time I walked out the door to greet Barb I was
up over 1.5 billion dollars since I had begun trading Bitcoin.

Since I had intentionally cut down my Investment Management
business a few years ago I was netting about $150,000 a year

before taxes, not counting money I made on my own investments. That's a fair sum, a lot more than most people ever make in a year. I looked it up, $150,000 put me in the top 7% of all earners in the U.S. Even if I didn't pay income tax, and I never spent any of the money, I'd have to work 10,000 years to accumulate the 1.5 billion dollars that I'd made in Bitcoin. And that kind of longevity doesn't run in my family.

I had an itinerary of activities planned for Barb and me. I was sure she was onboard for the activities. Nothing like getting engaged to build enthusiasm.

Because I didn't want to be disturbed with even thinking about Bitcoin until tomorrow morning, I had hedged the position. Simply, it was a time out, where I couldn't go up or down much.

A word about Hedging, without getting too technical. You can buy insurance for any kind of financial instrument for whatever period of time you want. Insurance for a day cost a lot less than insurance for a year. Think of it as buying auto insurance. Surely you'd pay less to insure a car for a day rather than a year, but it would cost something. But something strange was going on in the Bitcoin market. Because so many amateurs were currently playing in the Options and Futures markets for Bitcoin, the insurance for one day was free. There's a technical term to explain this: Stupid.

There was that one strange thing that happened at 11 am. The market just shut down for five minutes without explanation. Everything. Then trading resumed. CNBC said experts were looking into the glitch.

One Hundred Six
Moscow
The Lider's Apartment

The Lider placed a call to the President of the United States. It
takes a few minutes to organize such a call because in a
situation like this there are as many as twenty people listening
to the call on each side. Typically on the U.S. side there was
the translator for the President, people from the Departments of
State, Treasury, and Defense. This is no secret from either side.
But this time it was only the translator and General Goldstein,
Toni Anne Laudano, and Yuri Sokolov The Russians were
unaware of this. After very brief pleasantries The Lider
announced, "Mr. President, I am calling regarding the five
minute outage of your financial system today. As I am sure
your Cyber people are telling you, we were responsible for
that."

"Yes. We were about to call you with a complaint and a strong
warning," the President said.

"Your warning is noted, but I am certain that after talking to
your technical people, you will be changing your attitude. I
have something very important to announce to you," The Lider
said.

"We have a new Cyber weapon of which you are unaware. We
will unleash it in two days unless you meet our demands," The
Lider said.

"I find that difficult to believe, but go on," the President said.

"We showed you a miniscule portion of the new weapon's
capabilities when we launched the ransomware attack on
Baylor University. That attack was pitiful in relation to our
weapon's full capabilities." The Lider said.

"Go on," the President said.

"The Baylor attack showed our ability to include thousands of encapsulated micro-viruses within a larger virus," The Lider paused, as if to allow the President's advisors to explain this technicality, "but we sent only *one* identical type of micro-virus in the data stream. We have the ability to send literally *millions of different* micro-viruses in the data stream. You have no defense. It would take your experts years to fix this problem."

"So, we'll just retaliate," the President said. "How foolish to destroy both countries."

"You are getting ahead of yourself, Mr. President. I haven't told you the best part yet. Please allow me to finish, then we can have a rational discussion," The Lider said.

"Alright," The President said.

"As your Cyber experts have no doubt analyzed, our new viruses have the ability to not only shutdown your computer system, but also to reach in and seize all the assets within a Financial System, in this case your entire Financial System," The Lider paused again, to allow the President to get confirmation from his experts. "So not only will the computers in your financial system not work, but we will take all your money. Every cent in all banks, brokerages, insurance companies, and the U.S. Treasury."

"We will just issue new money," the President said.

"No, you will have no means to do so. Your financial institutions will be helpless, including the Federal Reserve and the Treasury. You would have no means of distributing the money. And any foreign branches of your financial institutions will be similarly disabled," The Lider answered.

"So why wouldn't I retaliate with a Cyber strike of my own?" the President asked.

"Because Russia is a backward nation. We are not a technologically advanced as you. So we are not so dependent upon the Internet. We have developed backups to run our financial, energy, defense and other systems that are not connected to the Internet, so your attack would cause some inconveniences for our citizens, but we would be up and running almost normally within a day. On the other hand, you would never recover. Millions of your people would die," The Lider said. "And Mr. President, I am fairly certain that you would not be re-elected."

The President was silent for thirty seconds. "You would leave me with no option other than to use Kinetic Weapons. We would unleash our nuclear arsenal," he finally said.

"I doubt that Mr. President, for two reasons. First, if you destroy us, you destroy the key to unlock your problems. Second, if you launch against us, I will be forced to launch against you. I am certain that your military experts tell you that while diminished, we still have the nuclear weapon capability to destroy your country many times over. I don't think you'll do that when I offer you a much more palatable alternative," The Lider calmly explained. "We simply require a ransom. A reasonable amount compared to the alternatives," The Lider said.

"Let's just suppose for a minute that we entertained your proposal. How much would the ransom be, and what assurances would we have that paying the ransom would be the end of it? What's to prevent you from an endless cycle of such behavior?" the President asked.

"Those are excellent questions. You are really getting to the heart of the matter. My compliments," The Lider said.

"And what are the answers?" the President asked.

"We don't require dollars or any national currency, or gold. What we do require as a ransom is Bitcoin. As you may know there are only 21 million Bitcoins outstanding, and that is all there will ever be. To be reasonable, we are demanding 20 million Bitcoins. It would be very difficult round up all the Bitcoin in the world. Some owners would not sell at any price. So we require just 20 million Bitcoins," The Lider said.

"And how do you propose that we do that? A direct payment from the Treasury?" the President asked.

"No. We will be sending requirements of specific amounts from all your large Financial Institutions. They will each have to acquire the Bitcoin however they can, then they will pool the total amount with your Treasury. You will then wire the Bitcoin to an intermediary, The Bank of International Settlements in Basel, Switzerland---"

"Yeah, I know where it is," the President interrupted.

"Good," The Lider continued. "That institution is as neutral an intermediary as possible. That gets us to your second question," The Lider said.

"Yes?"

"To assure you that we cannot launch an attack like this again, we will send your Cyber Command all of the code for this project, except the final algorithms that will unlock the viruses. As your experts will no doubt confirm, once a weapon like this has been used, and analyzed by an adversary, it cannot be used again. Defenses will be built against it," The Lider explained.

"Go over the timeline for me?" the President asked.

"Both countries will have representatives at the Bank for International Settlements. When your technical people are ready, we will send the final key. As soon as they verify that it is genuine, the Bank of International Settlements will wire the Bitcoin to Russia," The Lider said.

The President was silent. Finally The Lider said, "I am sure that you want to go over our proposal with your technical people. When you analyze all your options, you will conclude that our proposal is your only reasonable response. Otherwise millions of your citizens will needlessly die. The financial pain from this transaction will be digested in just few years by your vigorous economy. And Mr. President---"

"Yes—"

"We will be using much of our windfall to invest in your wonderful U.S. companies. Our two countries will end up being long term partners," The Lider said.

"It will take some time to evaluate your proposition, Mr. President," the U.S. President said.

"Unfortunately, due to the sensitive nature of this information, time is something you do not have. We cannot risk the news of this getting out. Therefore you have one hour to make a decision, and please call me back at that time. Otherwise 48 hours from now, your country will revert to the Dark Ages," The Lider said, then hung up.

One Hundred Seven
Moscow

Oleg Turgenev waited in an anteroom while The Lider was on the call with the U.S. President. The Lider's translator and assistants left his office and The Lider himself came to the door and said, "Come in the office Oleg."

The Lider sat behind his desk. "We are very close to consummating what may be the biggest event in the history of the world, Oleg. Wars are destructive, they just drain the resources of both sides. This method is so much better, even for the losing side."

Turgenev nodded.

"The one variable we don't have absolutely nailed down is Nakamoto, although we are much more confident with new information that has come in," The Lider said, "how do you assess the situation?"

"Sir, I have just carried out orders to the best of my ability. Surely you have experts on your Intelligence staff that can give a better assessment of that complex situation," Turgenev answered.

"Oleg, that answer qualifies you to join the mealy-mouthed bureaucrats that I am forced to spend so much time with. I have heard what they have to say. I want your opinion," The Lider said.

"Sir, we have interrogated everyone that the FSB has determined might know anything. Some of them were useless poseurs. The only things I know are:" Turgenev counted off the five points on his fingers;

1) Paul Glass talked to the CEO of Tesla. Glass then bought $5 million dollar worth of Bitcoin.
2) Later that day, Tesla announced that they would only accept Bitcoin for purchase of an automobile.
3) JR Johnson was summoned to talk to Cyber Command, but was uncooperative.
4) When Johnson returned to Austin from Washington he began aggressively buying Bitcoin.
5) Johnson visited Paul Glass right before Glass talked to Tesla.

When it became evident that Turgenev was done speaking The Lider asked, "and what conclusion do you draw from these points?"

"Sir, it seems Tesla and Johnson are confident in Bitcoin as a store of value, just as it is intended to be. Glass was just a minor player. He didn't know anything. He would have talked." Turgenev answered.

"Do you think The CEO of Tesla is Nakamoto?" The Lider asked.

"No, but it is possible that he knows Nakamoto. That was a bold move he made about only taking Bitcoin as payment for Tesla sales," Turgenev answered.

"And is this JR Johnson Nakamoto?" The Lider asked.

Turgenev laughed. "He does not possess the technical now-how, and he has no staff."

"So how do we move forward?" The Lider asked.

"Sir, I think that Johnson doesn't have any better idea of the identity of Nakamoto, or of his intentions than we do. And I think the U.S. Government believes that Nakamoto will not issue any new Bitcoins." Turgenev replied.

"Your opinion on the knowledge of the U.S. Government is based on—"

"Gut feeling, Mr. President," Oleg said, instantly regretting interrupting The Lider.

The Lider stared at him. "Your gut feeling is confirmed by our intelligence sources. Stick around Moscow until this thing is settled. I may need your services. You can go."

Turgenev turned to leave. "Oleg. Let's turn over every stone. Do one more interrogation. Let's see if Mr. JR Johnson can tell us anything."

"I'll make the call, Mr. President." Turgenev said.

One Hundred Eight
Washington, DC

An hour later the President of the United States called The Lider. The President told The Lider that after careful consideration his advisors had concluded that his only option was to accept the Russian proposal.

"Very well, Mr. President," The Lider said.

"One question," the President said, "why not just take a direct payment from our Treasury? Why go through the intermediate step of requiring each of our large financial companies to contribute to the ransom?"

"That is the way our experts have concluded it is most advantageous in the long run. That is not negotiable," The Lider said. "In order to make this process possible, we have decided to make the ransom demands only from your 15 largest financial institutions. Five minutes from now we will be wiring you the specific amounts that will be demanded from each institution."

"Very well," the President said. "You need to supply the technical information to our experts in Cyber Command."

"Yes," The Lider said. "Within minutes our FSB department head will call General Goldstein at Cyber Command in Fort Meade to make arrangements to fulfill that part of our bargain."

One Hundred Nine
Austin, TX

Barbara Jean suggested we have a roll in the hay prior to our poolside cookout. Sounded good to me. She was a damn good looking woman with her clothes on, half off, or bare assed naked, standing up, laying down. You get the picture.

When we had concluded our exercises she said, "Get up, lazy. Get the charcoal going, I'm hungry. Let's have some of those beers."

I love it when women talk like that. I mean, when my fiancé talks like that.

I had decided that the menu that night would consist solely of burgers on rolls. Ketchup optional. The Pearl beers were in the cooler on ice. Is there a better menu than high quality burgers with ice cold beer? I could skip the duck at the Tour D'Argent, even though I did plan to take Barb to Paris for our honeymoon.

"Barb, how'd you like to go to Paris for the honeymoon?" I asked.

"You mean Paris, France, right?" she asked.

We laughed. There was a Paris, Texas.

"Yup, Paree! You ever been there?"

"Yeah, I went when I was a teenager. I remember my father lingering in front of some of the nude paintings in the museums," she said.

"Well, I'm more sophisticated than that. Besides, I'd rather linger with you in some fancy hotel room. Could you bring that diamond studded bra on the Honeymoon?" I asked.

"I brought it tonight! You do realize that they're fake? I mean the diamonds, not me." she said.

"You're a very nice person," I said. "Why did I wait so long?"

One Hundred Ten
Moscow

Turgenev called Sierra Quinn. "We've got to find out if JR Johnson knows anything," he said.

"What's the time frame?" Quinn asked.

"As soon as possible," Turgenev said.

"It's a problem right now. He has bodyguards at his compound, good ones. We'd have a shootout just to get inside." Quinn explained.

"So what do you propose?" Turgenev asked, "He probably doesn't know anything, so it's okay with me if you kill him."

"We'll have to find a way to lure him out of the compound," Quinn said.

'Sometime within the next day," Turgenev said. "And if he takes a swim in the oil drum, make sure he's alive when we goes in the water. I guess Johnson has been a thorn in his side ever since New York."

One Hundred Eleven
Austin, TX

At five am the next morning Barbara Jean was ready to leave.
We were getting along just fine; it was just that she had to be
out at the ranch to help Alice take care of the cattle and
chickens.

I was wide awake, ready to go back into the free-money
universe and start trading Bitcoin. Barb gave me a little peck
on the cheek and said, "You keep the gun for now, but bring it
with you when you come out for the shooting lesson. Do you
think you can make it tonight?"

"Barb, if I do come out tonight I won't be able to stay over. I
just want you to understand that now. If that's not okay, I'll
wait a day or two," I said.

"Alright, JR. Hey, all this investing stuff you're doing. Does it
have anything to do with Bitcoin?" Barb asked.

"Why would you say that?" I asked.

"It's just that yesterday I saw how Bitcoin was going crazy on
the TV news. I don't understand Bitcoin," Barb said.

"Yeah, most people don't," I said, "we'll talk about everything
when this is all over. Soon."

"Yeah, okay. Listen I've got to go. Give me a call later," Barb
said.

One Hundred Twelve
Spicewood, TX

Sierra Quinn and Lev saw Barbara Jean's Corvette leave JR's driveway. They decided to follow her and drove undetected all the way to her ranch.

"Okay, we know how to flush out Johnson," Quinn said. Let's drive back and take care of the surveillance team in the car first. Then we'll come back here."

Lev grunted indicating his agreement.

Taking out the surveillance team would be the most dangerous, exposed part of their mission, but bold decisive action was not expected on a regular city street, and it had to be done.

When Lev drove the van back to Austin, the two man protection team was half a block from JR's house, parked in their plain Chevy Malibu in the shade.

Lev drove the van right into the back of the Malibu, hitting it hard, but not hard enough to cause any real damage to the van. The two agents got out of the car and walked back toward the van. Lev was raising his hands as if to say 'sorry'. Quinn got out of the van and shot both agents with her silenced Glock. They went down, dead. Quinn got back in the van, and Lev sped off. There had been no wasted motions, the whole thing took twenty seconds.

There was only one witness, an old lady with bad eyesight who couldn't help the cops much when they showed up. The old lady couldn't identify the type of vehicle the murderers were driving, and she wasn't sure if it was a man or a woman who did the shooting. She said she'd been looking out her window and it all happened so fast it didn't seem real.

The cops examined the two dead agents, who were carrying U.S. government credentials from an agency that the two Austin patrolmen had never heard of. The cops called their Lieutenant, who called his Captain. The Captain called the Chief of Police, who was attending an endless Prayer Breakfast. The Chief told the Captain to call the FBI. The FBI told the police to leave everything just as is, and went out to examine the crime scene. Because of this bureaucratic incompetence, no one called Cyber Command for hours, and Cyber Command did not call Bonnie and Eric until it was too late.

One Hundred Thirteen
Austin, TX

"Alright. Now we've got to get back out to the ranch. We'll see if the blonde knows anything, then have her call Johnson," Quinn said.

Lev drove at a speed that did not make him stand out from other traffic, and the van had only minor dents in the front, nothing that hampered driving.

Before the van got to the gate at Barbara Jean's ranch, Lev and Quinn switched seats, so Quinn was in the driver's side when she rang the button on the squawk box.

"Yes?" Barbara Jean said.

"Ma'am it's an emergency. JR Johnson sent us to protect you. Is there a camera on this device?" Quinn said. She knew there was no camera.

"No," Barb said.

"Oh. Well I'm holding up my FBI credentials. My partner and I will explain as soon as we get to your door." Quinn said.

Barbara Jean hit the button, and the gate buzzed open. Quinn drove fast to the house, and she and Lev went quickly to the front door. Quinn held up her wallet, flipped open, as though she had FBI credentials. When Barbara Jean opened the door, Lev punched her in the face, knocking her down on her side.

"You may have just guessed that we're not really from the FBI, " Quinn said.

One Hundred Fourteen
Fort Meade, MD
Cyber Command
Windowless Room

General Goldstein joined Toni Anne Laudano and Yuri
Sokolov. Just the three of them sat at the table.

"Yuri, as you know, just we three and the President know the
plan. The President has asked me to read in the Treasury
Secretary to an extent. We need him to handle the banks and all
the Bitcoin transfer and so on. But that will be it. No one else
will know, not even the President's Chief of Staff," Buck
Goldstein said. "Are you ready on your end?"

"Yes, General," Sokolov said.

One Hundred Fifteen
Washington, DC
The White House

The President called the Director of the FBI. "James, I am sending over a list of the CEOs of the 15 largest financial companies in the United States. We have the highest level emergency. I need the FBI to locate and apprehend each of these individuals and bring them by the fastest possible manner to the White House. I don't care what they're doing, whether they're screwing their mistress, or attending their grandchild's baptism. If you have to pull them out in handcuffs, do it. No questions, that's it."

"Mr. President, that's highly irregular. I'm sure it's unconstitutional. Their lawyers are going to go ape, there will be court challenges---"

"James we go back a long way. I need you to do this. I repeat- this is a National Emergency of the highest level. If for some reason you cannot carry out this order, then resign and I'll order your deputy to do the job. Can you carry out this order?" the President asked.

The FBI Director paused. "I'm only doing it because it's you."

"Okay James, I'll take all the heat for this. You'll understand in a couple days. That's all I can tell you. Now get your agents off their asses and go get these guys to the White House. The list is on its way. Now!"

"Yes, Mr. President," the FBI Director said.

One Hundred Sixteen
Spicewood, TX

Lev was an expert at hitting people. He had intentionally not broken any bones in Barbara Jean's face. Her mouth was bleeding as she sat up on her terra cotta tile floor. Barbara Jean was a brave determined person, but the suddenness and brutality of the punch stunned her.

"What," Barbara Jean said.

"Do you want to get hit again?" Quinn asked. Barbara Jean did not answer. "Duct tape her hands behind her back," Quinn said to Lev.

Lev did as instructed, then threw her on a leather couch.

"Well Barbara Jean Parker, you're going to tell us what we want to know, and do what we tell you to do. If you cooperate we'll let you live, and you can appreciate this nice house. If you don't cooperate, your life expectancy is about five minutes." Quinn said.

Barbara Jean just looked at them.

"Who is Satoshi Nakamoto?" Quinn asked.

Barb laughed. "What is that- gibberish? You might as well just shoot me now, if you're going to ask questions like that."

"What do you know about Bitcoin?" Quinn demanded.

"Nothing," Barb answered.

Lev was searching around the huge living room. He came over to Quinn with Barbara Jean's iPhone.

Quinn said, "Alright, we're going to make a phone call to JR Johnson. Tell me your iPhone password. When he picks up, just tell him someone wants to talk to him."

Quinn dialed Jr.

Quinn put the phone up to Barb's ear. Lev pointed his gun a Barb. "Don't do anything stupid," Quinn said.

One Hundred Seventeen
Austin, TX

I was on the phone with Toni Anne. She told me it was just about time to sell. "I'm doing you a favor. You'll see Bitcoin skyrocket from here---"

"Skyrocket from here?---"

"Yes, you dope. You ain't seen nothin' yet. But you want to be out at the end of the day at the latest. Don't get stupid and greedy." Toni Anne said.

"Hey, who do you think you're talking to?" I asked.

"Somebody who has the potential to get stupid and greedy," she said.

"Okay, got it," I said.

"I have to go. I'll be busy. Look, just get out of Bitcoin, sooner than later, but don't do it all at once. There's some major buyers coming in. You won't believe how much it's going to go up today, but be out by the end of the day. I didn't have to call you, but I feel like we owe you. Alright?" Toni Anne asked.

What I then did was to unwind all my hedges. That means I closed out all the option and futures positions, so that when I did sell the Bitcoin there wouldn't be any exposures left dangling in my accounts, I'd just have all the cash I had made. For the next 20 minutes, Toni Anne's prediction didn't come true. Bitcoin trading was quiet. It didn't move much in either direction.

The phone rang. Caller ID said: Barbara Jean.

"Hi beautiful," I said.

"JR, it's Barbara Jean." She sounded out of it.

"Yeah, I know---"

"JR, just listen, someone else is picking up," Barbara Jean said.

Huh?

"Johnson, it's Sierra Quinn. Listen carefully, otherwise Barbara Jean gets her brains all over the nice tile floor here, and then we'll come after you," Quinn said.

"You're as charming as ever. What do you want?" I said. I tried to keep my voice calm, but my heart-rate must have doubled. I felt panicked and ashamed. *What had I gotten Barbara Jean into? I had to get her out of it.*

"Come out to her ranch now. Right now. Don't tell anybody, don't bring anybody. If we even suspect that you're not following these instructions, we'll kill her," Quinn said.

"Alright. I'll be there as soon as I can. I will follow the instructions as you dictated." I said.

"Don't take too much time," Quinn said, then she hung up.

I didn't know what else to do, so I did as instructed. I told Bonnie that I had to go out, just have the surveillance team follow me.

One Hundred Eighteen
Austin, TX

In my haste to leave my house I almost forgot to bring Barb's gift, the SIG Sauer she had given me. I doubled back and got the gun off my dresser and stuck it down my pants because I didn't want Bonnie and Eric seeing me leave with the weapon.

As I left I couldn't get over the feeling of guilt. How could I be so stupid as to expose Barbara Jean? I should have done something when I saw Sierra Quinn, maybe told Barb to go on a one week trip somewhere. I'm not saying that I didn't care what happened to me, but Barbara Jean was Priority One. I had handled trading Bitcoin, that was something I more or less knew how to do. But how I would handle whatever arose when I got to the ranch, which would almost certainly include violence where I was out of my league. I decided just to improvise.

While Gabrielle and I were driving to the shoot-out with Banks in New York, Gab the Army Ranger combat veteran had told me that it's great to plan before a firefight, but once the shooting starts the plan usually goes out the window. I decided it would be okay to lay down my life for Barbara Jean, but only if she made it out alive.

When I was stopped at a light I slid the SIG Sauer from my waistband and laid it on the seat beside me. Then I picked it up and racked the slide, which chambered a round, as Barbara Jean had taught me that day behind the barn. It was ready to fire, and I remembered that she had told me that this weapon did have a safety. I located the safety and practiced switching it on and off.

Don't put it on the trigger unless you mean to shoot. That lesson seemed like a hundred years ago, not a few weeks. A half hour ago trading Bitcoin seemed like reality. That was moving make-believe money around, fantasy land. I was headed for probable exchange of high velocity lead. I was a rookie dealing with a professional assassin. I couldn't build a mental scenario that didn't end up with me dead. I had to go. That was my reality now.

One Hundred Nineteen
Spicewood, TX

I got to the gate at Barb's ranch, and hit the button on the speaker box. Without any conversation the gate buzzed open. I wondered about the two guys who tailed me. How far behind me were they? If they got here, how would they get in? Couldn't count on them now, so I drove to house as fast as was safe. I saw a white panel van parked in front of the house.

I decided to be upfront and walked in with the SIG Sauer in both hands at about chest level. With my index finger on the side, I switched off the safety. I didn't want it to go off by accident, and I was nervous enough to perhaps jerk my finger.

I was standing maybe fifteen feet from the front doors.

Both doors flew open. I could see Barb on a couch. It looked like her hands were tied behind her, and blood was streaming down her face. A heavyset man was pointing a gun at her head. Standing just inside the doors to my left was Sierra Quinn, pointing a gun at me. She looked like she knew what she was doing, I was playacting.

"You have five seconds to carefully put the gun down in front of you. Or she dies. Then you die," Quinn said.

Seeing no alternative I did as Quinn said. "Okay, now take five steps back," she said.

After three steps I tripped and fell on my ass. I wasn't embarrassed, I thought Quinn would shoot me, but she laughed.

"Slowly get to your feet." She commanded.

I did.

Quinn came forward and picked up my gun. "Nice. SIG Sauer. Very upscale. I prefer the Glock, more of the Honda Civic of handguns."

She now had a gun in each hand. "Go over to the van, and open the back door, Real careful."

I did as she said. Then Quinn added, "get the oil drum out of the van and spin it over there," she gestured with the gun in her right hand to a spot ten feet to the left of the back of the van.

I rolled the oil drum to that spot. "Go back to the truck and face me," Quinn said. When I was in position Quinn switched the guns so that my gun was in her right hand. She fired ten shots, the whole clip, at the oil drum. "Those bullet holes are so the drum will sink with you in it. We wouldn't want you bobbing around for hours if it comes to that." Quinn chucked my now empty SIG Sauer 20 feet to her right.

"Lev, bring her out." Quinn said.

The man, short, stocky, bald, looked like the evil Russian psychiatrist in the *Manchurian Candidate.* For some reason the though went through my mind that this could be the last old movie reference I made to myself. Ever.

As Barb got shoved out the doors and I got a better look at her, I could see that in addition to the bleeding, Barbs face was badly bruised with a puff right eye. She looked shaky on her feet. My guilt was almost overwhelming. I had to get that out of my mind for now and focus on something, anything, that would get us, or at least Barb, out of this mess.

"So *Lev,*" I said. "You go around beating up helpless women?"

Lev grunted.

Quinn spoke, "We're convinced that she doesn't know anything. You better start telling us what we want to know."

"Alright," I said. "But you have to let her go."

"Not going to happen. Here's my offer. We'll put her back in the house. Then you start talking. If I'm satisfied with what you have to say, we leave her alone. And maybe we even let you live," Quinn said.

I didn't believe Quinn, especially about letting me live, but I didn't have a lot of bargaining power. I also didn't know much, but Quinn didn't know that. I thought about the shooting lesson from Barb, and my chambering a round and taking the safety off. So much for my gunfighter career, which lasted about five seconds when Quinn had her gun pointed at me and was threatening to shoot Barb.

"Okay. Put her back in the house, and close the door." I didn't want Barbara Jean to see me get killed. "Then we can start talking."

Quinn motioned with her head for Lev to take Barbara Jean back in the house. He did so, then closed both doors before he returned to stand near Quinn. "Get the crowbar," she told Lev.

"Put your hands up,' Quinn said. I did. While I was standing like that Lev smashed me in my right ribcage. The searing pain made me drop to me knees.

"Get on your feet!" Quinn ordered. I managed to get up, but could not stand up straight. When I tried to take a deep breath the searing pain came back.

"Are you Satoshi Nakamoto?" Quinn asked.

I laughed, which brought back the intense pain.

"Answer the question," Quinn said.

"No."

"Before I ask the next question, keep in mind that if I'm not satisfied with the answer, Lev is going to hit you again with the crowbar in the same area of the ribs," Quinn said. "If you don't put up your hands as instructed, he will break your arm first, then hit you again in the ribs." That got my attention.

"Boy, you're strict. It's surprising a warm friendly gal like you isn't married," I said. What the hell, I was certain they were going to kill me anyhow. I might as well go with some style points.

Quinn surprised me by smiling. She was an attractive woman, especially when she smiled. "I find this work more satisfying than being married."

"Fair enough," I said.

"Do you know who Nakamoto is? Can you get in touch with him?" Quinn said.

"That's two questions, and the answer to both of them is no,' I said.

Quinn paused. At least she didn't order Lev to hit me again, yet. "Why did you go to Cyber Command?"

"They made me come in, threatened me," I said.

"What did they want?" Quinn asked.

"They asked me the same questions you just asked me. I told them the truth, the same as I told you." I said. I was bullshitting now. I figured the longer I talked, the better chance that somebody would come and rescue me.

"Why did they ask you those questions?" Quinn said.

"I don't know. I asked them why. They told me to shut up, that they were asking the questions, and I was giving the answers," I said.

"Then they let you go?" Quinn asked.

"First they had this woman, Laudano, pretend to be friendly and give me a tour of the place. At the end of the tour she took me aside, threatened me again, said if they found out I was lying they had the right to detain me without trial." I said.

"What does this have to do with Gabrielle McHugh? She was staying with you, then she went to work for Cyber Command. Don't tell me that was a coincidence." Quinn demanded.

"During the time she was staying with me I was looking into trading Bitcoin, doing research on the internet, stuff anybody could find. McHugh and I ended up not getting along, and the next thing I know she went back in the Army, to Cyber Command. Then I get threatened, made to come in on my own dime to get interrogated by Cyber Command. I think she turned me in somehow, for something I didn't do." I said. "I think she was using me to make a name for herself."

Man, I was just pulling stuff out of thin air! Maybe a couple cracked ribs helps bring out the sense of urgency. But it sounded convincing to me. I hoped Quinn was convinced.

"So why did you start buy Bitcoin so aggressively, if you didn't know anything?" Quinn asked.

"I just figured if they were so interested, something major must be going on. I didn't buy big at first, but when it kept going up I got more and more aggressive," I said. "I have an idea."

"What," Quinn said.

"I've made a pile of money. How about I cut you in for, say, $200 million? We'll each slip your buddy Frankenstein here a hundred bucks, give him a bucket of fish heads, and forget the whole thing," I said. I pointed at Lev.

"I would have a hard time staying alive long enough to spend the money," Quinn said. "That's looking like a problem for you."

At that moment Quinn's phone rang.

One Hundred Twenty
Washington, DC
The White House

The White House Cabinet Room is adjacent to the Oval Office.
It was filled, not with Cabinet Members, but with the CEOs of
the 15 largest financial institutions in the United States. They
were not a happy group.

"I demand to know what is going on!" shouted a portly 55 year
old, as he stood. He was not pleased about being literally
pulled out of his country club by FBI agents and put on a
government jet without explanation. Most of the fifteen, all
men, sat quietly at the Cabinet table, each seat equipped with a
land line telephone. Their cell phones had been confiscated
before they were flown to Washington.

The Treasury Secretary pounded his fist on the table, got quiet
in the room and said. "The President will be here in a moment.
I can tell you, as you may have guessed, this is a situation of
the gravest national concern, and you gentlemen are currently
sharing the highest risk. However, you will be a major part of
the solution."

That silenced the group. Into that atmosphere the President
entered.

"Gentlemen. Let me first assure you that the U.S. Government
is completely backstopping every company here. That means
we are taking on all the risk, and that any losses accrued by
your companies will be fully compensated by the U.S.
Treasury. That being said, we need your full cooperation," the
President said.

He nodded to the Treasury Secretary, who passed out a single
sheet of paper to each of the fifteen attendees. The paper was a

simple list of two columns, the name of each institution, in order of asset size and next to the institution there was a number. JP Morgan was first and the number was 2.8 million. The number got smaller in proportion to the asset size of each company.

"Mr. President, may I ask what these numbers indicate?" said one of the fifteen.

"Yes, of course. The numbers indicate the ransom necessary to pay to Russia to stop a complete, totally devastating Cyber Attack on our financial system by Russia. We have no defense for it. The five minute shutdown yesterday, which all your technical people are baffled by, was a miniscule demonstration of the power of the Russian Cyber capabilities. We have to pay. Our experts have determined that the Russian have the capabilities they claim. They are demanding that each institution, rather than the U.S. Government pay. We need to pay them."

The same chubby 55 year old rose to his feet again. "That's outrageous! Where are our tax dollars going? Are we not spending billions on Cyber defense? My bank is not going to pay $1.3 million to the Russians!"

"It's not $1.3 million," The President said.

Another CEO said, "1.3 million what then, Euro, ounces of Gold?"

"No, the number are not in dollars. The denomination here is Bitcoin. Each organization has to come up with that much in Bitcoin today, and then wire the Bitcoin to the U.S. Treasury." The Treasury Secretary then gave the specifics on how the funds would be wired to the Bank for International Settlements and so on.

"That's an outrage! My bank will not be part of this. I'm leaving!" The chubby CEO said and went to the door. He opened the door to find two armed Marines.

"Go back in, sir" one of the Marines said.

The CEO went back to his seat.

"You're holding us prisoner?" he asked the President.

"Here's the deal," the President said. "If we don't comply, the Russians will shut down our entire financial system, along with key utilities, like water and the electric grid. In my judgement, any of you who are faced with that and choose not to cooperate are mentally unstable, and will be removed for psychological evaluation at government facilities. Due to overcrowding in the D.C. facilities, the detainee will be flown to Gitmo to see our excellent doctors there. With that level of illness, who knows, the evaluation could take months. Have I made myself clear?"

The chubby man sat down and folded his hands on the table.

Another CEO was using the pencil that had been supplied for each seat at the table. "Mr. President, these numbers add up to 20 million Bitcoins. As I recall, there are only 21 million Bitcoins outstanding. And we will be bidding against each other, and driving up the prices."

"Yes," the Treasury Secretary said, "we know that. We think the Russians are doing that to inflict more pain. You each have a land line. Get on the phone and call whoever you need to at your institution to get the buying process started. I realize that it is not in your natures to pay whatever price the market demands, but you need to be done buying in a two, three hours tops."

"Again, the U.S. government will make good on all losses. Just go buy, whatever the price is," the President said.

The CEOs of the Wall Street firms picked up the phones first. They had risen from the trading floors and it was their natural instinct to beat the others to the trades to get the best prices.

"We have excellent kitchen facilities here," the President said, "please don't hesitate to ask. If you need to use the rest room, one of our efficient marines will accompany you. The Treasury Secretary will stay here. I'll be in and out. Get going."

The only CEO who hadn't picked up the phone was the chubby one. "I'll do it. But this just shows your gross mismanagement. Why don't we have defenses? I certainly won't be voting for your re-election."

"You fucking idiot! Don't you realize the existence of the United States, of the Free World is at stake?" the President said. "This isn't bullying your country club to get the White tees moved up because you can't reach the green anymore. Get on the fuckin' phone, or go to Gitmo."

There was something about being spoken to like that by the President, in the White House, in front of other people that got the man's attention. He got on the phone.

The President left the room. The chubby man said, "I'll do it, but this is ridiculous."

The CEO of JP Morgan said across the table to the chubby man, "Shut up and get the job done, or I'll punch you in the face. I've always wanted to do that anyhow."

One Hundred Twenty One
Moscow
The Lider's Apartment

"The buying has started in the United States. It's the big banks that are buying," the Finance Minister told The Lider.

"Are there any sellers?" The Lider asked.

"Our shell banks are selling to the Americans, but slowly. The Americans are buying at the market. That means they---"

"I know what it means. It means they have to own it, no matter what the price. It means that our plan is going to work!" The Lider said.

One Hundred Twenty Two
Spicewood, TX
Barbara Jean's Ranch

Quinn answered her phone, and listened for a minute.

"Ok Lev. We don't need Johnson's information that badly anymore. Go in and shoot the woman," she said.

"What?" I said. I tried to move toward Quinn, but my ribs hurt too much to make any aggressive move.

She looked at me. "Knock him out. Turgenev wants him to take a swim. We've got to put him in the oil drum. Not too hard, we want him to wake up so he knows what's going on when he goes for a dip."

Lev came over to me with the crowbar. He faked hitting me in the ribs, and as I moved my hands to block that, he changed direction and hit me in the head.

One Hundred Twenty Three
Washington, DC
White House

There was a frenzy at the table. Once the initial reluctance had
been broken, the CEOs were showing their collective
competitiveness by trying to be the first to meet their quotas in
numbers of Bitcoins acquired. These were men who got where
they were by being aggressive, and once they realized that they
were spending the Government's money, it became a
competitive game to see who would get to their goal first.
There had never been as much collective noise in the history of
the room, as the CEOs shouted at their subordinates over the
phone to just go out and buy, and keep buying.

A television had been installed in the room. CNBC was on the
ALL BITCOIN-ALL THE TIME mode. The price blew
through $400,000 per Bitcoin. Bitcoin didn't trade for minutes
at a time. It wasn't as though any regulator was halting trading,
there wasn't any regulator. It stopped trading because nobody
wanted to sell it. The price jumped from $410,000 to the next
trade of $490,000.

CNBC located the economist who weeks earlier had predicted
zero as the price target for Bitcoin. He said that after
recalculating his algorithm his new target price was: zero. He
talked about the Dutch Tulip Bulb mania of the mid 1600s. The
CNBC anchor was smirkingly dismissive, and got rid of that
economist as soon as it was marginally polite to do so.

The network got ahold of the Tesla CEO who had consented to
do a phone interview. He said he had no idea of what was
going on. The Anchor found ten ways of asking him the same
question, but The CEO finally said, "I don't know what's going
on. Sorry I can't help," and got off the phone.

338

In the Cabinet Room, the Goldman Sachs CEO had exceeded his quota of Bitcoin necessary to deliver to the Treasury. He began marking up the price of his surplus Bitcoin and selling it off to the other CEOs in the room. He was having fun.

The prices of other Cryptocurrencies also went up, but nowhere near the percentage rise in Bitcoin, as the day went on some of the other Cryptos had pullbacks. Not Bitcoin. It just went up. By the time the CEOs had completed their buying the final price of Bitcoin was $710,000 per coin. This was quite a performance from something that six years before had traded at $3 per coin.

The Treasury Secretary called the President who entered the Cabinet Room a minute later.

"Nice job gentlemen. I'm afraid you'll be our guests for the next day or so, until this transaction is complete. The Treasury Secretary will host you for dinner in the Navy Mess, and then you'll see a movie in the White House Theater. I've asked them to show *Jurassic Park.*

The chubby CEO said, "You can't hold us here indefinitely against our will!"

The President responded, "If you like, I'll check and see what movie is playing tonight at Gitmo. They usually show them with subtitles in Arabic." Then he left.

One Hundred Twenty Four
Spicewood, TX

Lev exited the front door of Barbara Jean's house alone.

"She's not there," Lev said.

'What do you mean, she's not there?" Quinn asked. "You put her on the couch, her hands bound in Duct Tape. Where could she have gone?"

Lev grunted. "I looked through the whole house. She's not there."

Quinn hesitated. "Let's not worry about her. We've got to get out of here. I'll help you put Johnson in the oil drum."

When JR was in the drum Quinn said, "Only tighten a couple of the tabs with the wrench. We want to open the lid when we get to the quarry. We'll try one more time to get him to talk, and then seal him up and roll him into the water."

While Lev struggled to get the oil drum in the van, Quinn had second thoughts about leaving Johnson's pistol lying in the dirt. She picked it up and threw it in the back of the van as Lev was closing the door. "No sense leaving any evidence," Quinn said to Lev. "We'll put the gun in the barrel when we dump him."

When that mission was accomplished, the rear doors of the van were closed. Lev drove while Quinn rode in the passenger seat. When they got to the gate Quinn got out and hit the release latch. Lev drove carefully away from the ranch. It wouldn't do to get pulled over for speeding. There was about a five mile drive to the quarry.

One Hundred Twenty Five
Spicewood, TX

Alice had been mucking out the horse stalls when she heard the shooting at the main house. She walked from the barn to the back door of Barbara Jean's. That had been when Quinn was shooting the holes in the oil drum.

Alice was inside hiding behind the bar when she saw the large man carry Barb and throw her on the couch.

Alice went over to Barbara on the coach and saw that her hands were bound, so she got a small knife from the bar and cut Barb's hands loose. With great difficulty Alice managed to help the wobbly Barb walk out the back door and travel the hundred yards to the barn.

There was a bench inside the horse barn. "Here, take this," Alice said as she handed Barbara Jean a glass of water. Barb took a sip, then poured the rest over her head. The water served its intended purpose, and Barb shook her head and regained most of her wits.

Alice and Barb went to the barn door in time to see the white van exiting the property through the gate.

"Alice let's go back to the house," Barb said. Alice held Barb's elbow this time, but she didn't need much help walking. They entered through the back door. A quick look around the inside revealed nothing of interest, so Barb walked out the front. Nothing to see. Barb walked back and unlocked her gun closet. She got two items out, a fully loaded Winchester 1892 rifle, and from a compartment behind a concealed door a piece of electronic equipment. The Winchester held 14 rounds, and Barb figured that would be enough. Her daddy had told her she was such a good shot with the Winchester that she could shoot the balls off a male mosquito at a hundred yards, quite the compliment from the proud father.

"Alice call the sheriff. Have him come here. I don't need him getting in the way." Their county sheriff would take about five minutes to get his fat ass out of his police car, Barb didn't want him around what she intended to do.

"Where are you going, Barbara Jean?" Alice asked.

'I'm taking the Corvette. Rescuing my fiancé," Barb said. "A good fiancé is hard to find."

One Hundred Twenty Six
Spicewood, TX

My head throbbed with shooting pain and I could see flashes of
light. I was trapped inside something. My knees were up by my
chest, and my shoulders pressed against the hard surface. When
I tried to stretch I discovered I was in something round. The
overpowering stench of oil made me gag.

I felt around with my hands. It was dark except for a few holes
of light. I touched one of the holes and it had a sharp jagged
edge that cut my fingertip. I jerked my hand back. Then I
reached up over my head and found a flat hard cold metal
surface.

I was imprisoned in an oil drum.

I pushed up hard with both hands. The top didn't budge so I
smacked the top of the can with the heels of both hands. I
fought the urge to panic, then I thought *screw it, panic is
appropriate sometimes, and it will give me more strength.* So I
panicked. I went crazy. Smacking the top once created no
result except for noise, so I smacked again and again, harder
each time. Finally the top popped clean off, wobbling onto the
floor. The act of raising my hands above my head created a
terrible shooting pain in the right side of my ribcage. Were my
ribs broken? I couldn't remember.

I tried to stand up straight, but I was exhausted by the sudden
spurt of effort. The pulsing pain in my head grew worse. I was
dizzy. My eyes tried to adjust to the sudden light. I realized I
was in the back of a panel van and it was moving.

The commotion I caused attracted the attention of a man and a
woman who were accompanying me in the truck. The man,
who was driving pulled the van over to the side of the road and

stopped. The woman got out of her seat and climbed over the front console and approached the oil drum. I couldn't focus my eyes, but she looked familiar.

"I didn't think this jerk would be waking up so soon after you hit him in the head with the crowbar," she said to the man. I didn't recognize him.

My fingers gripped the rim of the oil drum as I attempted to steady myself. At least now I knew why my head hurt. I panted with my tongue hanging out. My racing heartbeat sent steady pulses of pain to my head and chest. The woman aimed a gun at me.

"Don't kill him," the man said in what sounded like a Russian accent.

That was good.

"I'll give you one more chance. Tell me what you know about Bitcoin, about Nakamoto," the woman said to me.

"I don't know anything," I said.

"Remember, if he doesn't talk, Turgenev wants him to be alive when we dump the oil drum in the water," the man continued.

That was not so good.

I saw the woman taking a vicious swing at my head with the butt of her gun. Then everything went black.

One Hundred Twenty Seven
Fort Meade, MD
Cyber Command
Windowless Room

Toni Anne Laudano sat with General Goldstein and Yuri Sokolov. The others would be along in a minute.

"You were right, as usual, Toni Anne. Powers is in over her head as a General. When this crisis is over, I'll push her out, she'll get the choice of retiring at her current rank, or being demoted and being reassigned to some Cyber outpost in Alaska. I do need a visible woman in an important role. I'll promote Gabrielle McHugh. Eventually she'll be a General."

"Well she is a lot smarter than Powers. So, the Murder Bitch is getting her way?" Toni Anne said.

"We probably won't be calling her that in the official Press Release." Goldstein said.

"Well, I suppose I'd rather work with her than Powers. Anyhow, let's handle the current situation. Who cares about that other stuff right now." Laudano said.

In a minute the rest of the staff appeared. Sheldon said, "We've gotten all the information from the Russians. The smug bastards obviously don't know we've had their scheme figured out all along, but everything they sent checks out. Of course we could fix the problem right now."

"Yeah," Toni Anne said.

"I've got to tell you that it burns my ass to have to pretend that that these bastards have one over on us, to have to play dumb. I think I'm speaking for all of us." Sheldon said, pointing to the Team.

"That's understandable," General Goldstein said, "I think you'll all be pleased with how the situation resolves itself. Only Toni Anne, Yuri, the President, and me know our plan. We had to keep it that way. If it makes you feel better, please know that the Treasury Secretary is mighty pissed off that he hasn't been read in to all the details."

"What happens now, sir," Sheldon asked.

'We sit tight. You all have to stay here until the resolution. We wait for the final algorithms from the Russians. Then I tell the President, and we release the Bitcoin deposits at the Bank for International Settlement to the Russians."

"That's it? We lose on purpose?" Mike asked.

"I'm going to ask Yuri Sokolov to fill you in," the General said.

"As I have expressed, the Russians pride themselves as Chess Masters, and that is the foundation on which they build the philosophy of their Cyber Warfare. I came to General Goldstein and Ms. Laudano with something we might use. For now all I can say is 'why play Chess, when we have a mighty advantage?' The key was to make the Russians think they were playing Chess. We have invented a new game with rules they did not imagine. You will see how this plays out in a little while," Sokolov said.

'I don't understand," Sheldon said.

"You will," Toni Anne said.

One Hundred Twenty Eight
Spicewood, TX

Barbara Jean went to her garage and got into her Corvette. The
top was down and she was in a hurry. She used a device much
like a garage door remote to open the gate to the ranch.

On the passenger seat was her Winchester rifle and another one
of her toys. It was an electronic GPS tracking device. She had
chips installed on all of her guns, and the handheld screen
allowed her to specify which particular weapon she wanted to
track. She punched in the number of the SIG Sauer she had
given JR, and got a strong signal, which she then linked up
with the Corvette's Bluetooth system. On the Vette's
navigation screen a blip showed a blinking indicator of the gun,
and showed that it was moving on County Road 404.

Barbara Jean did spend quite a sum on her weapons and
associated paraphernalia. This was the first time she got to use
the GPS system. "I was wondering if I'd ever get to use this!"
she said to nobody as she floored the Corvette.

The panel van had a good head start on Barb. But on her side
she had a Corvette, the element of surprise, and the
Winchester.

One Hundred Twenty Nine
Washington, DC
The White House

The President got the call from General Goldstein. "Mr. President, the Russians have delivered the final algorithm of the code. It all checks out."

"Thank you," the President told Goldstein, and hung up. He then told the Treasury Secretary, who was holding with his representative at the Bank for International Settlements, to authorize the transfer of 20 million Bitcoins to Russia. The electronic transfer of the equivalent of seven times the annual Gross Domestic Product of Russia took a few seconds. Current value of the Bitcoin: Fourteen Trillion U.S. dollars.

"Why so glum, Mr. Secretary? Now the fun begins. Please review how we were able to establish our short position on Bitcoin," the President said.

"Mr. President, you do realize that we're on the hook to make up that sum to the banks, as well as any losses we might incur with the short position?" The Treasury Secretary asked.

"You know, I always get this backwards. Short position means that we're betting that Bitcoin will go down in value?" the President asked.

"Yes Mr. President! We are short $14 trillion worth of Bitcoin! That adds to our potential exposure if Bitcoin keeps going up. You're confused about that?" the Treasury Secretary asked.

"Relax. I was just having some fun at your expense," the President said. Then he laughed.

One Hundred Thirty
Spicewood, TX

Lev turned the van onto the dirt road that led to the Quarry. The road was rough so he drove carefully. Finally they arrived at the spot next to the embankment. Lev and Quinn got out of the van.

Lev opened the back doors and wrestled the oil drum out onto the dirt. It landed with a thump.

"Take the pliers and open the lid. Let's see if we can wake this guy up," Quinn said.

Lev pried back the metal tabs and removed the top, tossing it on the ground. He took an ammonia capsule out of his jacket and broke it, then waved it under JR Johnson's nose.

One Hundred Thirty One
Spicewood, TX

I felt the rush of ammonia in my nose before I smelled it, and woke with a start. This Russian thug was standing in front of me. I recognized him now.

I noticed oil all over my clothes, and felt like puking. My head hurt; the world seemed to be spinning. The thug shoved the ammonia under my nose again. It served its purpose, I was more awake, and felt the pain in my head and ribs more intensely. I didn't have the strength to try to get out of the barrel.

Quinn stood in front of me, pointing her Glock right at my head. I didn't think she'd shoot, but right that second I didn't care that much.

"All right, shithead. I'm giving you one more chance," Quinn said.

"A chance for what?" I managed to croak out.

"Tell me who Nakamoto is," Quinn demanded.

"I think you know already…I don't know. You just want an excuse to hit me again," I said.

"I don't need an excuse," Quinn said. She motioned to Lev. "Give him a love tap on the head. We want him to be a little awake."

Lev came at me with the crowbar.

One Hundred Thirty Two
Spicewood, TX

As Lev used the huge pliers to seal some of the tabs on top of the oil drum a yellow Corvette came into sight.

Barbara Jean stopped the car about one hundred yards short of the van, and hopped out, holding the Winchester rifle with one hand, right where the barrel met the wooden stock. Barb crouched down next to her open driver's side door, cocked the Winchester and fired. She hit Lev right in the center of his chest. Lev fell backwards, knocking over the sealed oil drum, which started to roll toward the steep embankment that led to the water.

Quinn ran toward the driver's door of the van, and before opening it spun to fire her Glock at Barb. Quinn knew she had little chance of hitting Barbara Jean at this distance, the shot was intended as covering fire while she got in the van. Quinn's bullet hit the front left side fender of the Corvette, then she got into the van and floored it, spinning up small rocks and dirt. The van disappeared down the dirt road.

The oil drum picked up speed as it rolled toward the water. Barbara Jean ran as fast as she could under the circumstances, but the barrel splashed into the water before she could get close. The oil drum began to sink as Barb frantically scrambled down the embankment.

Barbara was about to give up hope when the oil drum stopped moving. It was stuck on something below the surface and she waded out to it, still clutching her Winchester. She grabbed the oil drum, but realized there was no way she could move it closer to shore. Barb pulled as hard as she could, and the drum rolled maybe a foot toward shallow water before her hands slipped and the barrel rolled the other way, and began to sink faster.

Barbara took the Winchester and fired at the tabs on the top of the drum, and the top came off. Damn she was a good shot! The drum righted itself and began to sink again.

Barbara Jean threw down the Winchester and grabbed for JR who still seemed to be unconscious. She pulled him out of the drum just as the barrel sank into the seemingly bottomless mud pit. She dragged JR as far toward the shore as she could, finally getting him into about two inches of water. At least he was face up, and starting to come around. Finally he took a deep breath and opened his eyes.

One Hundred Thirty Three
Spicewood, TX

I woke up and opened my eyes. I saw the blue sky. My ears were submerged so I tilted my head forward.

I looked to my left and standing there was Barbara Jean Parker. It was the best sight I had ever seen in my life. She was wearing blue jeans and a white tee shirt and was soaked in water, mud, and slimy oil.

"JR, can you hear me?" she said.

"Yup." I propped myself up on my elbows. "You know Barb, if we ever fall on financial hard times, we could go around entering you in wet tee shirt contests. You're looking pretty hot right now, in a low rent kind of way," I said.

She looked down at herself. "Damn straight. I'm an all-around winner." She stepped over and fished her Winchester out of the water and placed in on dry land.

In a couple minutes we had half crawled, half walked, up the embankment. Thirty feet away was Lev, lying on his back. He wasn't going anywhere.

We walked over to inspect him, but didn't get too close, just in case. I kicked him in the head to see if he'd move. Nope. There was a lot of blood in the dirt, seemed like gallons, and a big hole in his chest.

"Good shootin' Tex," I said to Barbara Jean. I've said that to many people on the golf course over the years, but this was my first chance to say it to Barb in more serious circumstances.

"Thanks. Yeah, it was a good shot," Barb said.

We walked to the Corvette. "Look at that! That bitch shot a hole in the fender. You know how expensive it is to get the fiberglass fixed just right on one of these?" Barbara Jean said.

My head was still spinning. I got in the passenger seat. We decided to drive back to Barb's ranch instead of calling in the cops and waiting forever for them to show up. Barb drove up to Lev's body and stopped the car. "I'm gonna shoot him one more time, just to make sure."

I thought she might be kidding, but sure enough she got out, picked up the Winchester and shot him right between the eyes.

"He ain't going anywhere now," Barb said. "That shot was for trying to kill my fiancé and punching me in the face."

One Hundred Thirty Four
Fort Meade, MD

Toni Anne Laudano surveyed her group sitting around the conference table. She was excited. She and Sokolov had rehearsed what would happen next, but $14 trillion were in play, and this was the highest stakes game anyone, in the history of the world, had ever played.

Only Laudano, Sokolov, General Goldstein and the President of the United States knew what would happen after this transaction was concluded. Even the Treasury Secretary was in the dark. There were too many leaks at every White House. There had to be complete secrecy, or the plan wouldn't work.

Toni Anne addressed her technical team. "You all look like this is the worst day of your lives. Cheer up! The next half an hour is going to make it the best day of your lives! We have two more moves in store for the Fuckin' Commie! You ain't seen nothin' yet!"

One Hundred Thirty Five
Fort Meade, MD
Cyber Command
Windowless Room

General Goldstein addressed the group. "We don't trust the
The Lider to live up to the agreement. So we've had a separate
group working on a whole new firewall system, based on
Blockchain Technology that we are switching over to. It is
being implemented right now. It runs on a low level, below the
Dark Net. As far as the end users are concerned, like the banks,
the electric grid, the Social Media companies, nobody will
notice any difference."

Sheldon asked the General, "Who developed this? Is it
someone in our group?"

"No Sheldon. As you know, we had people working on
defensive technologies in Cyber Command. They did their
best, but the system they devised is just add-on stuff to our
existing system. They don't know this, but all their work was
just a straw man, never intended to be put into place," the
General said. "This was developed by a secret group working
in Hanford, Washington."

"That's all for now. There'll be no more discussion on this
until we formulate more strategy going forward. The first
people outside this room to notice this will be the Russians,
because in a few minutes they're going to go totally apeshit
and try to launch any and all attacks possible. Our new
defensive measures are so good that we estimate they are more
than 5,000 times as effective as the old measures," the General
explained. "Not just against the Russians, against everybody.
But since the Russians just gave us their best code, it will
probably take them years to catch up. They were willing to do

this because of the colossal financial payout they just received. We'll see how they feel about that in about half an hour."

Toni Anne continued, "That's just one shoe. Yuri's connections have lead us not only to the development of defensive system, but to our way of saying "Fuck You, Commies." I told you this was going to be fun. Since this was his idea, I'm going to ask him to go ahead and make the phone call to Omaha."

Yuri Sokolov stood and addressed the group. "You know the Russian think of this whole thing as a Chess Match. We let them win the Chess Match, but we invented a new game, with new rules. It didn't end with the Chess Match. Why play your opponents' game?"

Sokolov went on, "I made friends with a couple very wealthy guys several years ago when I did some work for their charitable foundation. On a lark, we combined to cook up the idea for the creation of Bitcoin. Honestly, we never imagined it would be as big as this, or that we could use it for this purpose."

Sokolov dialed his phone. In a moment it was answered. "Ok Warren, it's time to initiate Operation VICTOR LIMA ALPHA DELTA."

One Hundred Thirty Six
Omaha, NE

The two men sat in an office in Omaha. It was the office of Warren, the older of the two. His friend Bill had flown in for the occasion.

Warren spoke into his iPhone, "Roger that order, we'll start Operation VICTOR LIMA ALPHA DELTA. Alright Yuri, we'll take it from here."

Warren stepped away from his desk and gestured for Bill to sit in his chair. Bill did so and pulled the chair closer to the computer keyboard.

"People can't say that we didn't try to warn them. Oh well, some lessons are harder to learn than others. Okay Mr. Nakamoto, you have the controls," Warren said.

"Please, call me Satoshi," Bill said, as he limbered his fingers as if to play the piano. Both men laughed.

"Nakamoto promised that there would never be more than 21 million Bitcoins issued. I guess you should never take the word of someone who is so mysterious," Warren said. "How many Bitcoins do you think there should be now, Bill?"

"I've thought about this. Let's go big. How about 21 *trillion*? Nakamoto can just come out with a correction. He can explain that there was a typo in his original announcement," Bill said.

"Good thinking, Bill. Round numbers, it will be easier for traders to work out their profits and losses. I'm glad my company got their short position initiated yesterday," Warren chuckled.

Bill tapped a few keys and hit enter.

"You're very handy with the computer Bill," Warren said.

"I began at an early age," Bill said.

Using the same untraceable technology as his original statement had used in 2008, Satoshi Nakamoto announced to the world that his original projections had been a mistake. There were not 21 *million* Bitcoins, there would be 21 *trillion* Bitcoins available. Suddenly each Bitcoin was worth one billionth of what it had been worth when Bill had started typing. And nobody could do anything about it.

One Hundred Thirty Seven
Moscow

The Lider sat in his office with Oleg Turgenev and the head of
the Russian State bank. They looked at The Lider's computer
screen. It displayed their holdings in Bitcoin, and each line of
the screen showed the value of their holdings in the major
different currencies of the world. In the moments since they
have been wired the Bitcoin from Washington the value had
gone up.

"Mr. President, we have made $100 billion in the last minute.
The scarcity of Bitcoin is making our holdings worth more!"
the Russian Banker said, taking credit for it, as though it was
his doing.

"Maybe I'll spend some on fixing roads and bridges," The
Lider said, and they all laughed.

Then the screen started flashing rapidly. The trading looked
frenzied. The value of Bitcoin started to go down against all the
currencies.

"There must be something wrong with the machine," the
Banker said.

One Hundred Thirty Eight
Moscow

The Lider had been so confident in his plan working that he had directed his Treasury Department to pre-print checks showing their fractional ownership of Bitcoin, signed by himself, to each Russian resident the day before the deal was consummated, and the checks were mailed out. Some of the checks were intercepted before delivery, but some of the checks got delivered

So what had been worth $14,000,000,000,000 before the new Bitcoins were released was now worth $14,000. The Lider's windfall was worth $7,000 to him, the rest of the $7,000 was split among 145,000,000 citizens of Russia. The value to each Russian resident in U.S. dollars was around four one thousandths of one cent. It became popularly known as The Lider's *'Lomtik Khleba',* or 'Slice of Bread'.

The checks became a popular collectible and traded on Ebay for around $10.

One Hundred Thirty Nine
Spicewood, TX

The county sheriff never did figure out what was going on, so
when Barbara Jean drove her Corvette into the ranch he was
still there, sitting on the front stoop. He took a good while to
get to his feet and walk over to the car.

"Sheriff, I'm JR Johnson," I introduced myself. "I think you
know Barbara Jean Parker. We could use an ambulance to take
us to University of Texas hospital."

"Man, look what happened to you! Alice here has been filling
me in on what she saw. It's hard to believe," the Sheriff said.
After going over to see Barb, he continued, "I'm calling in the
Medical helicopter. It looks like you both could use getting to
the hospital pronto."

While we were waiting for the helicopter I explained what
happened as best as I could to the Sheriff. He knew where the
quarry was when I mentioned it. I thought of something. "Hey,
there's a dead body at the quarry. Barbara Jean plugged him.
It's a big old Russian. You'll recognize him right away. Looks
like Frankenstein. And he's dead."

"I've called the Texas Rangers, and they called in the FBI.
They're all going to want to talk to you. Don't worry, I'll hold
them off when you go to the hospital," the Sheriff said.

The exhaustion hit me, and I slumped in the passenger seat in
the Corvette. Barb never attempted to get out of the driver's
seat. I looked over at her. "You look so beautiful," I said.

"Yeah, sure," Barb said.

"I mean it. I think you're the most beautiful woman in the world," I said.

"Didn't you used to go out with the Most Beautiful Woman in the World?" Barb asked.

"Yeah, according to People Magazine," I said. "That's how I know what I'm talking about."

"You did get hit in the head with a crowbar a couple times today," Barb said.

"I did?"

We just sat in the car. In a few minutes we could hear the whirling of the helicopter. This time I earned my ride in the Care Flight the hard way.

One Hundred Forty
Austin, TX

We got Premium Level service at the University of Texas
Hospital Emergency Department. They took Barb one way and
me the other. I got a lot of x-rays and CAT scanned in a tube.
Doctors said "Hmmm," a lot. Then they put me back in the
room where I had started.

In walked Dr. John Good, brother of Tom Jr. Dr. John had the
good sense to still be a practicing doctor, but he was a Cardiac
Specialist, not an ER guy.

"They told me you were here, so I decided to come down," Dr.
John said. The doc was a client of mine, along with his
extended family.

"Why, are you going to tell me I'm having a heart attack, too?"
I asked.

"Nah, I was just wondering who was managing my money
while you were getting your brains knocked around," Dr. John
said.

"Yeah, I was thinking of you when they put me in an oil drum
and were rolling it toward the water, even though I was
unconscious at the time. I remember thinking, 'Hey I wonder
how Dr. John's account is doing.' You were utmost on my
mind," I said.

"You were really in an oil drum?" Dr. John asked.

"Yeah, I don't recommend it," I said. "That's why I'm all
musty and smell like the Exxon Valdez."

"Well JR, it looks like you're going to be okay—as okay as you get. I really just wanted to say hello. Your doctor will be right in," Dr John said, then he left.

My ER doctor came in and put some pictures up on the computer screen. "Mr. Johnson, you have a slight skull fracture, and bad concussion, and three cracked ribs. Other than some additional serious contusions, I think you're all right."

I laughed. Don't laugh when you have cracked ribs. "What do you mean?"

"Everything will heal. For the skull fracture and the ribs there's not much we can do. There's no surgery required, and we can't put you in a cast or sling. You say you got hit with a crowbar?" the doctor asked.

"Yeah," I said.

"The man who hit you with the crowbar either knew what he was doing, or you were very lucky. A blow of that magnitude a few inches in either direction could easily have been fatal," the doc continued.

"I think the guy who did it had advanced degrees in thug-ology," I said, "you won't be examining him."

"What?" the doctor asked.

"He had a serious case of lead poisoning. He got---"
I caught myself. I probably shouldn't be discussing this. "Hey doctor, can you forget I just said that. I think I'm into, uh National Security information."

"Really?" It was plain he didn't believe me.

"Anyhow, so what about me? Can I go home?" I asked.

"We're going to keep you in overnight for observation. Are you friends with Dr. Good?"

"Yeah,"

"Well, he made sure you are going to have excellent accommodations. The VIP Suite," the doctor said.

"The Governor must not be sick," I said.

One Hundred Forty One
Fort Meade, MD
Cyber Command
Windowless Room

Toni Anne Laudano addressed General Goldstein, Yuri Sokolov, Sheldon, and the others that made up the Group of Six.

"The General wanted me to tie this thing up for everyone in our group. You do understand that nothing said here today ever leaves this room, right?" She waited for everyone, even the General, to nod affirmative.

"Yuri and his partners never anticipated that Bitcoin would be as big as it was. They're real smart guys, so they decided to get us involved. They sent Yuri to the General, we cooked up this plan. Here's what we accomplished: We got Russia to use the big weapon they have been developing for years. Our intelligence shows us that they don't have anything like this in the pipeline. They were willing to shoot the whole wad because of the colossal financial benefit they, and particularly The Lider would get. It was so much money that they would be content to take years to get back into the Cyber big leagues again.'

Sheldon raised his hand. "How did we know our strategy would work?" he asked.

"The only way it would not have worked is if they found out who Nakamoto was. And there was no way they were going to find out," Toni Anne said. "One of the greatest things is we got to embarrass the Lider, big time. Of course, The Lider is one pissed off Commie right now. We should brace ourselves for whatever is coming next."

One Hundred Forty Two
Austin, TX
University of Texas Hospital

Barbara Jean got to spend the night with me in the VIP Suite at the hospital. She even got her own cot to sleep on. Barb got better pain meds than I did, because as the doctor explained to me, with head injuries they don't want to bomb you out too much, because they have to evaluate your condition every hour, performing complex medical tests, like making sure you're not dead.

So with a fractured skull and cracked ribs you don't sleep too well. But in the VIP Suite of the hospital they brought me a milkshake at 2 am when I had a hankering for that. I'm certain you wouldn't get that level of service in the Peon Wing in a Semi-Private Room.

At 7:45 Central Time Barbara Jean was still asleep. My phone rang. It was Toni Anne Laudano.

"JR are you okay?" she asked.

"Well, I'm pretty okay," I said. I was still groggy. I started to give her my medical report but she cut me off.

"JR, you don't have to do that. We've talked to the doctors," Toni Anne said.

"Oh. I forgot you're all knowing," I said.

"JR. I'm... sorry," Laudano said.

"Sorry for what?" I asked.

"I would have hacked into your computer, but I was too busy at the time. I should have gotten you out," she said.

"Toni Anne, you're not catching me at my tip top mental state. What are you trying to tell me?" I asked.

"Well, your charitable foundation is going to have to wait." Toni Anne said.

"Why?" I asked.

"You never sold your Bitcoin," she said.

"Yeah, I didn't have time," I said.

"Remember yesterday, is was worth $1.5 billion?" Toni Anne said.

"Yup."

"Today it's worth one fifty," she said.

"You mean only one hundred and fifty million dollars?" I asked.

"No, I mean $1.50," Toni Anne Laudano said.

"Well, when you're The Big Swingin' Dick these kinds of things happen," I said, "I guess the Dick swings both ways."

"Come on up to Washington when you're ready. I owe you an explanation," Toni Anne said.

"Okay."

Made in the USA
Middletown, DE
24 March 2021